THE
HORSEMAN'S
DREAM

To my dear friend Louise,
with lots of love,
B xxxx

A. J. Reid

DEDICATION

For John and Deborah Reid

And I saw heaven opened, and behold, a white horse, and He who sat on it is called Faithful and True, and in righteousness He judges and wages war.

- Revelations 19:11, *The Bible*

The horse misus'd upon the road

Calls to Heaven for human blood.

- William Blake

Row, row, row your boat,

Gently down the stream.

Merrily, merrily, merrily, merrily,

Life is but a dream.

- Traditional, 1852

1

For some time, Dr. David Hopkins had been thinking about searching his son's room. When he got home from the lab that evening, he set about doing so, knowing that Andrew would still be out. It was a scientific decision he was making. As long as he put everything back where it was, it would be ok. He had to find out what had happened to him in Syria.

Andrew's cheap aftershave hung in the air of the dark, empty room. Everything was always barracks-tidy since his return from service, but this was scant compensation for the damage done to the boy. Hopkins had taken care of the deafness with cochlear implants, but he couldn't find the cause of the psychological trauma without truth, which both the military and Andrew refused to provide.

On the chest of drawers sat a photograph of Andrew's mother, taken a few weeks before she died in the floods. Hopkins had fallen for her hard at university. She defied everything neuroscience and the world had made him believe. She taught him that some things would not reduce to reason and mathematics. Since her death, he found it hard to think about love, let alone say it aloud to anyone.

The photograph next to it was of Andrew's unit, taken in a desert somewhere on the outskirts of Damascus. Hopkins squinted at the nametag on their leader's uniform: Tappin. His eyes were narrow against the desert sun and his face, lean and cobbled with gristle. He held a large assault rifle as if he'd been born with it in his hand. Andrew stood next to him, eyes wide and skin pale, his rifle dangling from his neck like a metal albatross.

Hopkins rummaged through the neat piles of shirts until his fingers clinked against something. He took the half-empty bottle of whisky from the back of the drawer. Sitting on the edge of the bed, he rolled the bottle around in his hand, thinking about Andrew's therapy. When he heard the front door open, he dropped the whisky bottle on the floor, smashing it. Andrew didn't even look up as he entered the room, shambled over to the bed and sat down. As the boy leant against him, Hopkins felt a cold fragility, like porcelain.

'Do you ever think about Mum?'

'All the time.'

'I wish I could remember her.'

Hopkins put his arm around his son. 'She'd hate to see you like this.'

Andrew grunted.

'Why don't we try another session with Totem?'

'You said it wasn't working.'

'I've made some adjustments. I can drive us to the lab tonight.'

'I can't.'

'Let me see what happened. I have to know, otherwise I can't help you.'

'I don't want you to know.'

'You're all I have left.'

'What about Totem?' Andrew stood up and examined the broken glass on the floor.

'It's all for you, son. It always was.'

'And the millions the military are going to give you for it.'

'It's not about the money.'

'Another trophy to go on your shelf.' Andrew used his foot to push the glass into the corner of the room.

'I was looking for—'

'You're trying to save me.'

'You say that as if you don't need saving.'

'No, I said it like I don't want to be saved.'

Hopkins felt as if his heart had stopped for a moment. Where had his son gone? The old photos of Andrew's boyish face filled him with dread.

'I know that I've been in the lab a lot this past year. I thought it was the best way to help you.'

'Could have used a drinking partner.'

'You're eighteen years old.'

Andrew cast him a sideways glance and wiped his

eyes. 'Things have changed since you were eighteen, dad. Haven't you heard? Twenty's the new forty. Life expectancy in Britannia isn't what it used to be.'

'If you include all the provinces in a mean average with Sheffield, you won't get accurate results. The capital has hardly any disease or crime, whereas thirty miles down the road, you have Leeds. Then you've got Dartmoor and the other red zones to take into account—'

'I'm kidding.' Andrew rolled his bloodshot eyes. He always looked like his mother when he did that.

'Get some sleep.' Hopkins walked out and closed the door behind him.

'Dad?'

'Yes?'

'Doesn't matter.'

Hopkins waited a moment. 'You sure?'

'Yeah.'

'Night, son.'

Hopkins retired to his room and lay awake until exhaustion finally carried him off to sleep.

By 7 a.m. the next morning, Hopkins was already dressed, caffeinated and knocking on Andrew's door. Still worried by what he had said the night before, he wanted to check on his son before he left for the lab.

'Andrew?'

No answer.

Hopkins pushed down the handle and entered the room to find it as if Andrew hadn't been home at all that night. There wasn't a splinter of glass on the floor from the whisky bottle, although the tang of its contents remained in the air. He didn't usually get up this early.

Andrew's words kept coming back to Hopkins: *I don't want to be saved.*

Hopkins considered that he might be losing his own grip on reality. What if Andrew had never come home from national service? He lifted the lid of the laundry hamper in the corner of the room, relieved by the sight and smell of dirty clothes. The scent of boot polish drew Hopkins to the windowsill, where he picked up a few crumbs of the black, oily substance. Trying to ignore his peculiarly strong endocrinal response to the smell, the doctor picked up his car keys from the hallway and left the house.

Still perturbed by his son's words, Hopkins searched the village, but to no avail. Even the bookshop had not seen him that morning. Since the floods, Grosvenor's tabloids were all that most people read, but not Andrew. Hopkins thought of his bookshelf, which was forever in a state of near-collapse. Sometimes, Hopkins thought that all that reading might have done him more harm than good. He couldn't help thinking that ignorance might have served him better. Since Andrew had returned from his tour of duty, Hopkins blamed himself for his son's sensitivity. He considered the same old, worn-out mistakes as he approached the church. He shouldn't have encouraged the reading; should have told him to hit other kids back instead of turning the other cheek; shouldn't have told him that everything was going to be alright; should have spent more time at home and less at work; should have prepared the boy for a harsher world.

He turned the car around and headed back for another pass. After two hours of scouring the village and silently punishing himself, he gave up and headed for the lab.

The morning drizzled by as Hopkins reviewed Totem's most recent reports. Unable to concentrate, he tried phoning home to see if Andrew had yet returned. No answer. It was rare that Hopkins missed mobile phones or the internet, but this was one of those times. After trying the landline once more in vain, he slammed the receiver down so hard that it chimed. Resting his hands on the desk, he looked over his collection of books. Some of the shelves were so full that, like Andrew's, they bowed in the middle. He checked the neuroscience section and found several titles on mysticism and religion. That wasn't right. As he set about reorganising them, the rain drove harder against the window. The black clouds above drew a shallow sigh from the doctor. Even his assistant seemed grey as she handed him an envelope marked Grosvenor Media. He ripped it up without opening it and put it in the bin.

'You know what to do with those. I told Grosvenor months ago that we wouldn't sell.'

'That guy Chandler delivered it personally. Said they'd tripled the military's offer.'

Hopkins glanced at the bin. 'Tripled?'

'He was very specific that I should give it to you myself.'

Hopkins shook his head and went back to organising the books. 'When Andrew's recovered, we'll start fielding offers.'

'How is he? Last time, he seemed um, better.'

'I still can't get him to tell me what happened.'

'Doctor Hollis had no luck?'

'He didn't turn up to any of the appointments,' Hopkins replied, pulling a report from a drawer. 'I don't know what to do. Past these parameters, Totem might hurt him. I can't take that chance.'

'Henry in security keeps asking me whether the treatment is working.'

'Henry Beckley. Went to the same school. Phones the house sometimes, but Andrew never takes the call. Always asks if it's Arthur.'

'Who's Arthur?'

'He won't tell me. Says it's too dangerous.'

'Paranoid delusion?'

'I don't think so …'

A telephone rang in the assistant's office. 'Excuse me, Doctor,' she said, hurrying out of the room.

When she came back a few minutes later, she was as white as the lab coat hanging on the door. 'The police are here. They're at reception.'

Hopkins' hands trembled and his mind raced as he

calculated the possible reasons for this. He suspected another drunk and disorderly charge, but they'd never sent anyone to the lab before.

As he put on his jacket and headed for the lift down to reception, sweat began to seep from his forehead. Catching sight of himself in the steel doors of the lift, he saw that he had paled like his assistant. Arriving at the ground floor, he felt as if he was still sinking as the doors opened into the reception area. The detective looked grim as he approached.

'Good morning, sir. Is there somewhere private we can have a word?'

'Is it my son? Where is he?'

'It'd be best if we had some privacy.'

'Lab 2's free, Doctor,' the security guard said.

'Thank you, Henry.'

Hopkins led the detective down a long corridor until they reached a steel door. He held his eye to the retinal scanner and the latch opened. As they entered the lab, the workstation lights reflected off the giant gongs hung about the room. The detective leaned towards the largest gong and observed his alcohol-reddened face.

'This is our cymatics lab.'

'Lot of computers for one lab. We could use some of these downtown.'

'What is this about? Is my son alright?'

'You might want to sit down.'

'Just tell me,' Hopkins replied.

'A dog-walker found your son this morning in the

woods. It appears that last night, he took his own life.'

He shook his head. 'There must be some mistake.'

'There's no mistake, I'm afraid, sir. We already have results from forensics confirming his identity. I'm sorry.'

In the soundproofed lab, the silence was so absolute that it made Hopkins' ears ring.

'How did he—'

'Hanged himself.'

Hopkins leant against a workstation.

'Forensics wanted this, but I thought you should have it. It was found on his person, tucked into his left boot.'

The smell of the boot polish in Andrew's room came back to Hopkins in a sickening rush. 'Boot?'

'He was wearing his regimental uniform, sir.'

Hopkins took the envelope. 'I'd like to be alone now, please.'

'Sorry for your loss. I'll see myself out.' The detective left the room, letting the heavy door click back on to its latch.

Hopkins read the letter twice, but still couldn't believe that Andrew was dead. On the third reading, he felt the grief hatching inside him like a parasite. When he read it a fourth time, he flew into a rage, smashing screens and hurling the gongs to the floor. When he finally collapsed amongst the fallen circles of bronze and broken glass, he crumpled the suicide note against his face and wept.

2

Within a week of his son's funeral, Hopkins had sold his house, laboratory and research to Grosvenor Media. The military pulled their offer when they heard of Andrew's suicide, forcing Hopkins to sell Totem, too. Everything he'd owned had gone into the project. Without Grosvenor's offer, he'd have been on the streets.

Upon clearing Andrew's room, he'd found a stashed bottle of whisky and not stopped drinking since. He was about a bottle in one night, when he had the idea to buy the abandoned island distillery. He told everyone at the lab that he was retiring, but in truth, he was banishing himself. Most likely, he would die there if he carried on drinking and he was fine with that.

He was on his way out of the lab reception area for the last time, bound for Leeds docks by road and from there, the Highlands. Since the floods, no car could reach that far north, so Hopkins had bought himself a boat to complete the journey. He had this idea that it might capsize and save him the trouble of getting all the way up there only to blow his own head off or drink himself to death. The doctor contemplated his suicide with a poker face as he entered Reception. Henry Beckley the security guard half-smiled at him as he approached the main exit.

'Sir, about Andrew ... I tried to—'

'We all tried. Good luck, Henry.'

He strode through the freezing car park to his Range Rover and threw the bag of documents on the seat. He didn't even want them. He started the ignition and headed for Leeds, watching his laboratory fade in the rear view.

Hopkins couldn't help feeling glad that there was never anyone else on the roads since the floods. He hadn't been to Leeds since his university days when there were still traffic jams. Now, there were only Grosvenor trucks and security vehicles. Any private citizens on the roads were treated with suspicion. Two Grosvenor vehicles overtook Hopkins as he considered this, the occupants eyeballing him as they went.

Squinting through the rain, he recognised a bridge from his student days. The faded GOURANGA graffito was still there, translated from Sanskrit beneath as *everybody be happy*. Someone had crossed out the word *happy* and replaced it with *dead*.

The bottle of whisky in the passenger footwell clinked as he came to a stop on the quayside. Rain clattered against his windscreen in fat droplets as he stretched his neck. After he'd taken a drink, he got out of the car and posted a cash-filled envelope through the harbourmaster's letterbox. Peering through the salted window, he could see photographs of the man's family on his desk. He paused for a moment, despite the lashing weather. Feeling the car keys in his pocket, he posted them, too.

Hopkins ran back to the 4x4 and sat in the driver's seat, wiping the rain from his face with his sleeve. Once his hands were dry enough, he pulled Andrew's suicide note from the sun visor.

As he held the bloodied document, logic screamed at him to leave it behind, but his fingers would not let go.

An hour passed before he made up his mind and took it; the bottle of Laphroaig in his other hand.

Like most of the boats that had survived the flood, Hopkins' had a steel hull and a military history. The harbourmaster had stocked it with supplies for the journey. All GPS systems were useless due to the satellite blackout, so he had also left charts in the wheelhouse, to Hopkins' relief. Since the floods, sailing had become part of everyone's survival curriculum. He estimated that there were four times as many boats on the sea as vehicles left on the roads. A matter of physics. Displacement theory.

Boats float: cars don't.

Once he'd checked everything over, Hopkins sat in the captain's chair with his bottle, waiting for the tide. The rain outside was turning to sleet as he lit the hurricane lantern to survey the wheelhouse. He found a copy of The Serviceman featuring an article by Lucky Newman: a Special Forces veteran who had made some powerful enemies in Britannia. Most of the time, he was campaigning for peace in the Middle East, the abolition of National Service or the exposure of corruption in Britannia's ruling corporatocracy. In this piece, Newman was claiming that Grosvenor had not just profited from the blackout, but monopolised Britannia's media. According to her news outlets, solar flares were to blame, but Newman questioned this. He wrote of how shares in her media corporation had skyrocketed in the wake of the floods. Since she owned the only remaining analogue transmission equipment in the British Isles, this came as no surprise to Hopkins. The secret military weather control programs seemed a little far-fetched, but Hopkins read on anyway.

Hopkins briefly wondered whether he had made a terrible mistake in handing over Totem, took another drink and turned the page.

He did not doubt that most of what Newman wrote about Grosvenor could be true. She made her crooked father look like an amateur. Hopkins had once treated Alice during his tenure at a neuropsychiatric facility in Sheffield. His colleagues had been too afraid of her. He recalled that she had a slight impediment that made her sound like a snake when she introduced herself. After an hour of delving into her past and her psychosis, Hopkins understood his colleagues' fear. Running the risk of execution or worse, he told her the truth. Told her exactly what she was. How sick she was and why.

Surprisingly, she only fired him. Hired someone else to tell her what she needed to hear.

But she never forgot about Hopkins, it seemed. She had funded his retirement and her bouquet of flowers had arrived the day after Andrew's suicide.

She was prompt, if nothing else.

She'd been after the Totem research since the day Hopkins had started the project, but he had turned down her every offer. He was too busy with Andrew's therapy, not to mention reluctant to put his creation in the hands of someone as aberrant as her. Now that Andrew was gone, he didn't care whether the rest of Britannia sank into the sea.

Part of him wanted it to.

Grosvenor could have it all.

And he could have another drink.

As he rooted through his bag, he found a folder of the commendations and awards that he had amassed over the years. Hopkins leafed through the file, feeling the bitterness building inside him. He'd been able to help all these people, so why not his own flesh and blood? Should he have used sodium pentothal on his son to find out what happened in Syria? Pushed for more overtime from his staff? He opened the hatch of the wheelhouse and threw the file into the wind, scattering his achievements across the incoming tide.

After more whisky, he opened the suicide note and read the fading ink for the thousandth time, searching for answers that he knew he would not find.

Half the bottle was gone by the time he cast off at high tide.

He sailed past the lights of Scarborough Island and its famous fair, feeling loneliness descend upon him like a sea roke. The Big Wheel continued to turn in slow defiance. Its salvage by local trawlermen had been widely covered by Grosvenor News, turning it into a symbol of hope for the citizens of Britannia.

But Hopkins was all too aware that some things could never be recovered.

Anna had been working away in Canary Wharf when it happened. Her building was in the direct path of the tidal surge up the Thames. He had been holding baby Andrew in his arms as the news crackled through their kitchen radio in Queensbury, a small village up in the Pennines. The memory of his wife made his scalp tingle and his heart thud, so he opened a more recent copy of The Serviceman to distract himself. It was another article by Newman, outlining the reasons for his lying low:

Last night, I went to a bar in the business district. Low lighting, jazz piano and overpriced cocktails, that kind of place. Cruelty to animals is shitty, but there's a woman wearing a dead fox like I've never seen. She buys me a drink and asks me if I smoke. I give her one I rolled earlier; she invites me back to her place. In the alley out the back of the bar, her peach lipstick makes me want to puke.

Suspicious, since I quite like peaches.

I only realise that it's some kind of nerve agent when my face goes numb and my knees give way. She backs away from me and wipes her lips clean. Some guy sticks a fancy Walther in my face, so I grab it with my dead right hand. Back door of the bar bursts open and the bartender stands there looking at us, cigarette dangling from his mouth. I wrestle the gun towards his gut and thumb his finger down on the trigger. I don't know which way the bullet goes. Last thing I remember is the dead fox clacking away down the alley.

That's pretty much the statement I gave to the police, not that it will do me any good. Dodging a bullet is nothing new for me. It's how I earnt my nickname. In case you're wondering, my luck doesn't extend to card games.

I have no doubt this nasty business in the business district is a consequence of my criticism of Grosvenor's buyout of Totem. Sources suggest that Hopkins' research was for a cure for Post-Traumatic Stress Disorder. But we can be sure that Grosvenor intends to use it for something more sinister. We just don't know what yet.

If there's one person in these isles who has profited from the floods and the blackouts, it's Alice Grosvenor. With her dead father's fortune, she bought up every last propaganda machine across the isles; every printing press, every radio and TV station; every telecoms mast; every newspaper office. A keen eye might also note that Alice is the majority shareholder in the two pharmaceutical companies that supply Britannia.

Her latest and biggest venture is the development of drugs that put PTSD victims in a state of supposedly blissful catatonia, facilitating minimum contact with the patient and low staff expense. This barbaric practise demeans not only our youth returning from theatres of war, but also the thousands of flood survivors. It shames the medical profession, the luminaries and leaders of which have been conspicuously silent on the issue. These drugs happen to rank as the most profitable ever marketed to the British public for any illness, which speaks for itself.

To learn who rules over you, simply find out who you are not allowed to criticise. - Voltaire

Britannia is already a dictatorship. Capitalist sociopaths have been at war over the remains of our country since the floods, but none dare challenge Grosvenor. Where will it end? Who will effect the necessary change? Her poisonous propaganda is already deep in the veins of the British public. There's no end in sight to the deluge of blue pills raining from above, especially within the cushy utopia of the capital. While children are starving in the remote islands and provinces, Grosvenor and her cronies continue to profit. The Church is now nothing more than a quaint, toothless cult. Our foremost scientists are all on her payroll, all bound by confidentiality agreements. Our politicians are mere cheerleaders for Grosvenor, bought and paid for, taking breaks from counting their cash only to bend to her will.

So to whom does the responsibility fall?

It falls to those of us who have paid the cost of Grosvenor's rise to power. We have reaped no rewards except for a few trinkets to pin on our uniforms. The blood of children is no fair trade for oil or economic stability. Or for anything.

It is true that some veterans have signed up for Grosvenor's security forces, lured by more money for more killing. They do not represent Her Majesty's Armed Forces. We do not stand with them.

Meanwhile, her news teams are quite adept at silencing voices of dissent. Having been smeared in some lurid headline, Grosvenor's victims usually end up on remand for a crime they have never committed. Grosvenor's modus operandi sees an inmate or a guard dispose of them, making it look like an accident or a suicide. Through her media outlets, she will highlight the failings of our prisons, as she has done with our hospitals, schools, police and our armed forces. She intends to control every aspect of our lives. Why am I disclosing all this now? Because my time is short, it seems, and a libel suit is the least of my worries.

Some of us have done terrible things under orders on the battlefield. I confess that I am one of those men. When I can sleep at all, my nightmares are so vivid that I wake up unable to breathe, convinced that I am going to Hell. We have brought death to the innocent to serve the agendas of some of the most privileged and debased people imaginable. I only hope that my redemption can be found—if it can be found at all—in protecting the innocent lives that are at risk now. I ask you to do the same.

Our troops must come home. Our illegal wars must end. Grosvenor is feeding our youth into her war grinder and stuffing them into rubber cells upon their return, just for a tidy profit. Quite the hero's welcome. Any families not wealthy enough to pay the deferral fee will see their children suffer such a fate. Who can ignore that not one single conscript for front-line infantry has come from the capital in the past decade?

I have been calling on the politicians and the straw men of this country to halt this fascism for long enough. So now, I am turning to you as fellow servicemen.

All it takes for evil to triumph is for good men to do nothing. – Edmund Burke

Hopkins remembered hearing the first radio report in the aftermath of the floods. Soon afterwards, they came thick and fast, all reporting the same thing. According to Grosvenor's news outlets, solar flares had altered the magnetic fields around the poles. Basalt eruptions and the sudden melting of the ice caps had caused global sea levels to rise at speeds beyond all expectation or precedent. Later, everyone heard that tectonic plates had been rent asunder. One outlet put it down to a comet landing in the Atlantic Ocean. Misinformation. Disinformation. Every kind of information except the truth. All the science seemed to come from charlatans and stooges, desperate to please Grosvenor; to side with the powerful, to hide beneath the dragon's wing. Survivors were too busy grieving, rebuilding and battling the violent weather to care about something as trivial as the truth. Hopkins himself had accepted it, too traumatised by his wife's death to seek answers. Remote, elevated communities like Queensbury remained relatively civilised, but any surviving cities or towns outside of the capital became amber zones overnight, populated by desperate people who had left their old gods for dead in the floodwaters.

He sailed past where Glasgow had been, giving a password via radio to the sentinel battleship to avoid any confrontation. The voice that gave him clearance through the straits sounded Middle Eastern. Grosvenor's army of foreign mercenaries had been gradually replacing Her Majesty's Forces since the floods. Hopkins had seen them on the streets of Sheffield, sporting exotic weaponry and ballistics armour. Hopkins turned the next page to find out that a rebellion was rising in the provinces. Veterans and sympathisers were gathering in crumbling libraries to campaign against Grosvenor's government. Newman paid tribute to those who had been smeared or executed thus far, listing over a dozen names.

Hopkins wondered whether Lucky Newman was still alive somewhere out there. He stowed the empty whisky bottle with The Serviceman in the hold and checked his course as the Big Wheel faded into the snow-flecked blackness.

3

Alice Grosvenor removed the needle from the vein in the girl's hand and let it drop back on to the bed with a thud. She turned to her senior PR adviser, who quickly unclamped his own hand from his mouth.

'We've already got some ideas about how to spin it for you. A grandmother losing her daughter and grandson during childbirth should be an easy sell.'

'I don't care what they think, Chandler. Just make sure the package gets there.'

'We'll move the baby to the orphanage soon and report that he died with the mother during the birth. No-one will ever know any different.'

Alice moved the hair out of the young woman's glazed eyes. 'And the doctor?'

'He should keep quiet, but I can remove any doubt, if you'd prefer?'

'I'd prefer.'

Chandler nodded as if she had asked for more

sugar in her tea. He approached the bedside to look at the nineteen-year-old corpse of Jennifer Grosvenor.

'Such a waste.'

'It's not a waste. It's a sacrifice.'

Chandler tugged at his shirt collar with a nervous finger. 'It all seems—'

Alice glared at Chandler as she caressed the girl's dead hand. 'What?'

Chandler shifted from one foot to the other. 'She was a cute kid, that's all.'

'Is Muldoon dead yet?'

'Muldoon is still in solitary confinement. Has been since—'

'We found out she was pregnant,' she interrupted, smoothing the bed sheets over the girl's cold body.

'Well, since the last time we had someone try to shank him.'

Alice narrowed her eyes at her aide. 'Shank him? Learn that one on K-Wing, did you, Chandler?'

'We thought that he'd have done the job himself by now. I hoped that things would be tidier, like the others.'

'As my father used to say, every black cloud has a silver lining.'

'Would you like some time alone with her, marm?'

'I don't have time for that. We have to keep things moving.'

'What's next with Totem?'

'Are we ready for a subject?'

'The engineers say yes, but—'

'I have just the man for the job.'

4

Arthur Muldoon woke in total darkness, as he had done every morning for the past eight months. He retrieved the bread he had saved in his mattress, took a bite, and began his prayers. His son would be born soon, if he hadn't been already, so he spent twice as long praying that day. The idea of being a father had terrified him at first, being only eighteen years old himself. But since he'd received the news that it was to be a boy, he couldn't stop thinking about it. It made it real.

Under his bed was a small collection of suicide aids that the guards had pushed through the hatch, almost as if they had taken pity on Arthur. They delivered razor blades, pills and lengths of high-tensile paracord that looked like standard army issue. The pills were the ones given to conscripts in case the enemy caught them alive. They each bore a G for Grosvenor Pharmaceuticals.

None of his service to his country had counted in his favour during the secret trial. He knew they'd give him either a bullet or a jail cell for disobeying an officer's orders on the battlefield. Even if it was to go back and pick up a fallen comrade. He received neither when he came home. He thought he was safe, but when Jennifer told him she was pregnant, Grosvenor Security arrested and tried him in a secret court. Judge Higham sentenced him to indefinite solitary confinement, or ISC: the most feared sentence in the British penal system. A pathway to madness, they would do everything to keep a prisoner alive until he lost his mind, and then transfer him to the prison hospital at Exmoor. Last stop would likely be Dartmoor, but no-one ever knew for sure because the prisoners were never seen again.

Arthur had no-one to fight his appeal because he was the only one in his family to survive the floods. Once he was old enough for National Service, they plucked him straight from the overcrowded care home and put a rifle in his hand. Shipped him off to the desert, where he saw things that no-one could forget. Without Jenny and his unborn son to keep him going, there were some nights he might have used the things under his bed. He sometimes heard the guards talking about how long he had lasted: twice as long as anyone else they'd had in ISC. Meanwhile, Arthur would do press-ups, organise his rations and dream about his wife-to-be and their new baby. Although he hadn't known her for long, he had faith that Jenny would see him freed.

And if she couldn't, then God would save him.

Arthur ran his fingers over the cold metal door until he reached the series of gouges that made up his calendar. He took one of the razors from under his bed, and marked the fourteenth of February. As he finished the marking, the door opened, hitting him in the face and slamming him on to his back. In the blackness of the cell, the guards' torches seemed as bright as twin suns.

They dragged him down a long corridor, through two secure doors, and into another cell with a woman sat at a table. Even the immaculate hair and make-up couldn't soften Alice Grosvenor's face. Nor could her expensive perfume hide the faint smell of decay about her. Last time Arthur had seen her, she had been in the secret court, standing in silence like an elegant vulture. She bore little resemblance to Jenny with her hooked nose, strained neck and carrion-seeking eyes. Small wonder, since Grosvenor had adopted her from an orphanage. A care home kid, just like him.

'Hello, Arthur.'

'Ms. Grosvenor,' Arthur replied, his speech slurred and feeble from talking only to himself for nine months.

'I'm here to get you out. If you take part in a short experiment, you will go free to see your son.'

Arthur's eyes widened. 'Jen had the baby? Are they alright?'

'They're both fine. Jennifer has been asking for

you. Sign these.'

Arthur looked at the sheets of paper. 'I don't understand.'

'This is your only chance. I'm here to help you.'

'Is it a medical experiment? What's REM sleep? Dimethyltryptamine? Totem? I don't know what any of this means.'

'If you don't accept this deal, we have no choice but to send you to Dartmoor,' she said, holding up a photograph of Jennifer sleeping with their newborn son.

The stories he'd heard about Dartmoor were the stuff of nightmares. But it was the fear that he would never see his son that moved his shaking hand to the dotted line. He scrawled his name and dropped the pen on the table.

'You'll be removed from Exmoor Prison immediately, and flown to Sheffield. Full debriefing will be given on-site.' Her black eyes still giving nothing away, she stood up, clapped shut her Filofax and walked out of the room.

The guards walked Arthur down the dark corridor instead of dragging him this time. After half a dozen more secure doors and a staircase that took them up twelve levels, they finally reached a door with the words EXIT TO ROOF printed on it.

As the door opened, Arthur shielded his eyes from the blinding greyness of the British skies. On the helipad, he could make out the shape of a Sea King through the fierce wind and rain. Inside the helicopter sat two of Alice Grosvenor's security team: foreign mercenaries with assault rifles. Their dark eyes narrowed with contempt as the porcine prison guards struggled to frog-march Arthur to the helipad.

5

Hopkins moored up in the deserted harbour after seven nights at sea. He had endured the last two without whisky in order to navigate the dangerous waters leading up to the island. He fell on to the quayside, shaking so violently that he struggled to uncork the bottle, at first. The weather was still, but cold, and his hands felt like they would break as he twisted the seal. When he finally opened it and had drunk enough to calm the delirium tremens, he rolled on to his back to listen to the gulls' songs and the slopping of the water. The feeling in his hands returned as the winds died down, but the ground still felt cold enough to crack his spine. He stood up and hauled his duffle bag out of the boat and on to his back. The wet wood of the pontoon creaked as he walked across its planks, through the ghostly harbour and towards the distillery.

The wrought iron gates groaned open once

unlocked by the large black key in his pocket. Had Hopkins been less cold, he might have enjoyed the novelty of not having to hold up an eyeball to a scanner or a finger to a screen. His priority was to get to the fireplace in the distillery manager's house and warm up, dry out and cook some hot food.

The skins of the whitewashed buildings of the distillery had cracked and weathered since its abandonment. Hopkins picked at the flakes of peeled paint as he walked by. Looking east, he saw a small mountain range that protected the distillery from the brunt of the Siberian and Arctic winds. He staggered from one building to another, peering in through the leaded windows. There were several long, stone sheds full of brass intestines and copper lungs, with each wall whitewashed. The manager's house was redbrick, three floors and had two dead hurricane lanterns squeaking in the wind outside the front door. He flicked through his clump of keys and unlocked it, tripping over a pair of expensive-looking brogues as he entered the hallway. A tuxedo hanging in the kitchen alarmed him as he entered. As the twinge from the adrenaline subsided, he brushed his hand over the outfit. The silk of the lapel reminded him of the pre-flood awards ceremonies as he displaced a layer of dust with his shaking fingers.

In the room to his left was a writing desk holding various items of stationery and an oxblood chair. On the other side of the room: a small fireplace and a woodpile. He took a hatchet from his bag and made some kindling from the logs, feathering it so that it would catch. Once the fire was lit, he took another drink and moved the chair closer to the hearth.

Above the fireplace, photographs of the old distillery manager and his wife stood on a driftwood mantelpiece. Hopkins could tell the pictures had been taken before the floods. People didn't smile like that anymore, especially outside of Sheffield. He wondered if the couple were dead now. When he thought about being the first person to set foot there in years, he felt his neck hairs bristle.

Hopkins distracted himself with the chore of eating. From his bag, he took some salmon and fanned it out on its wrapping. Finding two long splints from the woodpile, he used these to cook the fillets in the fireplace. Eating it raw would have sufficed, but he wanted hot food to fight back the chill in his bones. Searching for tinned food in the kitchen, Hopkins found a full bottle of whisky with no label, indicating that it might be the distillery's own. He held it up to the light of the fire and found himself seduced by the flames dancing through the amber. Noticing the snow on the windows, he pulled his chair closer to the fire and unscrewed the bottle of whisky.

He woke early the next morning, upright in the chair with an empty bottle in his coat pocket. Sunrise had only just begun, but there was enough light to make a cup of coffee and the room was still warm, thanks to the smouldering fireplace. Hopkins had brought enough supplies for a month before he'd have to travel to the Scottish mainland to restock. Or start hunting. That was, if he wasn't already dead by then, but he'd come prepared for all eventualities. The harbourmaster told him that the sawn-off Beretta might save his life. Despite Hopkins' protests, the old man insisted that he take the weapon.

He picked up the shotgun, stuffed a handful of red shells into his pocket and set off exploring the island that he intended to be his mausoleum.

6

The guards grimaced as they clung to the brackets and rails lining the interior of the helicopter. The wind was bad and he could hear electricity crackling above him, but Arthur had faith that he was not going to die yet. Not before he'd met his son.

The Sea King landed on a roof near Sheffield Cathedral. Shortly afterwards, the guards delivered him to a cell with a flushing toilet and a bed.

For three days and nights, they gave him hot food. He was even able to see the guards' faces when they pushed it through the hatch. Although none of them answered his questions about Jenny or his son, he knew that they saw him too, and that was good enough. There had been times in the ISC when Arthur was not sure whether he had died out there in the desert. Whether he was stuck in some sort of purgatory. Or gone mad. His faith and the thought of being a father was all that had kept him from using the razors to open his wrists or the paracord to string himself up.

In the evening, guards led him to a large amphitheatre with a gurney in its centre. He began to feel less certain about his destiny as they strapped him onto it and disappeared. Dinner suits and evening gowns drifted into the seating areas. Arthur wondered whether he was having a bad dream. They drank dark liquid from champagne flutes between guffaws and what-ho's as if they were at a cocktail party. Alice Grosvenor appeared above him, shining a bright light into his eyes. Her voice was soft and unchallenged.

'You'll make history today, Arthur.'

'What is this?'

She glanced down at the tattoo of the crucifix on his right forearm. 'In Roman times, emperors would throw Christians to the lions. It was the mess that people liked.'

She traced its outline with her fingernail as the white-coated assistant stuck a needle in Arthur's other arm.

'We've moved on since then,' she said, shining the torch into Arthur's pupils. 'Somewhat.'

'Jenny ...'

Leaning closer to his ear, she whispered. 'Jennifer and your son are both dead. They died during the birth.'

Arthur mumbled, struggling to move his mouth because of the anaesthetic. 'You're lying.'

His heart beat harder against the tight straps of the gurney.

'In a hospital incinerator's ash tray, all because you couldn't keep it in your pants.'

She tidied Arthur's hair before the white coat began to shave it off. 'Sweet dreams, Arthur.'

As they scooped the last of his hair away with the blade, Arthur felt all hope leave him. The barber receded from view and more white coats moved in to attach electrodes to his naked scalp. They positioned a huge brass bell above his face, making the electrodes glow with blue light and his heart race. Champagne flutes rattled on the serving trolleys, silencing the chatter of the crowd. Arthur's hands and feet felt as if they were falling off as he lapsed into unconsciousness with the tang of hot brass on his tongue.

7

Lucky Newman was used to looking over his shoulder, but this was ridiculous. There were at least three people sitting behind him who had signed off on having him permanently silenced. It would be four when Grosvenor arrived.

The amphitheatre shook as the blue light from beneath Muldoon's gurney grew brighter.

Grosvenor's voice came through the speakers, 'Please make your way to the transmission area by following the blue lines to the exits. There will be a final scan for any glass or metal objects, so finish your cocktails before you leave.'

Lucky downed his drink, spilling a drop on to the lapel of his tuxedo. It was pretty good stuff - he felt a little woozy already. Wasn't quite roll out the barrel time, but he'd stopped giving a shit about the potential assassins in the room. Grosvenor wasn't desperate enough to try it right in front of the chief of police and the attorney general, was she? The two men stared at him over the rims of their champagne flutes.

A shambling, red-faced old man in a silk tuxedo startled Lucky.

Judge Higham looked wasted.

'Old chap, would you fetch me another?'

'I'm not your fucking butler.'

Lucky drained his glass and followed the blue lights to the transmission area.

The assassination attempts had come after Lucky refused Grosvenor's bribes and job offers. She wanted him to quieten down one way or the other. This was certain to be the last peaceful offering. He wondered whether she would use any of his ex-comrades from Commando 46 the next time she tried to have him murdered. And whether they'd be bothered it was one of their own. Perhaps it would be an old-fashioned cloak and dagger affair: polonium in the Earl Grey, then zipped up naked in a suitcase. More likely, he'd be paraded through the streets by her journalists like a witch to the pyre, but he had accepted that. They would frame him for something awful, throw him in Exmoor and banish him to Dartmoor eventually. But that was ok. As long as the truth was out there.

He'd decided to take his chances, as luck had already seen him through four such attempts. Since he'd been back in Britannia trying to readjust to civilian life as a journalist, death had continued to stalk Lucky.

Every one of Grosvenor's media outlets had labelled him a whistleblower. Some even called him a traitor, but he had always been a patriot. Not for the Britannia created by her, but for the country that it used to be. And not for the corporations that ran it, but for the people that suffered under their yoke. He was a patriot for his friends who had died out in the desert. For their mothers and fathers. Not for Alice Grosvenor or her vampires in their high castles and country estates.

Lucky followed the lights down a dark, low corridor, striding ahead of the excited guests. Upon entering the transmission area, he saw hundreds of egg-shaped, brass pods lined up on the bare concrete. In the centre of them all, there was a hundred-foot-high mast glowing blue. He scribbled diagrams and descriptions on his notepad as the attendant guided him to his pod. Bolted to the floor with tiny brass roots connecting them, the pods pulsed with blue light.

He saw that other guests were already locked in. Lucky sat back in his cot and the door clicked shut, making him wish he'd taken a piss when he had the chance. The light pulsed more brightly as Alice Grosvenor's voice counted down through the pod's speakers. He could taste the brass of the pod's wall, as if he were becoming the distorted reflection of himself.

The blue light grew brighter, even when Lucky

thought it couldn't.

5
4
3
2
1

ARTHUR MULDOON'S DREAM

Arthur Muldoon was lucky that it was a hot summer. His makeshift bed of dead grass and pine branches could not be too close to the fire, so he still felt the cold mountain air on his back. He stuffed some of the dry grass in the stinking green overalls and lay down in the dead field, enclosed by foreboding pine trees. The sky was purple and the birds sang as if dawn were breaking. As the hot suns rose, there were no bombs exploding, bullets whistling or children screaming, to his relief. The green overalls reeked of the previous owner's preoccupation with drinking, smoking and fixing tractors.

Arthur was 20 years old, strong and capable. His forearms bulged out of the rolled-up sleeves of the overalls, revealing a crucifix and several forces tattoos. He was aware of his youth; of his potential, but he worried that something terrible was happening beyond the tree-line of the field. He wandered through the dead grass, pulling out the odd handful of blades and throwing them upwards to see which way the breeze was blowing. Each time, the blades fell straight to the ground, but still the long grass of the field swayed back and forth.

He circled a patch of dry, cracked earth with the toe of his prison-issue trainer. A beetle emerged, so black that it reflected an iridescence of indescribable colours. Arthur brought the complicated sole of his trainer close to the head of the beetle and looked up to see a giant replica of his own shoe bearing down on him. He reached up and traced the rubber maze of the sole with his hand, stepping on the beetle as he did so. Sadness crackled in the air, stinking up the field. He knew that war smelled the same and cried out with agony as his bones, innards and colours squished between the grooves of the giant shoe. Despite his cracked body, he somehow raced through the dry grass, away from the thing that had crushed him. Each dead blade was as thick as a tree trunk, pushing its gold lance into the sky, the end of which Arthur could not see. When he had traversed a billion or so of these lances at speed, he came up against the roots of giant wooden pillars topped with green canopies.

Arthur pushed past the other insects and proceeded up the trunk of the tree with a thrilling velocity he had never known. He chose a branch facing outwards from the field, and followed it to its end. Wrapping his six black legs around the branch, he surveyed what lay beyond the tree-line. He saw a young family having a picnic in another field. Jenny and a young boy sat on a blanket with another man, eating cucumber sandwiches. This field was teeming with life: short, bright green grass, and there were flowerbeds of every conceivable colour. But something creaked and groaned through the air, sounding like it was near death. Further up, on the brow of the hill, Arthur heard the music of a carousel. Its silhouette seemed locked into perpetual, laboured motion against the two suns. He scraped his insect appendages against the bark of the branch in frustration.

The man told the young boy to go and play in the woods and began taking off Jenny's clothes. Arthur watched from afar with his shiny black eyes. He was ready to return to the field of dead grass, when he heard her crying out his name. Arthur descended the trunk of the tree and rattled through the leaves and twigs of the woodland floor, anticipating the hot green of the park grass. He heard a twig snap and found himself enveloped in warm darkness. The soft flesh smelled like cucumber sandwiches. The fingers parted, allowing his son to observe him in the shade of the pine trees. His son's eyes sparkled with the same colours as his own. When the boy smiled, Arthur felt that he was not alone in the universe. His son placed him on a succulent leaf and used his finger to transfer a single droplet of water from a nearby pool to its waxy skin.

Jenny called the boy back to the field, making Arthur's heart thud against his cracked shell.

Arthur wanted to say goodbye, but couldn't. He trembled with sadness, alone on the leaf of kindness, as John's footsteps faded away. His hopes soared when his son's hand scooped him up again. The red and white matchbox into which he was placed felt safe and warm. The stink of sulphur aside, he was ecstatic that his son still wanted to be with him. Arthur worried for his son: what would happen when he found out that his real father was a beetle? What would the other kids at school say to him about the thing in the matchbox? Better that than being the son of Arthur Muldoon, though.

Not the Arthur Muldoon?

Yes, the Arthur Muldoon.

They say he killed his wife and child.

That it must be true because they heard it on Grosvenor News.

He crawled out of his matchbox and on to Alice Grosvenor's pillow while she slept, trying to bite into her neck with tiny mandibles and no venom.

As the tang of brass filled the air, Arthur wrapped his hands around Alice's throat. The crucifix on his forearm bulged outwards as his muscles squeezed tighter. Her arteries throbbed against his fingers as he cracked her windpipe. She thrashed her legs against the bedside table and an alarm clock spilt on to the floor, beeping in time with her pulse, which had begun to fade. Her spit and tears were all over his hands, and her eyes had almost bulged out of their sockets.

Watching the life drain out of her, he felt freer than ever.

9

Slack-jawed Lucky Newman held the pencil over the paper, but his hand would not write. Too many words, and there was little chance he would make sense of them later on, but he scribbled anyway. He could see through the mirrored glass that other guests were being helped from their pods by white-coated attendants. The blue mast had dimmed, leaving only the soft illumination of the winding pathway. He watched the dignitaries and celebrities stagger along it like newborn foals. His egg cracked and Grosvenor was standing there, waiting for him.

'So, what do you think?'

'Am I normal?' he stuttered as he tried to see his reflection in the pod visor. He touched his fingers to his face, unsure whether it was real or whether he was still in the dream.

A white coat muttered as he scribbled on his clipboard. 'Yes, you're normal. You might experience mild hallucinations over the next hour, but nothing permanent.'

'Thank God.'

'No, Mr. Newman. You can thank me,' Alice Grosvenor sniffed with her sharp beak.

The guests followed the illuminated pathways back to their seats, glancing at each other for reassurance. Nobody spoke: there was only the shuffling of shoes and clothing. It reminded Lucky of the army chapel that he used to visit in the desert. He had been seeking respite from the sun to begin with, but the more time he spent there, the more he felt a strange attachment to something. He wondered whether the guests were contemplating their own strange attachments. He took the notebook from his pocket and read what he'd scribbled.

Epiphanies. Revelations. Miracles. Apparitions. Visitations. Visions.

He didn't remember writing the words. He had encircled "revelations" several times and didn't know why. Lucky was trying to recall where he'd put his standard-issue Bible when Grosvenor took centre stage at a podium.

'I bet some of you would like a real drink.'

Waiters appeared in the aisles with well-equipped trollies. Lucky took a single malt.

'What you have experienced is the future of broadcast entertainment, not to mention the benefits it will bring to our justice system. Post-transmission, subscribers will vote on whether prisoners are ready for parole. Judge Higham, you have known me since I was born and you were friends with my late father for 50 years.'

Judge Higham managed to raise his grim jowls for a faint smile.

'Did you enjoy killing me, your honour?'

The rosacea-cheeked old man looked at the floor while the audience waited in silence for his reply. 'More than anything, my dear.'

The amphitheatre hummed and buzzed with awkward chatter.

'Having experienced his consciousness, do you think that Mr. Muldoon should be released back into society?'

'No, madam, I certainly do not.'

Uncertain applause trickled through the theatre. Grosvenor's shills gave standing ovations and encouraged others to do the same. Meanwhile her agents took down the names of the unimpressed and unco-operative.

Lucky knew he was already on that list.

10

Arthur Muldoon woke in darkness. There was no temperature to the air. No texture to the floor. His breathing was shallow and uneven. Reaching out, he could just about feel the leg of his ISC bed in his numb fingers. Having hauled himself back on to it, the horror came back to him: Jenny and the baby were both dead. He felt as if he were watching himself through a television: he had no control. He sobbed as everything except his pain ceased to exist.

As the night wore on, Arthur's sobs turned to screams and he finally reached under his bed for one of the razors. He convinced himself that the only way to see Jenny and his son was to open the artery in his neck. There was a lot of blood, but Arthur understood a truth in his final moments: that he'd only borrowed it anyway. Whether it was on the floor of his cell or in his body, it wasn't his. Like everything, it belonged to God.

11

Hopkins walked through the deserted distillery with the shotgun loaded. In one pocket of his wax jacket, he had a box of shells; in the other, a pewter flask full of whisky. According to a dusty map he had found in the manager's study, on the other side of the estate there was the old chapel. He negotiated his way to the northern gate, which was hanging off its hinges. Its wrought-iron spikes aimed like harpoons into the blubbery clouds on the horizon. Lifting the shotgun, he pointed it into the deserted wilderness that lay before him and headed for the heather-spotted hills.

When he had descended the north face of the ridge, he came to a glen where huge pines formed a maze of creaking branches and moving shadows. Hopkins took a swig from his hip flask and proceeded.

It turned out that the glen provided some much

needed respite from the wind, allowing him to feel his fingers again. After an hour, he could hear the waves crashing on the rocks and was able to see the chapel through the trees. It lay about two hundred yards away from the cliff's edge on an elevated patch. The storms had almost ruined it, but the cross remained atop the spire. As Hopkins drew closer, he could see that there had been repairs made to the building, most of them somewhat shoddy. He pushed the heavy, riveted door open and stood in the vestibule, sniffing the air.

Smoke. Sweet, like pipe tobacco. Wooden Boards covered most of the stained glass windows, but there were still a few cracks, which created shafts of sunlight in the smoky air. Hopkins walked towards the altar, on top of which was a large and heavy-looking gold cross.

'Hello? Is there anyone here?'

From behind him came a voice. 'Don't move or I'll shoot you in the back.'

Sounded Glaswegian. The shadow on the red carpet in front of Hopkins was twice as wide as his own. He remained still while the shadow took a step or two closer.

'Beretta? Very fucking la-de-da. Put it down on the pew to your right and walk forward six steps.'

'But—'

'I wouldn't argue,' the shadow said, pressing the barrel of his gun into Hopkins' spine.

Hopkins placed the shotgun on the wooden pew

and walked forwards, closer to the altar's gold cross.

'Alright, turn around,' the shadow ordered and picked up Hopkins' shotgun.

Hopkins saw a hulking, wild-haired man in a ragged Crombie with a stick in one hand and the Beretta in the other.

'Much fancier than mine.' The man threw the stick aside and lifted the shotgun with both hands, turning Hopkins' insides cold. 'Now, what are you doing in here with this thing?'

'I bought this island. This is my island.'

'Suppose this is your church, as well?'

The waves crashed far below the cliff and the chapel door creaked as the two men glared at each other.

The Glaswegian's hands didn't tremble at all under the weight of the heavy shotgun. Like Hopkins, he was tall and in his forties, but carried the bulk of a rugby forward. His bulging overcoat bore shoddy repairs like the chapel. He shifted his army boots in the grit on the marble floor. The fact that they were shined to perfection suggested that he was ex-military.

They reminded Hopkins of Andrew, bringing the smell of his boot polish back to him.

'Get on with it, then. I don't give a damn anymore.' Hopkins sat on a right-side pew facing the altar, turning his back on the Glaswegian. He stiffened up, waiting for the boom of the shotgun.

The Glaswegian lowered the barrel. 'Don't be so dramatic, you wee bufty. Did you really buy this island?'

'Yes.'

The waves crashed while a torn union jack flag clinked on its mast outside the window.

'How much?'

'Five million.'

The Glaswegian burst out laughing. 'Things that bad on the mainland, aye?'

'For some people.'

'For you?'

Hopkins didn't respond.

'Drink?' The big man held up a three-quarter full bottle of Aberlour while still pointing the shotgun at Hopkins' gut.

'Got my own,' muttered Hopkins as he took a swig from his flask.

The Glaswegian sat in a left-side pew, opposite Hopkins. He rested the Beretta on top of some dusty hymn books and drank from his bottle. It wasn't that he didn't want the Glaswegian's whisky, but he needed his routine, his Laphroaig. Fluctuation either way in the volume of alcohol could upset the balance of the cosmos itself. He required consistency in his debauchery. Also, the stranger had pointed Hopkins' own shotgun at him. And called him a bufty, whatever that meant.

'Do you believe in God?'

Hopkins shifted in the pew and looked sideways at the Glaswegian, who was leaning forward to catch his eye. 'Maybe. I don't know. Give me my gun back and let me think about it.'

'Bit naughty, bringing this in here, don't you think?'

'What do you care? Who the hell are you?'

'I'm the chaplain, you cunt.'

The waves kept on crashing while dust settled in the stained sunlight.

Hopkins studied the man's face for any sign that he might be lying, but there was none. He was a few years younger than Hopkins, but he looked older around the eyes. He had that explosive air about him that Hopkins had seen so many times before when treating victims of trauma. The chaplain might have moved and talked like syrup, but men like him could go off like nitroglycerine.

'You ex-military? The boots give you away.'

'I was a chaplain for special forces out in Damascus when the floods hit,' he said, his hard features softening for a moment. 'Came back home and there was no-one left.'

'Sorry to hear that. I'm David Hopkins.'

The Glaswegian lowered the shotgun and reached out his hand cautiously, keeping his eyes fixed on Hopkins as he did so.

'Sorry about the welcome. I've been alone here a while. I'm McCole.'

'Why didn't you go back to work for the church on the mainland?' Hopkins shook his hand, but was already wondering how to get him off the island.

'They didn't want me back because of my service

61

record. Too many kills.'

'What about the military?'

'Not enough kills.'

'Why did you come here?'

'I've been coming to this chapel since I was a wee boy. My family lived in the valley over there.' McCole pointed to the empty expanse of sea. 'This is the closest to home I can get.'

Hopkins still wanted him off his island, but did not know how to say it. He could feel his plan going awry already.

'I can show you the best fishing spots all the way round the island.'

'I won't be here that long.'

'Just passing through?'

'Just passing through.' Hopkins took a drink from his flask. 'You can stay on the island as long as you respect my privacy.'

'No problem. Want me to show you those fishing spots?'

Hopkins picked up his shotgun and walked away.

'Shame. I've got an 18 year Laphroaig here I've been waiting to get rid of.'

Hopkins stopped in his tracks.

'Been sitting there since I came back here. Can't stand the stuff myself. I'll go and get it.'

McCole ran back into the chapel and emerged a minute later with the bottle. He handed it to Hopkins and slapped him on the back.

'You can't stand it?' Hopkins dusted off the label.

'What's wrong with you?'

'It's fine if you like drinking fucking cough medicine.'

'About these fishing spots … Have you got gear?'

'Stashed in the vestibule.'

The Laphroaig tasted sweet and smoky on Hopkins' lips as they walked the coastline to a large cove. He followed the chaplain over the cliffs and on to the rocks, fishing at different spots with varying degrees of success.

Later, they zigzagged back to the distillery full of whisky, laughing and smoking roll-up cigarettes. As dusk fell, so did the temperature, forcing them to stagger more quickly. A few snowflakes drifted by their faces as they arrived at the gates, which Hopkins unlocked with the key.

'Come on in and we'll cook this up,' he slurred, holding up the bag of salmon.

'What about your privacy?' McCole held on to the gate to steady himself.

'You can't even stand up.'

'Fair enough.'

They spent the evening eating, drinking and smoking by the warmth of the house's hearth. Even as McCole became more drunk, he still had enough manners not to pry into Hopkins' reasons for buying the island. Or why he drank. Or where his family was. This was the kind of respect for his privacy he had meant and he appreciated that McCole was good enough to honour his promise. Hopkins thought he had escaped any interrogation at all, when the chaplain broke the silence.

'How did you get here?'

'By boat.'

'Somebody brought you?'

'No, I sailed it myself,' Hopkins drained his glass and refilled it with water this time.

'Fuck off.' McCole slurped his whisky. 'From where?'

'Leeds.'

'So, you're Sigmund Freud and fucking Popeye all rolled into one?'

'I am what I am.'

Hopkins watched the snow piling up against the pane.

'You're welcome to stop here for the night, McCole, but I've got work to do in the morning.'

McCole was already asleep up against the wall in the corner of the room. His snoring forced Hopkins upstairs and into the master bedroom, where it was cold enough to see his breath. His muted complaints wisped in the icy air as he made a cocoon of the raggedy blanket. Despite having warmed to the chaplain over the course of the day's fishing and drinking, Hopkins slept with the shotgun loaded and the door locked.

12

Lucky still couldn't grasp what he had experienced. Everything had changed. Even the train on which he was travelling home felt like it was bound for some cosmic destination.

Colours.

Smells.

The feel of things.

All changed.

Grosvenor's arteries throbbing in his grip had felt more real than his own heartbeat. And now he felt hypersensitive to everything. It made him nervous that the medical staff had given guests personal alarms to activate should they feel unwell.

But he didn't feel unwell at all. He felt exhilarated and rejuvenated.. The laborious security routine to get into his apartment block was a welcome reminder of reality, having been somewhere so exotic. Retinal scan, thumbprint and good old-fashioned key. Not that the crime-rate was high in Sheffield, but it seemed to be that way around Lucky lately. Since the imposition of martial law, crime rates had fallen to almost zero in the capital. The rest of the country was a different story, though: the farther away from Sheffield, the more lawless it became. According to the Grosvenor Times, the red-zoned Isle of Dartmoor was the most dangerous place of all. The article claimed that the island still held inmates from the prison. And that they had survived by eating the villagers.

After the floods, Sheffield had expanded to accommodate almost five million refugees and Lucky was glad to be one of them. Better than being crab food or clinging on to life in some wintry outpost in the Highlands, waiting for the next natural disaster.

He pushed his kitchen door open and went straight to the fridge for a beer. Flicking through the endless channels of Grosvenor's shit on the TV, he came across an advert for Totem. The irony of seeing it advertised on a screen, powered by electricity and seen by the physical eye, made Lucky laugh. It all seemed so primitive compared to what he had just experienced. He felt as if the top if his head might come off and spill out thoughts and feelings like paint all over the floor.

In a deep voice, the advert ran thus: Grosvenor Media is proud to present the next step in reality programming with Totem. Like nothing you've ever seen. Live the dream.

Lucky's 1980's hamburger phone rang and he picked up the receiver, handling the antique with care, as he always did:

'So, can we do a deal, Mr. Newman?' Alice Grosvenor's voice sounded more serpentine the older she got. 'I want you to come and work for me. For Totem.'

'I still have questions.'

'Questions?'

He pulled a recording device from his desk drawer. 'Any adverse effects on the subjects themselves?'

'There is a risk, of course, but prisoners' enrolment in the Totem programme is entirely voluntary.'

'What kind of risk?' Lucky clicked the record button on his dictaphone and held it to the earpiece.

'Serotonin depletion can cause problems post-transmission. And some subjects have displayed sensitivity during the transmission process … To certain frequencies.'

'Sensitivity?'

'Cardiac sensitivity.'

'You mean heart attacks?'

Silence.

'What is the survival rate for subjects?'

'Eighty per cent during the process.'

'What about after transmission?'

Silence again.

'Hello?'

'Forty per cent,' she responded. 'But no ill-effects

for those tuned in to the transmissions.'

'And what does David Hopkins think about this bastardisation of his work?'

'Mr. Newman, I would urge you to think before you come crashing down on us with your typewriter. Think about what this could mean. I'm sure Doctor Hopkins would have no issue with our implementation of his work. We've simply amplified his design.'

'How will you monetise it?'

'We have already installed more than 100 Totem masts in the most populated areas across the Isles. The closer the user to it, the more intense the transmission.'

'What is the transmission? A dream?'

'Halfway between an NDE and a dream, to put it simply. If you want those details, you should speak to—'

'NDE?'

'A Near Death Experience.'

'And how do you simulate that?'

'Dimethyltryptamine and MAOI inhibitors. IV needle for the subject; champagne flute for guests; gas canisters in the pods. The brain recalibrates to bring about the synchronisation of wave patterns.'

'You've lost me.'

'Think of starlings in flight: they align, synchronise and appear to fly as one.'

'A murmuration …'

'How do you feel?'

'Murmurated.'

'But no ill effects?'

'Not yet.'

'We need you on our side, Mr. Newman. It's a big leap forward. We need you to make it work: the public trust Lucky Newman to tell them the truth more than anyone.'

'I still have questions.'

'Wheels are in motion for the first public transmission this Saturday. Should we keep your pod for you?'

'Who is it?'

'Sociopath up for double murder. Used to work for the intelligence services.'

'If he worked for intelligence, surely there's a danger he might disclose sensitive information?'

'We take steps to ensure that doesn't happen.'

'You can control the dreams?'

'It's a filtration process. In the interests of national security, of course … Should we expect you, Mr. Newman?'

Lucky didn't answer.

'Let bygones be bygones, Newman. We aren't the big bad wolves you've made us out to be in the past.'

'You tried to have me killed.'

Lucky heard his staircase creak. He pulled a snub-nose .38 revolver from his desk drawer and pointed it towards his front door.

'My father always said that one should let sleeping dogs lie.'

'Spare me, Alice,' he replied, cocking the hammer.

'Whatever you might perceive our previous misunderstandings to be, I think you can see the potential in Totem now.'

Lucky knew that it was going to change everything.

'I'll be there.'

He put the receiver down, but not the gun.

Not until the footsteps creaked away from his front door and back down the staircase.

13

Orphans didn't come much younger than John Muldoon. The newborn smiled at his pink toes as he breathed the warmth of his incubation chamber. Looking past the wires and bleeping machines, he watched the white ghosts floating past the doorway. A darker figure stopped at the door, looked both ways and came into the room. The shadow came close enough to block out the light from the corridor, then sank back into a chair and held its head in its hands. This was the third time that the shadow had done this and walked away shaking its head. This time, the shadow spoke into a telephone.

'Marm? Chandler. It's done.'

It picked up the clipboard at the end of the incubator, ripped a sheet out and clipped another in place. The shadow clopped away for the last time.

John continued to observe his toes until he fell

asleep.

When he woke up, John saw myriad shapes and colours as shadows wheeled him out of the warmth. The flashing blue lights and the continuous burble of voices made him smile. The burble turned to laughter every time he did it, so he kept smiling.

'How could anyone abandon him?'

'It's getting worse in Leeds. Half a dozen abandoned a week there and they're just the ones we hear about.'

'What will happen to him?'

'Care. Social Services. You know.'

The other shadow was silent.

'Listen, you can't do this every time. Stop thinking about it.'

'I know, but that word care. You hear such things.'

'Are you going to take in every baby that turns up on the hospital doorstep?'

'No, but I ...'

'Look, I know you're new to this, but you're gonna have to toughen up, ok? Let's just do our jobs.'

The green shadow rested its hand on the other's shoulder before calling ahead to have the orphanage open the gates.

'Row, row, row your boat gently down the stream.'

'Merrily, merrily, merrily, merrily …'

When the ambulance's engine died, John Muldoon felt a biting coldness. Fear covered him like a blanket as they wheeled him into the dark building. He cried to let the shadows know that something was wrong, but nobody answered his pleas.

'Life is but a dream.'

14

John walked towards the cluster of other kids to get a look out of the window on the top floor of the care home. Most were frightened by his scars and the stories they had heard about him. When he asked if he could have a look, they stepped aside and stared at the seams of dark, puffy tissue running across his face. He tried to smile, but that seemed to frighten the little ones even more.

Looking out of the window, he saw a long black car parked by the care home. It was that time again already. John's cheeks became wet with tears and his hands shook as the same woman as last time got out of the car. She wore sunglasses on her hooked nose and bright red lipstick on her thin lips. He raised his finger to his right eyebrow and pretended to smooth it to hide his tears, but the other kids knew. They'd already cleared a six-foot radius around him.

'What if they take one of us this time?'

'It's always him.'

'What do they do to him?'

'He never tells.'

'Why do they do it?'

'It's because he doesn't have a real name.'

'John Doe isn't his name?'

'That's what they call someone when they don't know it.'

The soft voice of one of the carers called out from the doorway. 'John, come with me, love.'

Miss Roach held out her pale hand. John turned to the other kids, but they were all looking at their shoes or pretending to tidy their beds.

'It'll be alright, I promise. No-one's going to hurt you.'

John put his trembling hand in hers and walked with her out of the room, looking back to see if everyone else was still staring at their shoes. Sure enough, they refused to look at him.

In the corridor, Miss Roach broke into a run, pulling John along with her. They ducked into one of the rooms halfway down, leading into an office full of books that John had never seen during his year at the care home. A big, old desk looked out over the grounds. Good for hiding underneath. On it were various dusty books and antique stationery.

'What's happening, Miss Roach?'

'I'm getting you out of here, John. I won't be a part of this. I won't let them hurt you anymore.'

'They'll hurt you.'

Footsteps clomped and creaked on the main staircase in the hallway. Her hands were shaking so much that she could barely get the key in the lock for the door. Beyond was a wrought iron fire escape leading down to the landscaped gardens of the home. The key didn't work, so she tried another.

'They won't catch us.' She turned a key in the lock. As it unlatched, a big man in a suit burst in from the corridor.

'Give the boy to me. Police,' he said, holding out an ID wallet as he stalked closer.

John noticed how white his teeth were. 'You work for Grosvenor.'

The man lunged and spilled all three of them out on to the small metal balcony. He had one hand grabbing John's collar and the other around Miss Roach's throat, sliding her over the 40-foot drop on to the concrete below. Her legs thrashed against him so much that one of her shoes came off and fell over the edge. John realised that the man only had a grip of his hoody, so he unzipped it and wriggled free. Miss Roach's legs spilled over the edge and she screamed, but managed to hold on to the railings. John took a letter-opener from the desk and buried it in the man's back, creating a bloody patch in the smooth fabric of his jacket. While their attacker struggled to extract the knife, John knelt down to Miss Roach, who was now clinging on to the iron platform by her fingertips.

'Run.'

As she said the word, she lost her grip and fell to

the ground. John took to the spiralling steps of the fire escape. On his descent, he could see that the circle of blood around Miss Roach's head was growing. The foot that still had a shoe was twitching and she was making a sound like she was drinking the last of a milkshake. As he reached the bottom of the staircase, he looked up and saw the man in the suit clanging his way down the iron spiral. Doing as Miss Roach had told him, John ran as fast as he could into the maze of sculpted hedges and walled gardens. As he rounded his third corner at speed, he crashed into a kneeling groundskeeper, knocking a garden fork out of his hand. John picked up the fork and backed away, pointing it at the man as he did so.

He wasn't going back to the home. No way. He wasn't sure if he actually said these words to the man, but he was thinking them. The groundskeeper held up his hands and smiled at him before John carried on running further into the maze.

'Your next stop will be the borstal, lad,' he called after John, which made him run even faster. Even the older boys in the home were scared of borstal, especially the one in Leeds. John continued towards the setting sun until he couldn't run any further. He slowed down to catch his breath and listened for any footsteps chasing him. Apart from his panting and the birds singing, there was nothing.

He tried to run, but the man in the suit erupted from the hedgerow and lifted him off the ground. John thrust the garden fork into the man's face and felt it sink in and stick there. The man yelled and dropped him, clutching at the wooden handle sticking out of his bloody eye socket.

John hurtled through the dusk's shadows to the end of the maze. His heart felt like it stopped when he saw the long black car and three more men in suits waiting for him.

A. J. REID

15

Hopkins looked at his watch. McCole was late again for his shift at the distillery. Sighing, he checked the temperature of the mash and took his wax jacket from the peg by the door. He had to walk all the way across the moor to the church, where the oaf still insisted on sleeping. Hopkins thought of how many mornings of the last sixteen years he'd had to do this and shook his head. Sometimes, he felt more like McCole's father than his business partner. And friend, Hopkins begrudgingly admitted to himself.

When he reached the chapel's door, Hopkins noticed that the oak needed varnishing again already. He'd thought that renovating the chapel for McCole would stop him drinking, but it had been to no avail. The chaplain had continued to drink at least a bottle every day since Hopkins arrived on the island all those years ago. And lately, it had become worse. Two bottles a day were now going missing from the crates in the warehouse and he wasn't showing up on time, if at all. Hopkins knocked on the peeling wood.

No reply.

He pushed the door open and saw McCole lying on the altar. An empty bottle of whisky rested up against the first row of pews. The fact that his snoring wasn't reverberating about the place concerned Hopkins. Usually, he was able to hear him on approach to the church, even through the thick stone walls.

Hopkins called into the silence. 'McCole?'

The chaplain lay motionless, one booted leg trailing down the red-carpeted steps leading to the altar. Hopkins began to fear the worst: that he would be left alone on the island, having failed to prevent yet another suicide.

He shook the chaplain's shoulder. 'McCole?'

Hopkins held his ear to the chaplain's mouth, but there was no breath. He rested his fingers on the carotid artery to check for a pulse and was relieved to feel the thud of blood under the cold skin. Hopkins rolled all 300 ursine pounds of the unconscious McCole on to his side and thumped him between the shoulder blades. The chaplain's boiler suit heaved as he retched and vomited all over the altar, unblocking his tongue from his airway. Hopkins wondered whether anything quite as absurd as this might be occurring elsewhere in the world at that moment.

'Jesus Christ,' spluttered McCole.

'Only me,' Hopkins replied. 'You're late for your

shift. Good job you're already dressed.'

'Fucking slave driver.'

'No-one else would have you.' Hopkins tried to hide his relief at McCole being alive. 'I'm docking you the morning's wages.'

'Are you for real, Hopkins?'

'And I'm moving you into the house with me.'

'No way.'

'Until you stop drinking so much. We were down two bottles on Friday.'

'Matched your record then, didn't I?'

'I never swallowed my own tongue,' Hopkins countered.

'I've never swallowed my own tongue either.'

'You did just now. If I'd arrived two minutes later, you'd be brain-dead.'

McCole tried to peel himself off the altar and brought the cross and candlesticks clattering to the stone floor. 'Bollocks.'

'Not that it would make much difference.'

'Fuck off, Hopkins, you cheeky bastard.'

McCole tried to extricate himself from the altar. He stood on one foot to free the snagged fabric in his boot, but lost his balance and toppled into the choir stalls with another crash. When the last stall had fallen, a faint groan emanated from beneath them.

'Pack some stuff and bring it with you. You can have the spare room.'

McCole remained under the fallen choir stalls. 'Why won't you let me die in peace?'

'Just returning the favour. And by the way, my record is three bottles in one day.'

McCole reached out from beneath the choir stall. 'Gis a hand.'

'I've got to get back to the mash. See you back at the distillery.'

'You're a fucker, Hopkins,' McCole shouted after him. 'Cheers.'

Back at the mash-house, McCole entered sheepishly, closing the door behind him. 'Sorry, Hopkins.'

Hopkins didn't take his eyes off the mash. 'It's alright.'

'If you want me to leave the island …'

'You say that every time. Where would you go?'

'I don't know.'

'Just lay off the drink. It's no good for either of us.'

'You want me to go cold turkey?'

'We've tried it every other way,' Hopkins shrugged, adjusting a lever. 'Or do you think faith might not carry you through?'

'Passive-aggressive twat.'

'Just saying you should practise what you preach.'

'Fine. I'll go cold turkey, but if I drop dead, it's your fault.'

Hopkins didn't look up.

'I didn't mean anything by it.'

'It's fine, McCole. We'll square this batch away and

go have some dinner. When was the last time you had a good meal?'

'Last time I was at the house, which was ...' McCole counted on his thick oil and tobacco stained fingers. 'Christmas.'

Hopkins had set the table with three tall candles, which flickered and made the cracks in the ancient oak look like dark ravines. They cast a magnified shadow of McCole against the far wall as he pushed his food around his plate.

'Not hungry?'

'It smells good, Hopkins. I'm just not feeling well.'

'You want some more water?'

'I wouldn't mind a proper fucking drink, I'll tell you,' he said, holding his shaking hands in his lap.

Hopkins didn't look up from the glass into which he was pouring the water.

'I said I wouldn't mind a drink,' McCole repeated, louder this time.

'I heard what you said.'

'It needs salt.' He tried to weave a shaking hand between the candles for the salt cellar.

'Here, let me help you.' Hopkins reached out his hand to pick it up.

'I don't need any help.' McCole snatched for the cellar, knocking two of the candles over and spilling their wax into the gravy boat.

Hopkins felt particularly aggrieved by this as he had gone to some trouble over the gravy, a luxury he rarely enjoyed. Still, he held his temper. 'Don't worry.'

'I'm not worried.'

'Here's that salt you wanted.'

'I don't want any salt,' McCole sulked as he cut a boiled potato in half, scooped up some gravy and forked it into his mouth.

There was silence for several minutes while McCole chewed each tiny morsel in turn.

'How's that gravy?'

'Tastes like arse.'

'If you can't even be civil anymore,' Hopkins said, placing down his cutlery and wiping his mouth with his napkin. 'Maybe you should leave the island.'

'Let me have one last drink, Hopkins. I'll be fine after that.'

'No. We agreed.'

'You think that if you dry me out, the nightmares about Andrew will stop.'

'Don't you dare,' Hopkins warned. 'Not tonight.'

'I'm not your salvation, Hopkins, nor your project.'

Hopkins blushed with anger as he smoothed his eyebrow.

'Or is this about Totem again? Grosvenor's miracle machine? She couldn't have done it all without you,' laughed McCole. 'Nice job, Doctor.'

'I didn't know …'

'You could have guessed. Bright bloke like you. Didn't you used to be that famous scientist, Doctor David Hopkins?'

'It's not like despots have never used religion to get what they want. Burning witches at the stake in town squares? Remember a little thing called the Spanish Inquisition? Your lot did worse than Totem.'

'Burning witches was more humane.'

'Don't be absurd, McCole.' Hopkins shook his head and forked another potato into his mouth.

'Some of the horror stories I've heard about Totem, I don't know. Maybe there is no redemption for you, after all?'

Hopkins stood up from the table and threw down his napkin. 'It's a drink you want, is it?'

'With ice.'

Hopkins went to the sideboard cabinet, withdrew a bottle of their own whiskey and slammed it down on the table. 'You can have that, but it'll be the last bottle of whiskey you drink on this island. I want you gone by noon tomorrow.'

'Fine,' McCole said, unmoved by Hopkins' outburst.

'You can take the Starry Night. There's enough fuel in her to get you to the mainland. I suggest you get a good night's sleep: it's a long trip.'

McCole uncorked the whisky. 'I'll sleep fine now.'

'Good luck.' Hopkins reached out for a handshake from McCole, who obliged as he chugged from the bottle of scotch. 'And goodbye.'

McCole nodded from behind his bottle and tipped his head back further to drain more of the whiskey.

Hopkins stormed out of the dining room and

climbed the stairs to his bedroom. Each step brought him closer to an even more desolate existence alone on the storm-battered rock. The past sixteen years babysitting McCole had been testing, but at least he was still alive. Hopkins had come to this island to die, but McCole had somehow prevented that. When the oaf wasn't too full of whiskey, he sometimes betrayed the considerable wisdom knocking about in his thatched head. Especially when it came to Andrew's suicide.

After he lay down on his bed, Hopkins heard McCole creak across the landing and into the spare room, slamming the door behind him. Hopkins pulled his blanket over his shoulders and rolled over. The dusty shotgun stood in the corner as usual - as if it were nothing more dangerous than an umbrella.

Hopkins remembered the first time they had a successful run at the distillery. The pair of them danced on the cobbles of the courtyard when they tasted the batch, it was that good. Every few months, they would load the Starry Night and sail her to the mainland to barter for supplies from locals and cash from the taverns. There hadn't been any need for hunting or fishing since they'd been trading, which saddened Hopkins, but their whiskey was making money, at least. He even bought a Lynx helicopter to accommodate the demand, but McCole hated it. He swore that he would never set foot in it again after its maiden flight around the island, so they continued to deliver their product by sea. For years, this feat of engineering had remained wrapped in tarpaulin on the helipad. Hopkins smiled as he remembered how McCole had shrieked with terror when he banked towards a mountain on their first and only flight together. And the time that he nearly blew his own foot off with the shotgun. Only that morning, the man had destroyed his own altar. Hopkins' smile faded as he remembered that come noon the next day, his old friend would be gone for good. He struggled to drop off to sleep, worried that he'd made a terrible mistake.

Hopkins woke to the sound of the out-house door slamming, expecting the customary retching to follow from within the tiny stone shed. He lay on his back to listen with both ears, but there was no sound except the wind whistling and the snow patting against his window.

Ten minutes passed before he got out of bed and looked out. The out-house lantern glowed around the weather-warped edges of the wooden door. The latch rattled, but there were no shadows to indicate any movement. Hopkins lifted his window and braced himself as snowflakes blew into his shirt. Through the night came quiet sounds of anguish. Stifled sobs were coming from the tiny shed. Hopkins stuck his head out of the window to listen, but drew back when McCole came spilling out of the wooden box. From behind the curtain, Hopkins watched his friend stagger towards the house with the shotgun in hand.

Looking to the corner where the gun had sat for many dusty years, Hopkins saw that it was gone. As he heard McCole open the kitchen door to come back into the house, Hopkins closed the window as quietly as he could and tip-toed back to his bed. As he got under the covers, he heard his door creaking open. With his back to the door, he could see McCole's shadow cast on the wall.

It occurred to Hopkins that the disturbed chaplain might have decided to take the island for himself. He watched the shadow move silently to the corner where the shotgun had been. Just as Hopkins thought the shadow was about to leave, it stopped at the foot of his bed and lingered for a moment. Despite the adrenaline surge, Hopkins remained still and quiet until McCole finally left, closing the door behind him.

A few seconds later, Hopkins sat upright and peered into the dark corner of the room. The shotgun was back in its original position, its barrel catching the moonlight. He climbed out of bed and crept over to the corner to pick up the weapon. Breaking the barrel, he saw that it was still loaded. His heart raced as he considered what his life would have been like had McCole actually blown his own head off in the out-house. He pulled the cartridges out and threw them in a drawer, shaking his head at the terrible thought of McCole using them on himself. After locking the shotgun in its safe, he hid the key under his pillow and rested his exhausted head on top of it.

The next morning, Hopkins knocked on McCole's door to no answer. He opened it to find the bed made and the chaplain nowhere to be seen. He went back to his room, put on a pair of pants and ran downstairs for his boots and jacket. Opening the front door, he could see McCole's tracks in the snow and followed them down to the harbour. As he rounded the last building of the distillery, he saw McCole heaving a suitcase on to the Starry Night, preparing to set sail.

Hopkins shouted across the harbour as he jogged towards the boat, 'McCole, hold on.'

McCole ignored him and started hauling the anchor.

'Let that anchor back down. Just wait a minute.'

'I've been here too long.'

'Don't leave. I'm sorry for what I said.'

'Hopkins, you shouldn't be apologising to me. I was a bastard. And after what you've done for me all these years.'

'You don't have to stop drinking. You can stay.'

McCole stopped hauling. 'You're serious?'

'I'm always serious, McCole. You ought to know that by now.'

'I'll cut down.'

'And turn up for your shifts.'

'I'll be there early.'

'Small steps,' Hopkins replied with a cynical lift of his eyebrow. 'Pass me your suitcase.'

McCole threw the suitcase to Hopkins, who reeled

under its weight.

'What the hell is in this thing?'

Hopkins laid it on the snow-covered ground and unzipped it to find a dozen bottles of scotch wrapped up in straw. He glared at his friend.

McCole shrugged. 'Supplies.'

16

Sixteen-year-old John Doe woke up in complete darkness, as he had done for the past three days. His goal for today was the same as it had always been: to survive. He'd been in Leeds borstal since he was ten for pushing a carer off a fire escape and taking out the eye of a police officer. He was the youngest person ever to be admitted to a borstal facility.

This time, they were accusing him of something even worse, so they moved him to Exmoor for assessment. It was something so bad that they called in a psychologist, who wanted to find out whether John might qualify for Dartmoor, despite his age. He felt certain that he'd never murdered anyone, but John had learnt some time ago that this meant nothing. His own interpretations of reality could not be trusted. This had been hammered into his head by various authority figures wielding syringes, pills or gas canisters for some time. Sometimes, he had difficulty telling his nightmares from reality. He could not trust himself, but then he could not trust anyone.

Guards dragged John from his cell and sat him in a darkly-lit room with a table and two chairs. They shackled both of his hands to the table while a man in a grey suit with a mean, thin face sat down opposite him with a clipboard. He didn't look up when he spoke.

'Are you John Doe?'

'I don't know.'

'Why have you never chosen a name? It's your right, you know.'

'I don't know.'

The suit scribbled on his clipboard. Still he did not look up. 'Why did you kill the warden Thomas Parry?'

'I didn't.'

'How can you expect me to help you if you won't be honest with me, John?'

'They don't want me to leave. Ever. So they killed the warden and now they're pinning it on me.'

'Who are they?'

'Grosvenor,' replied John.

The man looked down at his Grosvenor ID badge.

'The woman with the black car killed my father.'

'How do you know that?'

'I saw it in a dream.'

The man rubbed his eyes and sighed. 'Paranoid delusions, John.'

'It's true.'

'What was your father's name?'

John did not answer. His fists tightened in the shackles as he remembered the consequences for speaking of his father last time.

'Then how do you know the man was your father?'

'I have the same dream every night. My father's not the only one. There's a boy. Older than me. She kills him, too.'

The man rotated and placed his clipboard on the table between John's shackled hands, so that he could read it. The details of each violent act were only words on a page to him. Crucifixion. Blood loss. Suffocation. DOA.

'What are you trying to achieve?'

'I want to know the truth.'

'That goes for all of us, John.'

John leaned his scarred face forward into the light, causing the psychologist to recoil. 'Does it?'

He didn't care whether they kept him in Exmoor or sent him to Dartmoor. In fact, he was hoping for Dartmoor. At least there, he would be free or dead. He'd always wanted to find out for himself whether the stories were true, anyway.

The man noticed that John had the fingers of his right hand crossed in the shackles. 'What are you wishing for?'

'Dartmoor.'

'This is no joke, John. You do realise that for a sixteen year old boy, Dartmoor is a death sentence?'

'Maybe that's what I want.'

'Look, if you work with me, I can get you into a

half-decent hospital facility, maybe even one on the mainland. If you don't, it's out of my hands.'

Silence.

'The Attorney General needs your co-operation; otherwise we have no choice but to send you to Dartmoor. We need details of your crimes. A confession would be the best thing here.'

Silence.

'It's no skin off my nose,' the man said, standing up with his clipboard. 'Good luck, John.'

John continued staring at the crossed fingers of his right hand as the man stopped at the door.

'One last chance.'

John uncrossed the middle finger of his restrained right hand and upturned it at the man.

Within three minutes of the suit leaving, John was hooded and sedated. While one guard teased John about the horrors of Dartmoor, another injected his left arm that crashed him out of consciousness in seconds.

17

John half-opened an eye to see that he was in a cage in the brig of a ship with two armed soldiers standing guard.

'Should just give the fucker a bullet now.'

'How did we end up doing this shit on Christmas Day, Davis?'

'At least the money's good, Biggs.'

'I make enough to get by. I can be doing without this on my conscience.'

'Yeah, right. Conscience,' Davis said, fiddling with the sight rail on his firearm. 'If he's lucky, he won't last the night.'

The ship rolled and the two men struggled to keep their balance. Biggs zigzagged over to the lockers and withdrew a small olive rucksack.

'It's Christmas,' Biggs said, stuffing various items from his locker into the bag.

'You'll get done for that.'

Biggs stared down Davis. 'Who's gonna find out?'

'Waste of good gear, if you ask me.'

Biggs hesitated for a moment before grabbing his machete from the locker and strapping it to the exterior of the rucksack.

'You can't be serious.'

'I have to sleep at night, Davis. Can't send him in there unarmed.'

'He crucified a warden on our watch. If it wasn't for this freak, I'd still have it cushy in Leeds instead of Exmoor. I'm sick of being this guy's babysitter.'

'I also heard that there was no evidence. Not a hair, not a skinflake. Fuck all.'

'Yeah? How come they're sending him to Dartmoor then?'

'Because this is the fourth murder he's been tagged for.'

'Jesus.'

Biggs raised an eyebrow at Davis. 'Yeah, he never denied or confessed or gave them anything, so here he is. No family, no name. Nothing. Sixteen years old.'

'He looks older.'

'You would too, man,' said Biggs, packing some large gauze dressings into the bag.

'Once he's gone, will they send us back to Leeds? Fucking hope so. Exmoor's a shit-hole.'

'Who knows?' Biggs shrugged. 'They'll do whatever they want with us.'

Davis changed the subject. 'You tuning in for the

transmission this Saturday?'

'I'm busy.'

'Yeah, right. Who's too busy for Totem?'

'Who is it anyway? Have they transmitted that minister yet?'

'No, that's next week. Shoebomb guy this week.'

'The one who ran into the Grosvenor building shouting Bible verses?'

'Solid gold nutcase. Should be good.'

'If he really was a nutcase, they couldn't transmit him. Could drive the whole country mad, as if things aren't bad enough.'

'You know what I mean.'

'I heard the guy never had any explosives on him at all.'

'Set-up? No-one gives a shit as long as it's a good transmission. He's not the first and he won't be the last.'

Biggs finished packing the rucksack from the locker and saw John standing up in the cage. 'Looks like someone's awake.'

Davis jumped back when he saw the boy.

'Water.'

Davis grabbed a plastic bottle of water from a locker and threw it into the cage like a lion keeper throwing meat. John unscrewed the cap and drank half of it in one go.

'Thank you.'

Biggs and Davis looked at each other before turning their backs on their prisoner and resuming guard positions.

'Are we going to Dartmoor?'

'We're under strict orders not to communicate with you, so shut up.'

Biggs pointed at John's face. 'How did you get the scars?'

'You're gonna get us both done. Chandler said no communication whatsoever.'

'This?' John raised his cuffed hands to his face and ran his fingers along the seams of the scars.

Biggs rolled up his sleeve and showed John the scar on his forearm. It looked like a rasher of raw bacon. 'Got this in Aleppo when I was captured. Lump hammer. Metal plate in there now,' he said, dinking at his arm with his knuckles.

John lifted his shirt and turned around to show the guards his back. Looking over his shoulder, he saw Davis balking into his hands, the MP5 swinging from his shoulder. Biggs gasped and the whites of his eyes shone in the brig's low light.

'I got these in a care home in Rotherham when I was seven. Bike chain. I passed out after the tenth stroke, but they kept going.'

While Davis tried to catch his breath, Biggs took his sidearm and stuffed it into the rucksack.

'I lost my family, too.'

'Grosvenor killed mine.'

'Grosvenor what? Grosvenor Medical? Grosvenor Security? Grosvenor Pharma? What?'

'The woman in the black car,' said John. 'She killed

my father. She did this to me.'

The guards stared at each other before Davis burst out sniggering. 'This guy's hilarious.'

'Shut up, Davis.'

John observed the guards. 'Do you know who Arthur is?'

'Last time he started banging on about Arthur, it cost us that cushy number in Leeds,' Davis complained. 'God help us if they ever run this guy up the Totem pole.'

'What's Totem?'

'You don't know what Totem is? Biggest thing since TV? You know what a TV is, right?'

'He's never been outside of an institution.'

John sat down in confused silence.

'Why do you keep talking about Arthur?'

'I think that was my father's name: Arthur Muldoon.'

'Your file says that you're a John Doe orphan. There's nothing to say you're related to anyone.'

The ship rolled, causing all three of them to stagger. Meanwhile, the steel hull groaned under the force of the storm outside.

'It was in my dream.'

'Must be true then,' Davis rolled his eyes and turned his back on John. 'Come on, Biggs. Let's leave him alone. It was you talking to him about this shit that got us red-flagged in the first place.'

'Did you do the things they say you did?'

'I don't know.'

A voice crackled through Biggs' radio, alerting all personnel that docking the ship was out of the question due to the weather. The voice then requested volunteers for the lifeboat mission.

Biggs was the only one.

'Merry Christmas, John Muldoon,' Biggs sighed, picking up the rucksack.

The two marines opened the cage and escorted John above deck, where the capsule lifeboat was ready for launch. Davis chained John to a seat at the rear of the craft, while Biggs took the captain's position, keeping the loaded rucksack by his feet. He waited until a voice crackled through the radio and pulled a lever, thrusting the capsule forward into the water below.

The landing was so rough that John's wrists bled in the handcuffs, his skin torn by the unforgiving steel.

Through the port hole, he saw that the craft was upright, at least. Biggs pushed the capsule into gear and steered towards the landing dock at the prison. John could make out the black building through the wind and rain against the grey skyline. He thought that he heard a baby's cries as they arrived in the shelter of a small landing dock.

No-one answered them.

Biggs opened the hatch and moored the craft next to a rusty ladder covered in green sea slime. He helped John on to the barnacled concrete and undid the handcuffs as per protocol. John rested his hands on the ladder as instructed, while Biggs strapped the rucksack to his back.

'Don't open this until you've reached the top of this ladder.'

'Thank you.'

Biggs shrugged. 'It's the best I can do. God's speed.'

John clasped the slimy bars and hauled himself upwards into the rain and the aching, grey light. Halfway, he looked down to see Biggs climbing back into the lifeboat capsule. He climbed up the ladder until he spilled out on to the sea wall, a sprawl of white, institutional pyjamas on grey concrete. The landing dock was next to the prison, with the first building about half a mile inland beyond a series of wire fences sporting inmate-sized holes. Some contained souvenirs of the jailbreak in their razor wire: little pieces of orange cloth torn from the uniforms of the inmates. The rags blew towards John, so he knew that he was downwind from any predators, at least. Snowflakes whipped into the pyjamas and plimsolls he was wearing, making him shiver violently.

John knew he had to find shelter, but the prison looked so black and foreboding that he couldn't bring himself to approach it. Crouching behind the wall, he rummaged through the rucksack. His fingers brushed a cold metal object. He withdrew the gun and held it up to the light to inspect it. He'd only ever seen them on the belts of various guards when he was being transported from one hellhole to another. It was heavy, cold and fit into his hand perfectly. So much so that he didn't let it go whilst rummaging in the bag for food. He found a waterproof olive green poncho, which kept him warm and dry while he ate the ration biscuits and tested the torch. He strapped on the rucksack and walked away from the prison, keeping the setting suns on his left cheek and the pistol in his hand. The only living creatures John saw or heard were the seagulls fighting above the sea wall. Looking inland, he saw a barn standing alone in a field. He'd been walking for hours, so he calculated that he must be at least a few miles from the prison. He climbed over a rusty gate and began walking towards the barn under the crescent moonrise.

John pushed open the rusty corrugated iron door, walked into the darkness and lit up the barn with the torch. The respite from the wind and rain was welcome as he sat and shivered on a large brick of dry, yellow grass. He laid the gun to his right and the rucksack to his left, hopelessly trying to warm up by pulling the dripping poncho closer around him. He dug further into the rucksack for more clothing, but found nothing. Instead, he found a small metal box, which broke open to reveal a white brick, a box of matches and an instruction leaflet. John followed the instructions and set fire to the corner of the brick. His hands stopped shaking as he absorbed the heat. Later, he found that by adding the dry grass, he could make it warmer and brighter.

Searching the barn, he found a rusty barrel and an old wooden beam leaning in a corner. He used the big knife on the beam, creating splinters mostly, but enough to keep the fire burning in the barrel so that he could get some sleep. John curled up on one of the huge yellow bricks of grass and pulled his poncho tight about him.

He dreamt of Arthur Muldoon again that night, as he had done every night since leaving Leeds. He dreamt of the times that had never been: Muldoon holding him as a child, teaching him things, walking with him, smiling at him. The dream would always end the same way, though: in darkness and pain, allowing John to hear but not answer his father's screams. As with every dream of his father, John would wake in the early morning with a thirst for vengeance.

18

Lucky Newman's nickname had become a millstone around his neck. Every time something like this happened, the irony was like salt in the wound. As he chased after the seagull carrying off his last chunk of bread into the grey skies, he rued the day that he turned down Alice Grosvenor's offer. Sixteen years he'd lasted on the streets of Leeds. Most only made six months, at most, before the whisky or the weather took them. The others on the streets thought he had lived up to his name, having stuck it out this far.

How wrong they were.

One of Muldoon's guards had leaked Lucky a video in exchange for a small bribe, but he had been unable to watch to the end. Arthur Muldoon's suffering appalled him, and Lucky knew that his conscience would not allow him to gloss over Grosvenor's crimes. He didn't show up for the next transmission and pulled no punches in detailing his reasons why in the following issue of The Serviceman.

He never thought that the article would put him on his knees in some dirty alleyway in Leeds sixteen years later, sobbing over a seagull flying off with his dinner.

He wiped his tears away, checked both ends of the alley and took the opportunity to shit while he could. As he squatted and strained, he could see the Totem mast glowing blue in the city centre, meaning it was Saturday night. Sixteen years ago, he had a girlfriend, bank account, identity, a life. Saturday night would have meant cocktails in a plush downtown jazz lounge. Or peacocking about some wealthy hypocrite's charity event in a tux. Now it meant time to find a nice, soft copy of the Grosvenor Times and head for the nearest alleyway.

The Totem toilet session had become something of a custom. It was the only time Lucky could guarantee that there would be no-one on the streets except other vagrants looking for a place to have a quiet dump. When the transmission mast glowed, those who could afford it would strap themselves into the pods around its base. Waiting with open mouths for the exotic pleasures of Totem; for their glimpse into the cosmos through another's consciousness. Those who couldn't afford it were in a squat position, contemplating the stink of their existence. One group in the filth; the other in the light.

That fucking light.

Lucky's stomach felt like it had shrunk to a walnut. The past few days, he had chosen whisky over food and now he felt like all he could manage was a cigarette. He'd planned to smoke half of it after his dinner, but since that was in some seagull's gut, he opted to smoke it now anyway, whilst no-one was around. He was fucking hangry, and that screaming gull was making it worse.

He reminisced about his favourite Chinese restaurant in Sheffield: always warm and low-lit, the air filled with the smell of spices. Everywhere Lucky went in the daydream, there were symbols of decadence. Duck pancakes with the strips of cucumber and spring onion. Beautiful hostesses with perfumed cleavage. The opulent golden dragon statues and the bottles of champagne on every other table. It was only a dream. Only a dream.

How different could seagull be from duck? He knew that pancakes, spring onions and tits were too big a request, so he forgot all that. Perhaps another day.

As for that screeching fucking gull, though.

It was all too much for him.

Lucky wiped with the newspaper and pulled up his pants. Flicking open his lock-knife, he headed in the direction of the high-pitched cries.

After his meal, Lucky returned to the canal covered in blood. The other hobos huddled around the flaming barrel didn't appear to notice. Even

Dickinson didn't look up from the fire dancing through his whiskey bottle as he spoke.

'Any luck, Lucky?'

'Seagull,' Lucky belched.

'You ate a fucking seagull?'

They laughed at Lucky as he retired to his sleeping bag in the old canal tunnel. 'Oi, Newman. You're not going to bed yet. We've still got some canal pike left over. Nice and greasy.'

'Fuck off.'

'Got some smoked bass left over from the shore yesterday, too.'

'Fucking fish. That's why I went: to get anything else.'

'You couldn't do better than a seagull?'

Lucky pulled out his lock-knife and washed the blood off in the canal. 'It pissed me off.'

'It's a seagull, mate.'

'It wouldn't shut the fuck up,' Lucky said, pretending to threaten Dickinson with the knife, and then vomiting into the canal.

'Hang on.' Dickinson rushed off into the darkness of the tunnel. He returned and held out a handful of heartburn tablets to Lucky.

'Ah, fuck that. Get us a drink. I need some whisky.'

'You don't need whisky. I'll get you some water.'

'Get me whisky as well!' Lucky burbled through the vomit, his head almost in the canal as he leaned over the edge.

Dickinson appealed to the others for whisky in vain, leaving Lucky to contemplate his reflection in the murky water. His hair had grown long and his face was gaunt and patched with raw dermatitis. Some days, he couldn't even remember his own name. He was losing it.

He knew it.

Everyone knew it.

Losing it.

Grosvenor would be proud of her handiwork. She would be nothing short of thrilled to know that he was down to chasing and eating seagulls for dinner. Shitting in alleyways and sleeping in canal tunnels. It was only a matter of time before he ended up like Mac. When Mac started the Bible thing, everyone knew something was wrong. He'd stitch pages from Revelations together and hang them in the underpass. Lucky didn't doubt that it meant something to Mac, but no-one wanted to be dragged down with him. People without Totem had no escape from reality. From the filth. Mac thought he had found a way to deal with it. The guy took things to heart. He couldn't block out the bad, especially if it involved children; and on the streets, he and Lucky had seen a lot of bad stuff involving kids. Leeds had become a real sewer after they built the checkpoints around Sheffield.

Mac wouldn't shut up about it and wouldn't sleep because he was too afraid of his dreams, which meant that everyone became afraid of his dreams. Lucky tried talking to him through a dozen sleepless nights, but he knew that Mac was already a lost cause.

One day, he woke up to find Mac's sleeping bag empty. No sign of a struggle and his duffle bag was still there. It was as if he'd got up in the middle of the night and walked away. Everyone gave a shit the first day; the second, no-one cared; and by the third, they were glad that he was gone. Some said that it was long overdue. And that they never liked him because he was a coward. Lucky reminded them of what Mac had done during the war. That shut them up for about ten minutes before they continued their acidic, whisky-soaked obituaries.

Every time someone left the group, it was the same, but Lucky had a bad feeling about Mac's disappearance. Gower had gone to relieve himself in the canal in the middle of the night and come back shaking with fear, covered in his own piss. He claimed that Mac's dead, bloated face had appeared in the spot where he was about to relieve himself. He said that the corpse had no eyes and that dark leeches were crawling out of their empty sockets. Everyone got up and ran with torches, following Gower to the exact spot, but found nothing. They comforted him and offered him whisky, but he refused everyone, saying over and over again that he wasn't crazy.

The next month another man found Gower in that same spot.

And on it went. It would catch up to everyone, eventually. The machines would be the only survivors. They would develop compassion and understanding through complex equations inconceivable to us. They'd weld together the information of every science with the emotions of every art to compute the meaning of life itself. They would take the best of our thoughts and memories and multiply them like embryonic cells until they become reality. And who would write the algorithm for this process? God Himself, of course. Even at the last second, as fire or water consumed the Earth, it would be a blood-filled, human hand locking the vaults against the desperate hordes.

And maybe God would stop that hand. Maybe He would save Them: the meek and the hopeless.

Or that's how Lucky had it worked out, at least, in his whisky-addled mind, which felt like it had shrunk to the size of a walnut.

The only thing moving in mysterious ways right then was Lucky's gut. He climbed into his sleeping bag knowing his dreams were going to be nightmares. They always were whenever he had a fever, even before he went to war. Even when he was a kid, fevers would bring out that sense of otherness. That sense that words couldn't explain. It was like going through a tunnel at high speed with lights and familiar faces flashing by, on their way to other destinations. He used to think about it more often: nowadays, he had enough on his plate just getting through the day.

Yeah, enough seagull on his plate.

Lucky Newman, expert in not thinking about stuff, tried to muffle the seagull's death cries as he cradled his bony abdomen and drifted off to sleep.

19

As soon as he woke, John picked up his gun and rucksack and headed for the open moors. During the night, he had packed some of the dry grass inside his poncho and, because the morning was so cold, decided to leave it in there. He cut a piece of paracord and tied it around his waist to keep the grass in place whilst he rambled across the barren landscape.

By the third day on the island, John was beginning to wonder whether he was being punished or rewarded by his banishment there. He hadn't yet braved the prison, but he had explored most of the island and hadn't seen or heard another human being. He had enjoyed more freedom in the last three days than he had in his whole life. However, his rations had almost run out and so had his fresh water supply. He checked the fishing kit, packed empty water bottles and made for the river he had found on the moors the previous day.

It had been raining overnight and John had never smelled anything like the wet soil and trees. He breathed deep all the way to the riverbank and sat under an old oak to give him some cover, should one of the inmates come strolling by.

He'd had to gut fish in the borstal kitchens, so he had no trouble with that once he'd caught one. Cooking it was trickier, but after a few failed experiments, he had it worked out. He wrapped the fish in leaves and left it in the embers of the fire. It only took a few minutes before John was able to unwrap the leaves and pick out the pink flesh. The hardest bit for him was killing them. John didn't like taking life from another living thing, but he had to eat. In his other hand, he still kept a tight grip on the gun while he finished the salmon. He couldn't take anything for granted, but he was finding it difficult not to enjoy his new-found freedom. Based on what he'd been told about Dartmoor, John thought that he would be dead by now.

The next day, John explored the higher ground on the moors, finding the first sign of life on land: a wild, white horse drinking from a small pool. He stopped in his tracks and held his breath, but he was upwind of the animal and it smelled him almost immediately. It looked at him for a moment before galloping away and John wished that he could have had more time to look at it. He'd only ever seen them on televisions in the care homes.

On his fishing trip the day after, John was sitting by the river with his makeshift rod of birch, when he heard footsteps coming in his direction. He hugged closer to the oak on the river bank to conceal himself, dangling over the clear, fast water. The footsteps drew closer and stopped short of the slope.

Through the foliage, John saw the horse for the second time.

Peeling himself away from the oak tree, he moved into the horse's field of view, which startled it. He climbed the riverbank to see that the horse had not run off into the moors again, but was waiting under another oak tree about 20 feet away. It watched John as he reached into his poncho for a clump of the dry grass. He held out his hand, offering the grass to the horse. John's heart fluttered as the animal drew a little closer, then a bit more, until it was only a few feet away. He saw that the horse's legs and face bore long scars and ran his fingers over his own face in sympathy. The horse snatched a mouthful of the grass and disappeared into a nearby wood.

It was the happiest feeling he had ever known.

Over the next week, John fed the horse every day at the river and each time the animal flinched a little less and ran away a little slower. Eventually, John was able to reach out his hand and stroke the horse's neck.

One morning, he heard munching and sure enough, the white horse was there, helping himself to dry grass bricks for breakfast. He harrumphed in

John's ear and nudged him with his nose, stirring him into full consciousness. John felt a warm sensation in his chest and couldn't stop laughing at first, until his head sank into his hands and he sobbed with confusion. Whenever John had felt even the smallest happiness, it had always been taken from him in the cruellest manner. John had learnt not to make friends in the care homes because they were always taken away. Or worse.

He shooed the horse away, but he would not move, so he reached into the rucksack and pulled out the gun. Firing a shot into the barn roof caused the white horse to bolt out of the barn and back towards the moors.

He didn't eat that day because he felt sick at chasing away the horse, but he knew that it was his only choice.

The next day, John opened his eyes to find the horse staring back at him. Needing food and water, he grabbed his rucksack and started walking to the river, shadowed by the stubborn animal. No point in wasting another bullet to scare him off: it seemed as though John had no choice about this friendship. He stopped and touched the worst scar on his face, as he tended to in times of stress. It was just above his right eyebrow and felt like a piece of rubber to his fingertips, since there was no feeling in the scar tissue itself. With the same fingers, he slowly reached out and touched a scar on the horse's cheek. It felt the same: like pain. The horse lifted up his head to shake

John's hand away, but John persisted and spoke soothingly. After a bray of annoyance, the animal settled down and allowed John to stroke him.

They walked on to the river together, John smiling from ear to half-ear. The other half had been flushed down a toilet at the borstal in Leeds a while ago when he had been held down and stanleyed. Those two boys were dead by his hand, according to the wardens and the doctors. John tried hard not to think about any of that as he grabbed at his half-ear. He and his new companion walked side by side towards the river.

Soon, John was able to ride the horse. He'd fallen off a few times, but every time the animal had been there waiting for John to get back up and try again. After a few days, he was comfortable enough to ride out beyond the river. They travelled a few miles north and came upon a small village, which seemed as deserted as the moors. John drew the pistol from his rucksack anyway as they clopped into the main high street.

He thought that the tarmac would hurt the horse's feet, so he climbed down and walked alongside, holding the gun out in front.

Not a window had been smashed. Nothing looted. There was no sign of anyone. John wasn't about to complain, but it was playing with his mind. Surely an island overrun with inmates would bear some mark of the event? John had fantasised about revolution in every institution he'd ever been in. He'd imagined it to be bloody and fiery. No sign of that here. Even the quaint little bookshop was still intact, although the sign had weathered to the point of falling apart. John stopped and wiped the dirty glass so that he could see inside. What he saw filled him with joy: the shelves were stocked full of dusty volumes.

In the home, books had been few and far between: most went to the schools and universities that were still above water. The TV consisted mostly of programmes about war, disaster and disease. When this wasn't scheduled, John had overheard screws in the borstal talking about Totem, though. Where they had once talked about other people doing something mad or evil on television, they now talked as if they themselves had done it.

John didn't understand and had no real reason to try: surviving every day without a shank or a razor to a major artery took enough effort. After what Davis had said about Arthur Muldoon, John wanted to know more about Totem. Now, he had a chance: there might even be a picture of Arthur Muldoon in one of the books.

Maybe he would recognise him straight away.

He shouldered the shop's door and the damp wood gave way at the hinges. The place smelled of ink and tobacco.

'You wait here, Arthur,' he said to the horse, whilst proceeding into the dusk-lit bookshop.

The floorboards creaked and the studs in the oxblood leather couch glimmered like deep-set jewels. The shop was a maze of shelves, filled with exotic treasures. Each book that John picked up made his head tingle with new information. He couldn't believe his luck. He placed one after the other into his rucksack and left the shop to find Arthur waiting patiently in the same spot he'd been before the suns had set.

They headed over the crossroads and came to a stone building with a wooden barn attached to it. Inside were more dry grass bricks on which Arthur could graze. In the adjoining stone building, John found all sorts of tools hanging on the walls and U-shaped pieces of metal strewn about the workbenches. A wood-burning stove made him remember the hours he'd spent chopping wood in the wind and rain as a punishment in the Rotherham home. One carer would make him do it without gloves in the snow, then cane his near-frostbitten hands when he had finished. John was glad to see a stack of firewood already chopped. He set a fire and warmed himself until he had embers on which to cook the leaf-wrapped trout in his rucksack.

Having eaten, he explored the rest of the building. He found a tin bath, a bed, some clothing and out back, a river. He made use of all of them over the following days. John learnt from the bookshop that the stone building was a blacksmith's forge. The same book taught him what the different tools were for, and he practised with them at the anvil to make shoes for Arthur. In a store room, he found a saddle, which made things more comfortable on their long journeys across the moors. He learnt quickly from the books, and it wasn't long before Arthur had his set of shoes.

Despite the many things he had learnt in the bookshop, John still had no further information on Arthur Muldoon. He wondered whether the dreams about Muldoon being his father were a withdrawal symptom from all the medication. A mere hallucination. A symptom of his madness.

As the weeks wore on, the dreams faded and John managed to push the idea to the back of his mind, as he did with many things. He thought about changing the horse's name, but couldn't think of anything else that suited him. Every night before bed, he would say goodnight to Arthur by holding his scars to the horse's.

John had never loved anyone or anything before, but when he thought of losing Arthur, he felt a sinking, sharp feeling in his stomach. He'd read about this feeling in poetry books from the bookshop, but had never known it. He learnt that the bond between humans and animals had always existed, with many cultures worshipping them as gods. And with that, John set about finding out what god meant. He read the Torah, the Koran, the Bible, the Bhagavad Gita, the Vedas and the Egyptian Book of the Dead, learning about different deities and rituals. And that people are mostly afraid of death.

John knew that there were worse things, though: and every night, he expected them to come knocking at the door of the blacksmith's cottage.

20

Lucky's nightmares were usually of the surprised eyes of freshly-bayoneted enemy insurgents. His friends' blood, bone and brains on his uniform as they were executed in interrogation. The feel of pliers on his teeth. Or any of the other hellish things that he'd experienced out there. The nightmares had faded over the years, but that night, fever had gripped his brain. He crawled out of his sleeping bag and staggered to the end of the tunnel, kicking a dead rat into the canal as he went. A few stragglers still remained, hands outstretched towards the fire barrel. They grunted at Lucky as he sidled into the circle. McClane – an ex-Marine from the valleys – was the only one still sober enough to talk, it seemed.

'You were making a right racket, Newman. Nightmares?'

'Fever. Food poisoning, I think.'

'Yeah, I heard. Seagull not cooked through?'

'I've got to dry out here.' Lucky leant closer to the

flames in the rusty drum. 'Or I'll die of pneumonia.'

'Remember Collins? Nasty way to go.' McClane rummaged in his bag and threw a sweater to Lucky. 'Here, put this on.'

Lucky took off his damp T-shirt and hung it over the smouldering barrel. The size of the sweater was a stark reminder of how much weight he had lost. McClane was still doing alright – carrying the malnutrition well, even a decent bit of muscle mass, but Lucky had become skin and bone. The group hadn't dared steal any food since Grosvenor Security shot several of them for attempting it. After two died from malnutrition, Lucky took part in a raid on a supermarket, but it was a disaster. Since Grosvenor Security took over, no-one could get anywhere near. He should have known. Lucky and McClane managed to make it out alive, but they were the only ones.

'We're gonna have to find food. You don't look well, Newman.'

'Going to the country. Baby, do you wanna go?' Lucky sang.

'You're gonna die of kidney failure before pneumonia gets you.'

'I only ever wake up out of habit anyway.'

'What about your plan? Revenge is something to live for, isn't it?'

'I'm away for a walk.'

'Whoa, whoa. You're not going into the city?'

'I don't care if they shoot me,' Lucky said as he staggered off into the night.

'Don't be getting holes in that sweater,' McClane shouted after him. 'I want it back when you're dead.'

Lucky wandered the neon-smeared streets of the west side, weaving between the natives. Hawk-eyed hookers looking for a john and sly-eyed hyenas looking for a mark. He crossed the road from the blood-tub ale-houses because he didn't want to get stabbed up and bleed out, if he could avoid it. He wanted to go out in a hail of bullets - or so he told himself.

A small part of Lucky still believed that he could take revenge against Grosvenor. The faint voice of optimism still haunted him, keeping him clinging to existence. Lucky knew the catalyst would come some day, but he had no clue that he would find it in a pissy alley in Leeds that evening.

The Sheffield sex tourists trawled up and down the strip, their guilty glances turning Lucky's withered stomach. Pampered CEOs, lawyers and doctors leered from their expensive cars at the kids pouting on the pavement. A few stopped and hoovered up the youngsters into their cars before driving off to satiate the needs that they couldn't within the walls of the capital. Lucky rifled through the bins of a takeaway in the hope of finding some discarded morsel that hadn't been gnawed or pissed on by rats, but without success.

Everything stank. Everything was toxic. Even the air itself in this part of town had a biological odour to it, which was putrescent and sexual in equal parts. Lucky balked as he thought of the acts that were taking place in concealed compartments within this reality. Behind the locked doors, the blacked-out windows, in the dark and steamy alleyways, under the floorboards, under and over the streets, they were all hard at work. What they lacked in morals, they made up for with a high work-rate: ejaculating, cannibalising, birthing, shitting and pissing through the night. Gnawing at the borders of reality, they hoped that one day the walls would crumble and the world would be theirs through attrition.

Lucky felt some degree of sympathy for the rats and their optimism. They didn't know what else to do except to keep gnawing and multiplying. It made Lucky think of some of the things he had done under orders during his last tour of duty. He didn't know what else to do at the time. In Hell, it doesn't matter which way you turn: you get burnt anyway.

The military had made him their poster boy, but he wouldn't smile for the camera - not after the last tour. He took the job working on the newspaper to rebuild his life, but Grosvenor put paid to that after she read his article attacking Totem. No creaking on the stairs this time. The guy was another of Grosvenor's foreign special-forces mercs. Either Latvian or Lithuanian, judging by his dying words.

After Lucky had killed the man, he fled Sheffield with no bank account and no citizenship, both of which Grosvenor had revoked. In the article, he'd suggested that Grosvenor intended to manipulate subjects into having violent or sexual dreams. That she wanted to use her colosseum to banish her political enemies to Dartmoor. He'd written that it was another phase in the normalisation of mass psychopathy that could only lead to dire consequences for society. Or something like that.

And here he stood, three feet away from a hooker lifting her miniskirt to piss all over her high heels. She shook it off all over his leg before running back out on the street. He had dire consequence all over his trousers and it reeked.

Drawn like a dying, stinking moth, he staggered to a caged pawn shop window where an old TV flickered. Lucky hooked his fingers through the cage and stared into the screen. He was old enough to remember the internet, satellite television and mobile phones before the floods. The masses were already halfway into the abyss even before Totem came along. They'd foamed at the mouth for celebrities eating insects and having doomed sex with each other on camera. Meanwhile, their sons were being earmarked for the desert. To suffer damage beyond repair; many never to return.

That was when they were still in possession of some modicum of innocence. Now that Totem had become so popular, their schadenfreude knew no bounds. Cruelty was just another genre. In fact, it had become the only genre. Across Britannia, a banal, yet sinister revolution had been occurring. Evil was normalising itself, preparing the way for greater evil. And now, Totem was more powerful than even he— its greatest critic—had feared and predicted.

He could have been riding high in the capital if only he'd given Totem a glowing review like every other journalist. They were all educated people: there was no way that they didn't realise how dangerous it could be. Now there was a mast in every town and village from Exmoor to Edinburgh, and 90 per cent of the population subscribed.

Still, they all fawned into the cameras about the next phase of our evolution. Published pictures of Alice Grosvenor hob-nobbing at various star-studded events. Broadcast good old-fashioned radio propaganda about the benefits of the new British way of life. Emphasis on how we must all aspire to be like those in the capital. And if we couldn't aspire to be like them, then we must yield to them.

Lucky could hear a citizen yielding at the far end of the alley, squeaking against the cream leather interior of a new Range Rover. He tried to focus on the Totem special that was being shown on the TV. They were showing what looked like a picture of Exmoor Prison.

Grosvenor Media has stunned the nation by announcing that they intend to transmit one of the most dangerous inmates in Britannia. Fresh from the notorious Exmoor Prison Hospital and the Dartmoor Pathway, The Horseman is sure to create a sensation. Confirm your subscription fees are up to date by calling the number below. Caution advised for those suffering from any nervous disorders or heart conditions: this programme is likely to contain scenes of violence and other graphic imagery.

The squeaking in the Range Rover had turned to screaming. She sounded young. Small hands pounded on the steamed rear window. His diamond-encrusted wedding ring clicked against the glass as he throttled her.

'Ah, shit.'

Lucky wished he hadn't seen any of this. He had to keep a low profile. He approached the car and pulled the back door open. The pervert took his hands from around the girl's neck and glared at him with a glass eye. Lucky pulled her out of the car, allowing her to flee into the night.

'Do you know who I am? I'll have you locked up within the hour.'

The pervert spoke in his public school accent, stepping from the car. Obviously juiced up, his biceps strained against the fabric of his designer suit. Not a hair out of place, perfect white teeth and a spray-on tan: the uniform of the average Sheffield male. Lucky would have guessed banker from the tie, but the glass eye made him think he might have seen some action.

'You shouldn't be doing that.'

'Who are you? My fucking father?'

'Stay back. Don't do it.' Lucky wrapped his hand around the lock knife in his pocket as the banker-soldier approached.

'What's your name?'

Lucky started walking away with the thug followed

him. His expensive shoes echoed off the cobbled street and high buildings.

'You Lucky Newman?'

Lucky quickened his pace, but was stopped in his tracks as he felt a sudden pressure around his neck. The stranger smashed him into the nearest wall and pinned him there by the throat. Already, Lucky's eyes were bulging and he could feel his windpipe beginning to crack.

'Think they'll put Lucky on your headstone?'

Lucky released one hand from the giant forearm of his attacker and fumbled in his pocket for his lock knife. No time to lose. He flipped it open and jammed it into the man's armpit twice, causing him to let go. The man leaned against his car, one hand under his arm. Both his eyes widened—even the glass one—as the blood stained up his fancy suit from the armpit outwards. Lucky knew he'd hit the axillary artery just by the colour of the guy's face. He was already draining as he staggered to the dark end of the alleyway, clutching the wound. Lucky shook the dying man's grip off his ankle as he jumped in the driver's seat of the Range Rover.

Lucky realised that the pervert still had the keys on him, but didn't want to see him die. He waited until the clawing at the driver's door stopped before opening it. When the guy had bled out, Lucky rifled through the pockets of the tailored suit. He found car keys and a wallet stuffed with security passes marked Grosvenor Media. Once he'd buckled himself in, he looked backwards to reverse out of the alley and saw a large gym holdall and an aluminium briefcase on the back seat. Grosvenor's agents would descend on the city when the body was found. No time to check the bags. He had to get out of there. Since the canal tunnel was on his way out of the city, he headed there first.

Lucky pulled the Range Rover into the far end of the tunnel. The sun wasn't up yet, but it wouldn't be long. He found Dickinson and McClane with no trouble and woke them up with the news of the Range Rover. They didn't believe him until they saw it for themselves. Lucky didn't even need to ask whether they wanted to join him in getting out of Leeds.

'Where do we go?'

Dickinson cracked open the aluminium briefcase. 'Holy shit.'

He rotated the case, so that Lucky and McClane could see inside from the front seats. Wads of large denominations were neatly banded and stacked together.

Dickinson handed them the briefcase and opened the holdall, which was heavy.

'Fuck me,' Dickinson said, as Lucky and McClane flipped through the wads of cash to check that it was all real.

'What? More?'

Dickinson pulled the bag open wide to reveal a

cache of weaponry enough to arm half a regiment.

'Who was this guy?'

'Creep was gonna kill some kid he'd bought on Water Lane. Then he tried to kill me.'

Lucky handed McClane the wallet he'd taken from the dead man.

'This guy works for Grosvenor Security?'

'Doesn't surprise me. He should be more tooled up, if anything.'

Dickinson pulled a photograph from the glove compartment. 'Newman, you're in deep shit.'

'I was in deep shit anyway.'

'How many more have they got out here looking for you?'

Lucky realised that maybe had finally lived up to his nickname. He smiled for the first time in a long time. No-one was laughing at him now and seagull was off the menu for good.

'I'm leaving. You coming?'

McClane nodded.

Dickinson rooted through the bag of firearms and explosives. 'Where are we going?'

'Snowdonia.'

Dickinson looked back at the cold, damp tunnel as the sun crept over the horizon. Lucky turned on the heating in the car and Dickinson was sold. 'To the mountains, then.'

'Hot food first, then the mountains,' said Lucky, turning the car heater down a notch.

No-one argued.

Lucky estimated that it would take a few hours for the Grosvenor thug to be discovered in Leeds. Probably another 24 for him to be processed and ID'ed, by which time he would be in the heart of Snowdonia, where Lucky had completed his basic training. He knew the wilderness there: places where they could lie low. Once they'd been off the radar long enough, they could use the money to rent somewhere, but for now, he was going to let his paranoia lead him. That was why they were going to burn out the Range Rover in the hills and walk five miles to the ferry terminal in Buxton.

'Why can't we take the car aboard the ferry? They won't even find the guy until the morning.'

'Can't take the chance.'

'Fuck's sake. I've only just warmed up.'

'How much money is in that case?'

'Half a million, I reckon. I'll be fucked if I'm counting all that,' muttered Dickinson. 'Will they have heating aboard the ferry?'

'We're not getting the ferry. Too risky. We'll get our own boat.'

'What?'

'There's a boatyard down on the shore in Buxton. We'll go down there and offer them cash for a little yacht or something.'

Dickinson looked at McClane, then back at Lucky.

'Come on, it's the most sheltered crossing in Britannia. Anyone can do it. No way we'll get that holdall past the ferry terminal security. Do it this way, and we can keep the guns.'

Lucky turned off down a dirt track on the borders of the Peak District and parked the car in the corner of a muddy field. There were no houses in sight and it was well-concealed from the road, so he ordered everyone out and set about twisting a rag into the tank of the Range Rover.

'You sure you wanna do this? Why don't we just hide out here in the hills?'

McClane handed Lucky a lighter. 'Too close.'

Being the biggest, McClane took the holdall of weapons on his back, but Lucky put it down again. 'We should do this now. You two have any preferences?'

'CZ75 will do me.'

'I don't care.'

'Where's the ammo?'

'Usually stowed under the back seats in these things. I'll check.'

McClane and Lucky were agog at the hardware at their fingertips. It had been a long time. Dickinson came back from the car with two large plastic ammo boxes.

'9mm, nothing else. Hollowpoints, though.'

'Why doesn't that surprise me?'

In the bottom of the holdall, empty magazines clinked against each other as Lucky laid the weapons on the grass. Beretta 92FS, Walther PPQ, two CZ75s and three Heckler and Koch MP5s. The others were eyeing up the MP5s, but Lucky wanted something that he could conceal. He picked up one of the Czech pistols, stripped off the fancy bits and loaded up two mags with regular 9mm rounds.

Dickinson held up the red box of shiny brass rounds. 'You don't want the hollowpoints?'

'No,' Lucky said, remembering a hollowpoint execution he'd been forced to watch in Homs.

Dickinson put down the box sheepishly.

McClane loaded the last round into the magazine, slid it into the pistol, cocked the slide and flipped the safety off and back on again. He found a webbing shoulder holster in the holdall and asked if anyone else wanted it before attaching it to himself. Lucky kept the gun and extra mag in his coat pocket, while Dickinson followed suit with the Walther and stuffed it into his jacket.

'You can't do that.'

'What?'

'Stuff it in your pocket like that. No safety. There's another holster there. Use that.'

'Shit.' Dickinson removed the Walther carefully from his jacket. 'Just give me a gun made of metal: none of this plastic and pottery bullshit.'

Lucky handed him the Beretta, which he'd already loaded. McClane heaved the remaining gear on to his shoulder and walked Dickinson clear of the soon-to-explode Range Rover. Lucky lit the rag in the fuel tank and ran clear to join them.

They couldn't even see the smoke from the burning vehicle's carcass once they'd arrived at the boatyard. They were almost safe, but Lucky knew he would not relax until they were in the wilderness of Snowdonia. The yard was about 100 metres long with a slipway leading down into the water. Various tired-looking boats lined either side of it, chocked up or on trailers. Some of them looked as if they were about to give in and tip over. A corrugated iron shed stood at the top of the yard, accompanied by a free-standing wooden out-house. The sounds of a biological skirmish came from within, followed by a flush and the creak of the opening door. A small old man in a blue boiler suit with rolled-up sleeves stepped out. His knotted arms were covered in Royal Navy tattoos.

'Alright, lads. What you after?'

'Anything for sale in the yard?'

'It's all for sale, mate.'

'Got anything that will get us to Wales?'

'And some whisky,' muttered Dickinson.

'How much experience have you got?'

McClane stepped forward and pulled up his sleeve to reveal his Marine Commando 46 tattoo.

'That'll do,' the boatbuilder said, raising his white eyebrows. He stroked his moustache and looked around the yard.

McClane pointed at a small fishing boat. 'How much?'

The boat builder climbed aboard, drew back the tarp, checked the cabin and gave them a price. Lucky had already taken twice the amount out of the briefcase in anticipation. He handed it to the boat builder, who clutched the wad of cash as if it were about to bite him, keeping it at arm's length.

'This is too much.'

'Have you got any supplies you can give us?'

'I can get them,' the boat builder said, looking down at the money in his hand.

'When's the tide due?'

'Two hours from now.'

'Money's yours if you can get us stocked and on the slip for this tide.'

'And some fucking whisky, please,' Dickinson whined.

'I can do that,' said the boat builder, stuffing the money into his boiler suit and setting to work. He spun his fat set of keys and climbed into the ancient, mud-caked machinery by the shed. Black clouds rolled above and a few heavy drops of rain hit the tractor's windscreen. 'Looks like you might get some weather, though.'

With McClane at the helm, they managed to negotiate the first few miles of their trip with only a few bumps. The bruised sky thundered, but the wind gusted only a few times, rolling Dickinson out of his makeshift bed in the cabin. Eager to breathe clean air for a change, Lucky and McClane sat on deck, eating flapjacks that the boat builder's wife had baked in a hurry.

McClane stuffed his face. 'God bless that woman.'

Lucky mumbled in agreement, crumbs falling from

his mouth.

The sun was sinking behind the Welsh mountains. He smiled at the iridescent fingers of light poking through the black clouds as he breathed the sea air.

'Wonder when we'll wake up?'

'Hmm?'

'I'm sure I've had this dream before.'

Lucky spluttered as a wave splashed into his face. 'Feels real enough to me, McClane.'

McClane smirked as Lucky spat out the saltwater and bits of flapjack. While he steered the boat into a small cove, a seagull that had been following the boat since the slipway continued to taunt Lucky with its cries.

When they landed on the beach, it was dark, but the boat-builder had equipped them with torches. They made use of an old pack of cards while they waited for the tide.

'Game of shithead?'

'Go on then.'

'Why don't we just stay here one more night on the boat?'

'Let's get into those mountains and take it from there. From here, it's only ten hours on foot at an easy pace.'

'But we've got bunks here, man. Where are we gonna sleep?'

'Dickinson, you've been sleeping in rat shit by a canal for the last two months. One more night roughing it won't kill you,' said Lucky, picking up the heavy bag of guns. 'Let's go.'

Lucky took another wedge of cash out of the briefcase before they headed into town and arrived at a surplus store. He bought them everything they needed to hold out in the mountains for a few weeks. The clerk was only a young kid who didn't take his eyes off McClane's special-forces tattoos as he rang the stuff through the till.

Lucky wondered where the kid would end up one day. To which hellhole would he be assigned for his national service? That spark in his eye would go out soon enough. Maybe the first time he saw a toddler with his intestines blown across his legs would do it. Or interrogation. It'd get to him, one way or another. Lucky wasn't about to draw attention by lecturing the boy on the evils of war. He paid him and sent Dickinson to the corner shop down the road for food.

The only people around seemed to be farmers in rusty old tractors rumbling by and a few drunks swaying outside the tavern, smoking their cheap tobacco into the cold air. Lucky noticed a few stragglers wandering into the parish church, but apart from that, the town was dead. Despite the peace and quiet, Lucky was still anxious to get into the mountains.

'Sirs, you forgot your dry-sacks,' the kid came stumbling out of the run-down building holding three bags in one hand and working a crutch in the other.

He hadn't noticed at the checkout because the kid

was stood behind a till counter, but he was missing a leg. Lucky took the bags and gave him a handful of cash.

'How old are you?'

The kid stared open-mouthed at the cash in his hand. 'Seventeen, sir.'

'How'd you lose it?'

'Lost it on my first tour of duty last year, sir.'

'Sorry to hear that.'

'But every Saturday, I get to have two legs like everybody else. Unless they transmitted another amputee, which would be weird.'

'How's that?'

'Totem, of course, sir. Since they put a mast here—'

'They put a mast here?'

'A few years ago.'

'You tune in every Saturday?'

'Everybody does.'

'Where is the mast?'

'It's the old TV mast. See the one with the six red lights?' the kid said, pointing to the north. 'Well, that stays on all the time, but every Saturday, you'll see it light up blue while Totem is transmitting.'

'We weren't here, ok?' Lucky nodded at the wad of cash in the clerk's young hand. 'You never saw us.'

They headed into the woods to share out the kit, the guns and the money into their new backpacks. Dickinson's eyes lit up as he received the cash, but McClane seemed less enthusiastic.

'This is your money, Newman. You killed the guy.'

'McClane, just take the money. This is the best way, trust me. Dickinson doesn't need asking twice, see?'

'Fucking right, I don't. Nice one, Newman.' Dickinson stuffed the money inside a plastic bag. And that inside the dry-sack, and that inside the waterproof pocket of his bag.

All three heaved on their rucksacks and headed up the mountain in silence.

By the time they reached the vicinity of the hideout, Dickinson was drunk. He'd already polished off a bottle of whisky from the corner shop, now he was barely able to stand under the weight of his rucksack. The three of them stood in darkness near the top of the mountain until Dickinson collapsed on to a tuffet of moss.

'McClane, you wait here with him while I find this door. Keep your headtorch off and your gun drawn.' He pulled a machete from his backpack and headed into the undergrowth, taking a few practise swings along the way. The vines and branches had grown thick since he had last been there. A good sign that they would find the place deserted, as he'd hoped. Lucky swung and chopped his way to a heavy metal door that looked like it came from a submarine. In the deep, dark woods halfway up a moonlit mountain, it appeared surreal. It was marked as property of Her Majesty's Royal Navy, which dated it. The navy hadn't been Her Majesty's for years, but this was more likely to have been surplus from Cammell Laird shipyard. Like Buckingham Palace and the monarchy, it had been underwater since the floods. He whistled to McClane, who stepped out of the undergrowth. The big man took Lucky's rucksack in one hand and Dickinson's in the other: the half-conscious, whisky-soaked Dickinson still attached.

'Help me with this, McClane,' Lucky said, pointing his headtorch at the handle.

McClane wrapped one massive hand around it and opened it first go, to Lucky's embarrassment. The two of them pulled the door outwards against the vines and brambles. Inside was a metal ladder leading downwards beyond the range of their head torches.

McClane shook Dickinson awake. 'Get it together.'

Dickinson snorted and grabbed the metal ladder, insisting that he go first.

'Let me go ahead, Dickinson: I know this place.'

'Fuck that,' Dickinson slurred as he climbed down the ladder. Halfway down, he lost his footing and clanged on to a metal platform. Lucky and McClane followed, taking extra care on the slimy rung that caught out Dickinson.

They dropped into a room that looked like a kitchen with a hob, sink and steel surfaces.

'Oh my God, it's a bunker. A fucking nuclear bunker,' said Dickinson, creating echoes off the walls as he staggered about.

'Told you we'd be safe here.' Lucky offloaded his backpack on one of the creaky wooden chairs in the kitchen. A dusty cathode-ray TV stood in the corner, bouncing the light from their head torches back at them off its smeared, dead screen.

McClane set a fire in the log burner, while Dickinson snored on top of his backpack in the corner of the room. Lucky made coffee and smiled to himself. The place felt like home already.

21

Hopkins collapsed on to his bed, exhausted from the morning's work at the distillery. Whenever he had nightmares about Andrew, the next day was always full of unanswered questions and sorrow. That morning, he had been walking through the still house and seen a reflection in the sunlit copper bulges. The figure even cast a shadow on the stone floor. It was Andrew standing there, smiling at him.

It had only happened on three or four occasions over the last few years, but every time, it took his breath away. Lately, it had been getting worse. The sightings had begun to develop into full-blown panic attacks. His nightmares were bad enough that he considered rejoining McCole on the slope into alcoholic oblivion, to numb himself. Reflections and whispers in the quiet corners of the distillery continued to haunt him and recently, his son's face hadn't been the only one. Another young man's face had been appearing. Although Hopkins didn't recognise him, he recognised the desperation. The terrified young man was always screaming silently. As he pleaded for help, his scarred features would contort in a terrible anguish that haunted Hopkins.

He loosened his boiler suit collar and concentrated on his breathing. Eyes closed. Knock at the door.

'Hopkins?'

'What do you want, McCole?'

'You greeting again? Fuck's sake: have a drink.'

'That's not going to help.'

'Fucking might.'

Hopkins picked up the receipts and other assorted paperwork on his bedside table. He pretended to read them to avoid making eye contact.

'Andrew would have liked this place.'

'He didn't even like whisky before he went to Syria.'

'When are you going to forgive yourself?'

Hopkins responded only with a brief, contemptuous glance.

'You said you wanted to go back to practice: why not leave the distillery to me for a few months?'

'Because it'd fucking blow up.'

'Where's the trust?' McCole pulled his friend up off the bed and into a hug. As ever, it remained unrequited by Hopkins, who kept his arms stiffly by his sides.

'You've put weight on,' Hopkins observed as McCole released him.

'Wanna go fishing later, mister fucking charisma?'

Hopkins didn't respond.

McCole thumped him in the chest, half-winding him. 'Aye?'

'Aye,' Hopkins groaned.

'There's something else. It's about Alice Grosvenor and Totem.'

'I don't want to know.' Hopkins cast a glance at the framed photograph of Andrew on the bedside table.

'I'll get the fishing stuff together then,' McCole said, creaking out of the room and towards the staircase.

Hopkins sat on the bed, brushing his right eyebrow with his finger. He couldn't contain his curiosity. 'What the hell is she doing with it now?' he shouted to McCole, who creaked back into the room.

'Heard it on the radio earlier. They've been cleared to transmit that inmate.'

'Inmate?'

'The one from Exmoor. The guy with the scars. Supposed to be a total nutter.'

'They can't transmit anyone who's been certified. Did you say scars?'

'Grosvenor's legal department said they found a loophole.'

Hopkins ran his fingers over Andrew's tattered suicide note in his jacket pocket while he made calculations. 'Do you realise what could happen? The trauma of that transmission … We're talking mass schizophreniform disorder.'

'Yeah, that sounds bad.'

The face from his recurring nightmare flashed into Hopkins' mind. 'Did you say the one with the scars?

'Yeah, the one with the scars. Guy looks like Buckfast Bennie. All sliced up.'

Hopkins stared blankly at McCole.

'An auld mate. It's not him, just looks like him,' shrugged McCole. 'Anyway, thought I'd tell you before you heard it on the wireless and had one of your moments.

Hopkins stared at the photograph of Andrew. 'Help me get the helicopter ready.'

'You're having a moment anyway. That's great,' McCole sighed. 'What do you want that thing for?'

'I'm going to the capital to see Alice Grosvenor.'

'Yeah, right,' McCole laughed. 'What about the distillery?'

'We shut down everything for a few days. I have to do this.'

'You're serious?' McCole picked up a photograph of Andrew while Hopkins pulled a suitcase from atop the wardrobe. 'It's not gonna bring him back. When I was talking about salvation, I was thinking ... you're really going back to the city? Hopkins, they won't even remember you.'

'You don't have to come. Stay here and blow up the distillery, by all means.' He took clothes from the wardrobe and wedges of cash from the safe before packing them into his case. 'I'm going to Sheffield.'

'Oh, aye. You'd love that: something happens to you and I'm the one left with a guilt complex. Pull the other one.'

'You'd better get packing then, Reverend. Don't forget your dog collar,' said Hopkins, handing him the safe key. 'Or the shotgun.'

Once they'd locked down the distillery and loaded their gear into the Lynx, the two men climbed into the cockpit. Hopkins attached his headset and adjusted his microphone while McCole yanked furiously at his safety belt. Hopkins took an instruction manual from the compartment above his head.

'Very funny.'

'I need to brush up on a few things first.'

McCole finally wrangled his seat belt into place. 'You're fucking serious? I thought you knew what you were doing.'

'Have faith. Isn't that what you're always telling me?'

'Shite.' McCole closed his eyes and clawed the armrest as the rotor began turning.

Hopkins radioed ahead to the sentinel ship Edinburgh for clearance on their flight path and to Totem HQ to request a landing on their helipad. Both answered in the affirmative, so Hopkins pulled the throttle for take-off. Once in the air, he was careful only to make small compensations as he steered them south towards Sheffield. Despite the smell of fear and stream of expletives coming from McCole, Hopkins' racing mind slowed down during the flight. There was something meditative about the details and the unforgiving nature of the physics involved. He had no time to think about anything else when he was flying.

The setting sun lit up the cockpit of the Lynx in a strange golden light whilst the glass dials sparkled in the half-darkness. Soon, they would be flying over the walls of the capital, into streets of glass glowing with Grosvenor's ruthless propaganda.

22

Alice Grosvenor was not afraid of anything or anyone since her father had died.

Except them.

Everything had happened exactly as they said it would. She had doubted them once and they made sure that she never doubted them again. She never dreamed that she would have to endure such servitude on her rise to power. She couldn't run and she couldn't go back.

She could never go back.

At least Totem had given the wretches of these isles something to live for. Still they didn't love her for it. But they kept giving her money, making Grosvenor Media the richest corporation in Britannia. She didn't want their love anyway: she wanted their submission.

She deserved an award. And she had them. Every

morning, she liked to look at her reflection in her trophies while she drained her first cup of coffee. But even this ritual of self-congratulation couldn't calm her after what she had just heard.

The antique Bakelite red phone on her huge office desk was still chiming because she couldn't help slamming it down. It wasn't often that they used the phone to contact her. Only when they wanted every word as clear as possible: no static or dropouts. She couldn't shirk her duty through claiming to have misheard them, which is exactly what Alice wished that she could do.

It wasn't that she felt any pangs of conscience: Alice simply hated being in anybody's thrall. The whole point of a rise to power is so that you can control others, not be controlled yourself.

Or so she thought.

She'd searched for angles on members of the Board, but how do you blackmail someone whose face you've never seen and whose name you've never known?

Alice had always been the smartest. Smartest in her family, smartest in her class, in her lectures at university, in press conferences, but this was one riddle she could not solve. All she knew was that they could do a lot worse to her than the brainwashed, unwashed rabble ever could.

Ten years before, the Board made an example of someone who had questioned their virtues. Alice recalled that it was a bright spring morning. About seven o'clock, she heard a loud thud outside her office window. The whole building was sealed off while Lord Hammond's impaled body was removed from the spiked railings. The crime scene resembled a photograph that they had sent to Alice the day before. He was wearing a red tie and a black bowler hat in the photograph, as he was when he landed on the spikes.

When Alice first saw the body, she became aroused. She had never revealed this to anyone, except one or two quacks during her dalliance with psychotherapy. She found the violence to be intensely erotic and their anonymity only made them all the more intriguing. Now she had her chance to become one of them: to claim her rightful ascension.

But she could not run and she could not go back.

She could never go back.

Her father had taught her that.

She had reached the point of no return upon sacrificing her newborn grandson John Muldoon to the Board: wheeled into an institution as an orphan with no name. He was an offering, a blank canvas for them to paint with colours of fear and loathing. Alice didn't even care that it was her own flesh and blood, as long as she got that promotion. Only now could she see the true horror and scale of what they had planned. Once again, she found herself giddy with excitement at the thought of shocking new terrain to explore.

She picked the most sycophantic shrink she could

find in her Filofax and called him to book an urgent session. He would tell Alice that her dead father's psychopathy had made her the way she was. That she'd had no choice but to do the awful things she had done. That she wouldn't go to Hell. That all leaders have to deal with collateral damage. That sacrifice is necessary to fulfil any high ambition. If she gave them enough money, they'd tell her anything she wanted to hear. Over the past two decades, she'd been through every quack in the capital and they were all the same.

Morons.

Alice checked her appearance in the large mirror hanging behind the desk. She pinched and pulled her surgically-altered skin and brushed her salon hairdo back from her face. She looked more like a woman in her thirties than her fifties, but she booked a consultation with her plastic surgeon anyway.

She took the elevator to the ground floor of the smoked glass Grosvenor Mail building. Two bodyguards stood up and followed her through the reception area to the limousine parked outside. The driver was Joe, one of Alice's favourites because he never spoke, even to greet her. Too coarse and stupid for meaningless social convention, here was a mind that she could warp on a casual, regular basis. She could abuse employees like Joe as much as she wanted and the next day they would return, too terrified to quit their job. No-one wanted to leave the capital. And in the capital, you pretty much had to work for Alice one way or another. In public, she often referred to Sheffield as being ultra-civilised, when what she really meant was enthralled. The citizens weren't complaining though. Just like they didn't complain about the checkpoint shootings or the Totem fatalities. As long as they were protected and entertained, she could do what she wanted. As long as she wasn't sending their kids off to war, she could do what she wanted. The policy of conscripting only those born outside the capital walls had been in place since the floods. Most citizens considered Sheffield to be a utopia, according to her PR chief. He agreed that the capital should not be sullied with the burden of trauma and rehabilitation. He even called Alice a visionary. That fork-tongued cretin would say anything for a raise, though.

If the people of Britannia knew what she planned to do to them, they would revolt, no doubt about that. Totem had so far served as the perfect distraction while she prepared to deliver her coup de grace. After transmitting John Muldoon, the entire population would come crawling to her pharmaceutical companies for relief from their waking nightmare. She wanted them as damaged as he, stupefied by their trauma. Gloriously pliable to her will.

'Take me to headquarters,' she demanded as the bodyguards made space for her in the back seat of the limousine.

As they passed between the tall buildings on the

busy streets, Alice considered the possibility that she had been remiss in allowing David Hopkins to live once he'd sold Totem to her. She dismissed it quickly, as she always did. It would have drawn too much attention to kill him as well as his son. The boy's fake suicide had certainly worked in prying Totem away from Hopkins, but she hadn't expected him to live this long. Now the Board were making angry phone calls to tell her that he was returning to the capital, as she always knew he would.

The only critics that dared speak up against Totem so far had been outspoken members of the Church and a few retired headshrinkers. They claimed that the average mind cannot cope with the intense pain and pleasure of such delusions. It becomes dissatisfied with everyday life and seeks fulfilment in ever more risky ways until violence ensues.

Alice had handled the medical naysayers, but the Church was a different matter. They had been a thorn in Alice's side since the very first transmission. She had reduced them to a crop circle cult under a mushroom cloud of propaganda, but now people were starting to listen to them again. Outside the capital, abandoned churches were being restored. Attendances were up while Totem subscriptions stalled. One priest had even dared to start up a pirate radio broadcast from his church, which soon burnt to the ground with him locked in the vestibule. After that, there weren't so many problems with the clergy, as the Board had demanded.

They had told her that Hopkins would be arriving by helicopter at Totem HQ to meet with her. He was asking to counsel the inmate before and after the transmission. Of course, the Board wanted it spun into a story. If they had simply told her to dispose of Hopkins, her hands wouldn't have been shaking.

Alice began scheming how to get the helicopter shot down without them finding out it was her who had ordered it.

She worried that they had heard that thought.

'Are you alright, marm? Your breathing—'

'I'm fine. Don't speak to me again.'

The driver glanced in his rear view to check the bodyguard's reaction, but there was none.

As they drove along Church Street, Alice imagined the outlines of the buildings she had razed for the headquarters. They'd needed a legion of bulldozers just for the bones in the graveyard. Citizens cared little about the sledgehammers on the headstones. Or about the names on them, broken up into meaningless marks on jumbled old bits of rock. Least of all her.

She thought that she had crushed enough of her past to make it unintelligible, even to David Hopkins.

But now he was back.

The limousine rolled down to the parking garage in the basement. A sacred crypt once full of human remains, now stuffed with expensive vehicles belonging to Totem staff. The driver remained in the limo while Alice and her two bodyguards called the elevator. She instructed them to radio for two more armed security personnel. They were to wait by the helipad on the roof for Hopkins and escort him directly to her.

She pictured Andrew Hopkins' eyeballs bulging and his urine-soaked legs thrashing in the woods that day. She remembered how the steaming liquid had run quickly off his freshly-polished boots. It still gave her butterflies. His firm, athletic body was useless once it had been strung up. Alice had tingled when it was happening and she still tingled every time she thought about it. Even as she was being driven away from the scene that day, she couldn't help looking back for the final few twitches. Not only had it given Alice the most delightful memory, it had also forced David Hopkins to accept her offer in his unhinged and unmanly grief.

Sometimes, you have to crack a few eggs to make the omelette, her father would say.

Alice Grosvenor sat in her office and waited for Hopkins, contemplating how best to kill him before he uncovered the truth about his son.

23

'Don't underestimate this woman, McCole.'

Hopkins adjusted his headset microphone. The rotor throbbed above as they passed over the city wall and into the capital's airspace. He tried not to think about how many surface-to-air missiles were trained on them at that moment.

'Evil, you said.'

'No, that's what you said: I said high-functioning schizophrenic and secondary psychopath.'

'Proper wrong 'un, then.'

'Don't believe anything she says and don't give anything away.'

'I know how to deal with psychopaths.'

'Special forces?'

'No, from supporting Rangers.'

'Is that some kind of paramilitary outfit?'

McCole sighed. 'They were a football team,

Hopkins.'

Hopkins radioed for clearance to land on the helipad as they soared over Sheffield and its bustling streets of screens and holograms.

The landing was rough, but Hopkins managed to get them down eventually. The two men unstrapped themselves and hung their headsets in the cockpit. Beneath the still-turning blades, they headed for the group waiting for them by the fire exit. Their reception party wore sub-machine guns on shoulder straps over immaculately tailored suits.

'We take you to Grosvenor,' one of the suits shouted above the whine of the helicopter's dying rotor.

In went the first suit, then Hopkins and McCole. The rest of them crammed their shoulders and firearms through the door before slamming it shut.

The lemon-scented stairwell led to another door after only one flight. This door required a thumbprint, eye-scan and finger-prick before it would open. The guard opened it and led them into a corridor where they were scanned for weapons or toxins. Hopkins considered the paranoia required to keep an office this close to a helipad with all those security measures. Being Alice, it was probably justified, considering her history. He wondered whether McCole was starting to take everything a bit more seriously yet.

McCole held up his flask. 'Anyone want a drink before I declare this?'

The guard glanced at McCole's dog collar. 'No,

thank you, reverend.'

'Nothing to declare but my faith,' he belched and handed the guard the empty flask.

They walked through more scanners which, when satisfied, opened another door leading to a bar. McCole's eyes widened when he saw the bottle of Aberlour amongst the other bottles on the counter.

'Please help yourselves to any refreshments. Ms. Grosvenor will see you shortly.'

McCole had already drunk a glass of the whisky before the guard had finished his sentence.

'Thank you.' Hopkins sat down in one of the leather armchairs. He hoped that McCole wouldn't ask him.

'Want one, fucking Airwolf?'

'I'm not sure that's a good idea.'

'Who's gonna pull you over?'

'Why are you here again?'

'I'm a representative of the Church,' McCole said, adjusting his collar and rolling his eyes. 'I didn't think they'd knock down the fucking cathedral, did you?'

'I didn't see that one coming, either.'

'Because whisky?'

Hopkins fired McCole the same glare he'd been firing at him for sixteen years. 'Because I was grieving.'

'And whisky,' McCole replied, raising his glass. 'Judge not, lest ye be judged.'

'What would I do without you?'

'Kill yourself out of self-pity. Fucking

embarrassing, man.'

'At least I'm not the only one. Don't think I've forgotten the episode in the out-house.'

'I couldn't hold my ale that night. Anyway, you know why I'm here, Einstein.'

'Don't call me that.'

The guards waved them into Grosvenor's office, which was made entirely of tinted glass that gave them a hyper-panoramic view of the city. Various icons and avatars glowed and whirred in the low light. Grosvenor was sitting behind a desk made of the same glass as everything else. Nearby, Hopkins noticed her personal Totem pod. Its sleek metal shell sparkled in the low light of the office, suggesting the presence of an unborn entity in the room. As she stood up behind the desk to greet them, she looked taller than Hopkins remembered.

'It's been a long time, David. How is the distillery?'

'We've shut down production for a few days and—'

'I'm Alice Grosvenor. A pleasure,' Grosvenor interrupted, reaching out her manicured claws towards the chaplain.

'Reverend McCole. The pleasure's all mine.' The reverend winked. Grosvenor withdrew her hand first from the shake.

The men sat in traditional office chairs, while she lounged on a throne of gorilla glass. The various swipe bars and menu icons on the armrests illuminated her face from below.

'So, primary counsel for the subject before and after the transmission?'

'That's not what I came here for, Alice. I came here to stop you from transmitting the subject at all.'

'We have the finest neuroscientists alive working for us – all except you. Why don't you join us, doctor? I'll even give you your old lab back.'

'It's dangerous, and you know it is. Not to mention a violation of every human rights and mental health act under the sun.'

'I know you've been gone a long time, David, but no-one really talks about human rights anymore. If you came here to stop the transmission, I'm afraid you'll be disappointed.'

'Who are you working for these days?' He focused on her irises, on the exact measurements of her pupils and the muscular movements in her face.

She clamped her lips together and looked downwards.

'That's very rude of you, Doctor. Please stop doing that.'

'It's my nature, Alice.'

Grosvenor looked up from her desk and met his eye with arctic coldness as she spoke. 'Your nature was always predictable. Be careful that it doesn't grow tiresome.'

McCole snorted with laughter and held his hand to his mouth. 'Sorry.'

'You've been gone a long time. What do you want?'

'To stop you sinking what's left of these islands with my creation.'

'Please,' Grosvenor guffawed. 'It's really none of your business anymore.'

'This transmission could cause mass psychosis. There would be chaos.'

'David, you've spent too much time on that island with your friend here. People can't get enough of Totem.'

McCole belched loudly. Grosvenor wrinkled her nose into a faint sneer.

'So is this it, Alice? The moment you've been waiting for?'

'I can give you the position as psychological counsel - that's it.'

'You can do anything you want. Your father's dead: he can't control you anymore.'

'David, you always knew how to smooth-talk me,' Grosvenor smiled, trying to draw attention away from her trembling hands. 'Take it or leave it: you'll head up the counselling team.'

Hopkins didn't take his eyes off her. 'I don't want your people interfering. I want to be his only counsel.'

'And whisky,' McCole added. 'We need whisky. This wetty wouldn't even let me bring a bottle for the road.'

'Sky.'

'Whatever.'

Grosvenor frowned at a blemish on her perfect claws. 'Done.'

'Have you chosen the patient yet?'

Grosvenor nodded.

'Any names, details?'

'Tune to this frequency tomorrow and give this code,' she said, handing Hopkins a slip of paper with pencil scribblings on it. 'A doctor at the facility will brief you in full on the inmate. He's a John Doe, but they call him the Horseman.'

McCole half-choked on the last of his whisky at the biblical allusion. He coughed and loosened his dog collar. Grosvenor was difficult to read, but Hopkins picked up a repetitive tell in her eye movements. There was something she was holding back.

She swiped one of the pads on her gorilla glass throne and two guards entered.

'Meeting's over. Feel free to make use of the bar area before you leave. It's been a pleasure, gentlemen.'

The sun had set by the time they reached the southern isles. An orange glow clung to the horizon as they flew over the clusters of civilisation still holding on in the ruins of Britannia. McCole remained silent as he peered down at the lights of the tiny villages. Exmoor seemed a long way from Sheffield.

When they arrived at the coast of the island, they saw only darkness below. Further inland, the lights of another village appeared. Hopkins flew low enough for them to see a tractor wheezing along a country lane. He landed on the roof of the high-security hospital to a reception committee of neolithic orderlies and a TV crew.

'Stay here and look after the helicopter, McCole. And keep that shotgun handy.'

'She seemed quite lovely to me.'

'She'll kill us both at the first opportunity.'

'I thought we had something.'

'Right now, she'll be working out how soon she can do it without creating a scandal.'

'I don't think people would care, as long as they get their next transmission.'

Reporters and cameramen edged towards the helipad.

'Stay in the helicopter. Don't move for anyone.'

'Ok, Mammy.'

When he disembarked the helicopter, a young reporter seized upon Hopkins and ordered her cameraman closer. The logo on the camera read Grosvenor News.

'Doctor Hopkins, how does it feel to be returning to Britannia after all these years?'

'I'm here to protect the well-being of the patient.'

The reporter turned to McCole, who sat in the cockpit, his headphones around his neck. She had to shout above the noise of the rotor blades winding down. 'Reverend, what interest does the Church have in Doctor Hopkins' appointment as counsel to the inmate?'

'I'm here to support the doctor in any way I can

and to ensure the boy's and the public's safety.'

Hopkins raised an eyebrow at his lucidity.

'The Church feels that there is a danger to the public? Please explain.'

'And I saw when the Lamb had opened the first seal and I heard the first of the four animals saying as with a voice of thunder, come and see.'

'That's from the Bible, right?' The reporter maintained her TV smile despite the wind wrapping her hair across her face. 'What does it mean?'

'It means that if this transmission goes ahead, we're all fucked.'

The reporter dropped her microphone in shock. She threw her hands up in desperation and stamped her elegant heel on the helipad's concrete. Hopkins entered the main building, smiling at the clang of their first spanner in Grosvenor's machine.

24

John Muldoon sat atop his white horse and looked over the moors. He couldn't be sure how long he had been on Dartmoor. He couldn't be sure of anything. In his time there, he had not even encountered another human being, let alone any cannibal savages. And still, Arthur remained as loyal as ever. For the first time in his life, John felt peace.

That morning, he made coffee, fed Arthur, tended to his vegetable patch and explored the isle for the rest of the day to search for new resources. It would have been paradise, if not for the looming shadow of the prison: the only place on the island that John and Arthur hadn't explored. John felt that it was better not to tempt fate. He'd heard the phrase used many times in the care home. And they had been right. He had once tempted fate and pleaded with a worker to save him. Even believe him. But no, the worker reported John and they punished him even worse.

He and Arthur continued to steer clear of the institutional building, to be on the safe side.

The more mornings John woke up to this peaceful life, the less terrifying his dreams became, until he eventually slept through a whole night. However, the departure of his fear brought with it a new fear: that his paradise might be set ablaze by the same demons that had been chasing him forever. How long before he saw that long black car pull up outside the prison. Or the blacksmith's cottage. His memories were like festering wounds in his brain. They never healed and scarred over like the wounds on his skin. Time had been his enemy. Everyone had been his enemy. Life itself had been his enemy.

But that's not how things were on Dartmoor.

Although the weather was cruel, and the seasons indistinct from one another, he had shelter and warmth in the blacksmith's cottage. Instead of enemies every which way he looked, John now had a friend in Arthur. Sometimes, he would press his ear to the horse's flank and listen to his heartbeat to remind himself that he was real. He was so grateful, but he didn't know who to thank. If it was God, then where had he been all these years? He must have heard some of his screams through the pillows and jackets held over his face.

Maybe he could thank Biggs, the marine who gave him the rucksack and the gun. He'd still never had cause to use it because he seemed to be alone on the island. Considering the number of inmates sent to

Dartmoor, he should have run into someone by now.

The suns were setting, so he and Arthur made their way back to the forge for dinner. As they rode over the moors, Arthur stopped in his tracks, spooked by something. His head turned and he snorted into the wind. John strained to hear the faintest sound of a rotor blade in the distance. He never forgot that sound because the wealthiest care home visitors would arrive by helicopter. And they were the ones to dread the most.

John rode Arthur to cover in a nearby wood and waited for the chopper to pass overhead, but it never did. When the rotors faded, they headed home. John ate in the barn with Arthur that night, as he did most nights, keeping the loaded gun to hand.

The next morning, John woke to the sound of the helicopter. It sounded like it was hovering overhead, but by the time he'd unlocked the barn and run outside, there was no sign of it. He saddled up and rode Arthur in the direction of the turning rotors, towards the prison.

As they rose up on the moor, John could look down upon the dark buildings and further out to sea. There was no chopper in sight, but he did see a dot bouncing around on the rough seas in the distance. It was the first ship he had seen since arriving on the island. The first sign of another human being.

It had to happen sooner or later.

Arthur reared up and grunted, disturbed by the

sighting. John soothed him by stroking his mane and whispering in his ear, before riding down to a nearby cove to watch the ship from a safe distance. From the chill shadows of the cove, he and Arthur watched the vessel creep towards them. When it was too close for comfort, they rode back inland towards the prison.

John saw one of the windows in the ugly building flicker with light and wondered who might be lurking in there. Any inmates would have devolved beyond the animal state into a more ruthless society, like insects. He imagined what kind of hierarchy might emerge, and who would be fearsome enough to reign over such a dangerous colony.

25

Hospital guards escorted Hopkins to a windowless office. They watched him shake hands with a man whose mean thin lips made him look and sound like a deflating balloon.

'It is an honour to host the eminent Doctor Hopkins, of course.' The man looked straight through Hopkins without an ounce of sincerity. 'My name is Mr. Chandler. Please take a seat.'

An unnerving array of high-tech weaponry hung on the wall behind the chief executive. A few of the devices were non-lethal and somewhat familiar, but most he had never seen before. Even when he had been working in high-security hospitals. Hopkins sat down opposite the nauseating Chandler and tried to remain neutral.

'I would like to see the files for the patient, please.'

'I'm afraid there is still a D-notice on those files, sir. Nothing I can do. Not for some time, at least,'

Chandler replied, tapping his pen on the desk.

'And who told you to tell me that, Mr. Chandler?'

Chandler stopped tapping his pen. 'I assure you that I take orders from no-one. I run things here.'

'Then I would very much like to read those files.'

'Do you understand what a D-notice is, Doctor?'

'It's a secrecy pact, based on the notion of national security being at stake. That ship sailed some time ago, if you hadn't noticed.'

'National security is more important than ever. I cannot release those files,' Chandler pinched his lips and inhaled through his beaky, bureaucratic nose. 'The legislation remains in force, as you know.'

'Then give me some background on him, at least. You expect me to counsel a patient blind?'

'I expect nothing from you, sir. You are here of your own free will. You would do well to remember that in the coming days,' Chandler said, his lips curling upwards into the faintest of smiles. 'Besides, inmate care is not within my purview.'

'Not within your purview? But you run a hospital.'

'I have no medical training, sir. I am a chief executive and therefore cannot comment on the inmate, nor his condition.' Chandler looked at his watch.

'Then what is your purpose here?'

'To maximise profits for the hospital, which is a good thing, I'm sure you'll agree.'

'So how much did she pay you?'

'Pardon?'

'How much did Grosvenor pay you to hand over one of your patients for transmission?'

Silence.

'A fraction of what she paid you for Totem, sir,' Chandler replied. 'I should thank you. Business has been brisk these last few years.'

Hopkins didn't rise to the bait. 'I need to know what's in this patient's head before Grosvenor transmits it into every town across the country. Do you know how dangerous this could be?'

'That is also not within my purview, sir.'

'Then to whom do I speak, Chandler?'

'You should talk with the head of C-Block: Doctor Charles. You'll have to be escorted.' Chandler spoke with perceptible relief, swiping at a glass surface on his desk.

The door opened and Hopkins stormed out with the two security guards in pursuit. The colourless corridors split like fractals into other colourless corridors. Each one lined with pastel-coloured, gel-padded hellholes for the insane.

After passing through several armed checkpoints, Hopkins found Charles' office. He knocked and the door opened into a dark room, with only a sliver of sunlight poking through the closed blinds.

'Please, come in and sit down. Doctor Hopkins, I am a huge fan of your work.'

'Hello? Doctor Charles?'

'Please forgive the lighting. You have caught me at a low ebb, I'm afraid. Migraines.'

'Migraines, hmmm?' He walked across the room and let enough light through the blinds to see a man lying in a blanket on an oxblood sofa. He was cupping his hands around his sunglasses.

'Please, no light. I might turn to ash.'

Hopkins let the blinds snap back.

'I heard that you were coming. I wanted to be back on my feet, but you're here sooner than expected,' Charles croaked. 'You came here to stop it, didn't you?'

'Yes.'

'I hoped you would.' Charles tried to sit up on the sofa. 'But everyone thought you were drunk or dead.'

'I haven't drunk a drop in 14 years.'

'Good for you, Hopkins. Good for you. But I cannot survive without these pills. The people have Totem, you have your whisky and I have these.' The doctor popped another two. 'Escapism is big business these days. How is the whisky trade?'

'Brisk.'

'Well, there you go.'

'Who is Grosvenor going to transmit?'

'Oh, I'm supposed to fill you in on details. Don't they say that God is in the details?'

'Some people do.'

'I've been doing this for 30 years and never seen anything like this patient.'

'In what respect?'

'We couldn't keep up with him. Every time we had him in for analysis, he would score off of our charts.

We had to create new ones.' The doctor sat up and pulled the blanket the blanket around his shoulders. 'All our results were inconclusive. He fit none of our criteria, and the trauma couldn't—'

'What trauma?'

'You've never seen him, have you? It was all unspecified in his paperwork, but you've only got to look at his face: half of it's scar tissue. He wouldn't talk about that or what happened in Leeds, so they sent him to Dartmoor. It was out of my hands.'

'You sent him to Dartmoor? Why in the hell would you do that?'

'We don't literally send them to Dartmoor, of course. It's the euphemism we use to describe the catatonia,' Charles sighed. 'He's right here in this building.'

Cold sweat crept down Hopkins' back as he glared down his nose at Charles.

'It wasn't my choice. This is now standard protocol for any violent or delusional inmate who has been in state care or is ex-military.'

'So this patient has received no counselling? You just drugged him and isolated him?'

'I insisted on scans to rule out any kind of tumour or physical trauma to the brain.'

'And what did you find?'

The doctor heaved himself to his feet and staggered over to his desk. In the dim light, he picked up a file that was already open on his desk and handed it to Hopkins.

'Officially, this doesn't exist. Chandler told me to destroy it.'

Hopkins examined the data and the images from the scans. He didn't even need to turn the page. 'This can't be right.'

'That's what I said. Amazing though, isn't it?'

'His whole brain's lit up.'

'Look at the readings.'

Hopkins parted the blind again, and Charles shielded his face with his arm.

'My God,' he muttered, scanning the information. 'What happened in the borstal in Leeds?'

'They say that he crucified a warden.'

'What?'

'On a metal staircase, the report says.'

'So you sent him to Dartmoor … Medicated him into catatonia.'

'Best place for him, Hopkins. He's in no pain there. This kid arrived here in full body restraints, shackles and a bite mask.'

'Why do you call him a kid?'

'You mean you don't know? I assumed that's why you came here,' Charles said, releasing his head from his hands. 'He's 16 years old.'

Hopkins made no attempt to hide his disgust. 'How do you live with yourself?'

'I've learnt to accept it. I started out running a hospital; now it's a battery farm. What can I do?'

'He's a child.'

'You're preaching to the choir, but Grosvenor

wants him and only him.'

'I want to see him as soon as possible.'

'The orderlies are weaning the inmate off his medication—bringing him back from Dartmoor—as we speak.'

'The patient, Charles.'

'We have to call them inmates by law now. Everything's changed here.'

Hopkins lowered the scans. 'I have earnt my right to speak up. So have you, Doctor.'

'I have a family to think about.'

Silence.

'I'm sorry. I didn't mean to—'

'So, you know what happened to my son?'

'Half the … we have here are veterans. National Service alone has tripled the strain on mental health in the last 20 years.'

'So you drug them and lock them up?'

'Even the families advocate it in most cases, since PTSD can never be cured. It's not that bad: not for Big Pharma anyway.'

'And what's your end, Charles? PTSD can be cured, by the way. I invented the cure.'

'And sold it to Grosvenor who turned it into Totem. You're as much to blame as me. What do you want from me, Hopkins? You want me to take them all on? What do you think I am?'

'You took an oath. You're supposed to be a doctor.'

'We might as well throw the Hippocratic Oath in

the sea, Hopkins. We're PR scarecrows, nothing more. You think I'm happy about it?'

Hopkins stood up to leave. 'When can I meet the patient?'

Charles slouched back on to the sofa. 'He'll be awake by noon tomorrow.'

'And you have no evaluation of his condition?'

'Only what you've seen in the scans.'

'And what is your conclusion on those?'

'Traumatised paranoid schizophrenics tend to show similar patterns, but never lit up like that. I don't know.'

Hopkins gathered up the documents. 'I'll find out tomorrow.'

'I'll have a full security team organised to escort you - and you'll need a radio. We'll have him restrained in his cell to be on the safe side.'

'No security. Just me and McCole. And leave the restraints. It's a plexi-cell, right?'

'Right, but—'

'Don't test me on this, Charles.' Hopkins opened the door with his thumbprint.

'Do you have somewhere to stay, Hopkins?'

'We'll find a guest house.'

'Take my car,' Charles said as he held up a set of Mercedes keys. 'It's the least I can do. I never drive it anyway.'

Keeping his eyes fixed on the shambling doctor, Hopkins took the keys. 'Thank you.'

Hopkins returned to the helicopter to find McCole somewhat out of sorts.

McCole slumped in the back seat with the Beretta laid on his chest. 'Took your sweet time. Been bored out of my mind.'

Hopkins climbed into the pilot's seat. 'They're transmitting a child. The Horseman is sixteen years old.'

'They put a kid in this place? What for?'

'Crucified a warden in Leeds borstal.'

McCole's cleared his throat. 'As in crucified?'

'Crucified. Nailed him to a metal staircase.'

'Bet that raised a few eyebrows,' McCole said, climbing forwards into the cockpit.

'This isn't a joke.'

'Well, what do you want me to say?'

'That you'll come with me tomorrow to assess him.'

'What use am I gonna be?' McCole frowned until it dawned on him. 'Because of the crucifixion thing. You think he'll talk to me. Fuck's sake. Want me to dress up in my robes? Bring some fucking holy water?'

'Don't worry: I'll do the talking. I just need you there. The dog collar will be fine.'

'Who is Grosvenor so afraid of? Who's running this show?'

Hopkins glanced sideways at McCole. 'I can't tell you.'

'Don't give me all that oath shit, Hopkins. Both

our arses are on the line here.'

'You wouldn't believe me if I told you, anyway.'

McCole narrowed his eyes and leaned closer to Hopkins. 'She takes orders from her toaster, is that it?'

'It's a Board of chairmen that instructs Alice in her actions, headed by her father.'

'Oh, aye.'

'No, really. It's her coping mechanism for the shame of all the things she's done to get where she is. They exist only in her mind. It's all her.'

'And how do you know all this?'

'I treated her … Once.'

'Just the once?'

'Back in Sheffield, after her father died. Trust me: the only person you ought to fear is Alice herself.'

McCole put on his headset. 'You're all over the news, by the way,' he said, making the radio squelch and whine as he tuned it.

Grosvenor Media announced today that they have retained the father of Totem, Doctor David Hopkins, to oversee their upcoming transmission of The Horseman. With the endorsement of Doctor Hopkins - who pioneered the groundbreaking technology - Grosvenor Media is confident that the transmission will be a ratings success. The doctor was unavailable for comment today, but has expressed his enthusiasm for the project and hopes that it will usher in an exciting new chapter in the evolution of Totem.

'She was always going to spin it.'

'That doesn't make you angry?'

Hopkins took the key from the helicopter's ignition. 'Like you said, McCole: no-one will remember me anyway.'

'I thought we were taking off again?'

Hopkins jangled the Mercedes keys in front of McCole. 'Doctor's lent us his car.'

'Thank Christ.' McCole unhooked his headset and hauled himself out of the cockpit.

26

John's dreams were full of horrors that night, like they used to be back in the borstal. They clamped cold electrodes to his skin and his freshly-shaven scalp as he stared up into a brass, black hole. In the metal's reflection, he could see the gurney on which he was lying and the white coats surrounding it. Blue light glowed in his peripheral vision, smearing across the brass and sliding into the darkness.

His mother's face appeared in the field through the blades of grass. He tried to focus and hold on to the details of her features, but they slid away with the blue light every time.

Sadness knotted in his stomach.

Then he was picked up by his giant eight-year-old self. Fingers like pudgy, pink zeppelins dropped him in a huge matchbox.

John woke up soaked in sweat.

The light was unnatural and the floor, metal. The

sand of the beach had disappeared beneath him. Engines hummed instead of the wind whistling and the waves lapping at the shore.

And Arthur was gone.

When he realised that he was back inside the cage aboard the ship, he felt like his heart was going to stop.

He grabbed the bars and pulled at them as hard as he could, unable to bear the thought of Arthur waiting for him on the beach.

'It's alright,' said a familiar voice from the other side of the bars. 'You're coming down. We'll get you levelled out, don't you worry.'

'Wish this kid would hurry the hell up.'

'Davis? Corporal Davis?' John spoke into the darkness.

'Yeah, Corporal. That's right,' Davis laughed.

'Stop that, Davis. Don't you listen to him. Take a sip of your water and have a lie-down. You'll be right soon.'

'My horse. I can't just leave him.'

'That's alright. He'll be fine. He can look after himself.'

'He's going on about that horse again. Jesus Christ, we should just send him back. He's round the bend. Have you forgotten the borstal, Biggs? He caused fucking mayhem.'

'Shut up, Davis. I'm trying to do my job.'

'Blood and shit everywhere. I know: I had to clean it up.'

'How come they never found any traces of anything under his nails, in his hair or in his cell then?'

'Because he's a clever little fucker isn't he? Creeps me out. You didn't see what he did to that other kid, nevermind the warden.'

'Just keep it to yourself, ok?'

Davis shrugged in the shadows, while John cried out for his horse. The pain in his chest was so great that it made his back arch and spasm. His face felt as if it was on fire as tears ran down his cheeks.

'What's he doing now?'

'Call the crash team, Davis. Looks like he's having a heart attack.'

John was still blind and couldn't breathe. His teeth clenched so tight he thought they would break, and all he could hear at first was the ringing in his ears. The bars of the cage felt cold and hard as he thrashed against them, breaking a toe and making his head bleed. He tried to call out for Arthur, but his voice would not work. Voices rang out in the distance, as if shouted across a wide gorge.

'Got to get him on his side or he'll swallow his tongue.'

'You're not going in there?'

'He'll die if I don't.'

The Plexiglas door flew open and John felt hands on his body pushing him around until there was a stab in his thigh. He was able to breathe and his heart stopped thudding in his chest so much. The door closed. He sat up against the wall and stared at the two familiar faces dressed in white uniforms behind the glass.

'Where am I?'

'Exmoor High Security Hospital. You're adjusting to new meds, that's all.'

'Where's my horse?'

The two men whispered between themselves before Biggs replied, 'Your horse is safe and sound. Don't worry about him. We transported him too.'

'We're not supposed to do that, Biggs. Let's just use a wake up can.'

'He's just nearly gone into cardiac arrest, Davis. Are you stupid, or do you really hate this kid that much?'

'Fine,' Davis sniffed.

'Just give him a few minutes.'

'I'll have to cancel the crash team now.'

'Jesus. Sorry for the inconvenience, Davis.'

'Why are you dressed like that?'

'Relax, just hospital rules. We have to wear this stuff.'

'Let me go back. I have to find my horse.'

'Shut the fuck up about your horse. We sold him to the glue factory.'

John stared blankly at Davis.

'You see? There's them dead eyes,' Davis said. 'Fucking told you so: absolute scum.'

'There are a few tests that the doctors need to do, John. Then you can go back.'

'Why tell him anything? You should have put the

bite mask and shackles on him while you were in there. What if he starts arresting again?'

'He's over the worst of it.'

John kept his eyes covered with his hands as he lay on his side on the floor of the cell. His white pyjama-clad body twitched.

'Keep your mouth shut, Davis. Let him be.'

John couldn't stop shaking. He tried to slow down his breathing and unclench his body, but it was no use. His mind was like sand. Every time he would start shaping a picture of his surroundings, the tide would wash it away. It was the same nightmare that had plagued him whilst he had been on Dartmoor: of a place with no air and no water. No grass for Arthur to eat and no rivers to fish. He was in a steel and plastic box with faces peering in at him. Orange fingers of gas came creeping through the vent. In the nightmare, there was always a noise before the fingers came to get him. Sssssht clank.

Spreading the fingers of his right hand a fraction, John peeked at the floor of the cell. It was the same gel-like material as the walls and when he tried poking his finger into it, he couldn't even make a mark. He turned his head to look at the Plexiglas window and the two white ghosts standing behind it. At least two inches thick. No chance of breaking out. He thought that if he could find a way to escape, he could wake up from this recurring nightmare. Make coffee and feed Arthur. But this nightmare seemed too real.

Panic set in and his body spasmed again. His eyes

pulled upwards into his brain as he clawed at his face. Sweat seeped into his pyjamas as he convulsed and thrashed on the rubbery floor. His teeth felt as if they were about to shatter and his temples about to cave in as the pressure in his jaw increased.

No release. No escape from the airless, colourless room.

Clink sssht clank.

The orange fingers reached towards him until they vanished, only for more to curl from the vent. As they wound their way around his body and up through his hair, they didn't even stop for the tender scar tissue. John winced as the fingers clawed him, raking over the map of pain carved into his back. He could feel the rubbery floor against his cheek. It was the most vivid nightmare he'd ever had. Why couldn't he wake up?

The ringing in his ears stopped and his breathing slowed down again. John squirmed in his wet pyjamas, and pulled himself to his feet against the rubber wall. His eyes felt as if they were sinking towards the centre of the earth.

'See? Right as rain,' Davis said from behind the Plexiglas, tossing the empty gas canister to Biggs.

Biggs dropped the can with a clatter and lunged for Davis, smearing his slimy face up against the Plexiglas. After a few seconds of struggling, Biggs had twisted Davis into an arm lock, from which he could not escape.

'You're getting sacked for this, you wanker. I don't

care who you know.' Biggs increased pressure on the lock. Davis squealed and smacked his free hand against the wall in submission. 'You'd better pray that boy's alright.'

When Biggs released him, Davis backed into a corner, holding his arm. 'You shouldn't have done that, Biggs.'

John ran his hands over his face, feeling the familiar curves and edges of his skull. The ridges of scar tissue, some of which had been there since he was little, were all exactly where they should be. It all felt so real, his brain didn't know which way to turn. If this was reality, he didn't want to be there. He collapsed on to his side and kept his eyes fixed on the colourless gel wall only because it was the safest place to look. He heard voices come and go, but could not understand what they were saying. The words held no meaning. John felt the drool coming from his mouth dampening his chest. The acrid smell of the gas. This was happening.

He had to find a way back to Dartmoor.

John hoped for the best: that Arthur had returned to the stables next to the forge. He'd left plenty of bales of hay in the nearby barn, which the horse would find eventually, and he certainly knew his way to and from the river for water. Arthur had survived on his own before John arrived on the island, so he could do it again, but he was still bereft. His chest ached and his vision swam as he tried to ignore the ghosts peering in and moaning at him.

27

McCole looked at his watch. 'I'm starving.'

'Get something from the canteen,' Hopkins said, not taking his eyes from John. The boy was still staring at the wall, as he had been for the past six hours.

'Have you seen what they're serving? I'd rather eat my own shite,' McCole leant back in his plastic chair and stretched his arms. 'Like the fella down the way there.'

To Hopkins' discomfort, McCole had turned the journey to the boy's cell into a sideshow, giving a running commentary on the tragedies behind each Plexiglas window. Hopkins didn't dare look: he couldn't be distracted from his task by those he had no chance of helping.

And he prayed to God that McCole would shut up about them.

'There's a woman pulling out her fingernails in this one,' McCole shouted from down the corridor. 'Why don't they do something about it?'

'They'll send them to Dartmoor, I should think,' Hopkins replied. He gathered up his documents in preparation to leave. 'Come on. Let's get some dinner.'

'God loves you, Hopkins.'

Hopkins put on his jacket. 'John, I'll be back tomorrow.'

As he left, Hopkins studied the boy's scarred profile. The worst of it looked like a blade injury running from the top of his head, down his left eye and through both lips.

He was lucky to have kept the eye, judging by the scar's trajectory.

Hopkins couldn't assume anything until John had emerged from the catatonia.

McCole was already wrapped up for the weather. 'Come on, Hopkins. Leave him for tonight. We'll come back in the morning.'

Hopkins thought of the morning he waved Andrew goodbye as he left for National Service. He'd never been the same again. That was the last time that he had seen his beautiful son. They only shipped back fragments of him in a man-shaped jar of flesh and blood. A botch job. Too many bits missing, like an old jigsaw puzzle.

Like this boy.

As the young guard buzzed them through the

security gate of C Wing, he caught Hopkins eye, but looked away too late. Hopkins had already recognised something in the young man's micro-expressions.

Halfway down the next corridor, he stopped. 'Wait here, McCole.'

'Seriously, I'll kick off if I don't get some food soon.'

'One minute.'

McCole grunted.

Hopkins approached the guard and cleared his throat. 'Do you know where I can find the orderlies that brought Muldoon back from Dartmoor?'

The guard, no older than twenty, looked behind him before he spoke to Hopkins through the steel mesh. 'Mr. Chandler suspended Davis and Biggs, sir.'

'On whose orders?'

'I can't say.'

Hopkins noticed his boots, polished to parade shine. 'Where did you do your service?'

The guard looked surprised at the question. 'Yemen.'

'My son served in Syria.'

'I know, sir. Sorry to hear what happened to him. I read it in The Serviceman.'

Hopkins tried to smile at the guard. 'Thank you.'

'I'm sorry I can't be of more help, sir.'

Hopkins drew closer to the mesh. 'Where would you look for these men?'

The guard made sure his radio was off before answering. 'Most orderlies live in digs on the other side of the island in Hawkridge. There's a tavern on the beach that sells cider. I'd ask around there.'

'I appreciate it,' Hopkins replied. Now he had to placate the hungry, scowling chaplain tapping his foot in the corridor.

'Sir?' the guard called after him. 'Don't go alone. Local farmers don't like strangers.'

Hopkins nodded to the guard before continuing down the corridor towards the car park.

'Let me drive.'

'So you don't want any cider?'

'Nowhere serves cider anymore.'

'This place in Hawkridge does.'

'You drive,' McCole said, already buckling himself into the passenger seat.

'Maybe we should go back to the guesthouse for the shotgun. The guard warned me about the locals.'

'Hopkins, stop being so paranoid, man. We're going for some cider. What locals anyway?'

'Farmers. And Grosvenor's men could already be there waiting for us, for all we know.'

Silence.

'It wouldn't hurt to stop by the guesthouse.'

The weather was warm for the time of year and the ubiquitous storm clouds had dissolved for the evening. There was even a sunset instead of the usual grey blanket wrapped around the islands. As the Mercedes climbed up the winding country roads to the peaks, Hopkins was able to see the entire island glittering under a red sky. A sheep caused Hopkins to brake, and McCole's grin appeared in his peripheral vision. It usually meant he'd remembered a tasteless joke or had come up with some other way to make Hopkins uncomfortable to amuse himself. He always started them the same way.

'Hey, Hopkins?'

'Yes, McCole,' Hopkins replied, as per their sixteen-year-old ritual.

'What do you call a farmer with a sheep under one arm and a goat under the other?'

'I don't know.'

'Bisexual.'

Silence.

'Let's try again. Why can't farmers count sheep to get to sleep?'

'Go on?'

'Because when they get to five, they've got to stop and have a wank.'

Hopkins sighed.

'How do farmers find their sheep in long grass?'

'Don't know.'

'Irresistible.'

'Maybe keep the jokes to yourself when we get to the tavern.'

'You're just no a people person like me.'

'We have to find out what happened to the boy.'

'Can't we just have a drink for tonight?'

'No-one's stopping you.'

'No farmer from round here is even going to

understand what you're saying.'

'Stow it for now, McCole: we're here,' Hopkins said, turning the Mercedes into the cobbled courtyard of the ancient tavern.

Its walls were painted white and the roof was neatly thatched. In the courtyard, a dozen 4x4 vehicles and two tractors sat. Hopkins parked the Mercedes behind them.

'Not the most inconspicuous choice of vehicle, Doctor.'

'If we're going to be assassinated, we might as well go out in style, Reverend.'

'Assassinated?'

'Grosvenor will try it sooner or later. She'll make it look like an accident and spin it for the transmission's PR campaign.'

'Yeah, but what about me? What have I done to deserve an assassination?'

'You're collateral damage.'

'She'd have a man of God killed just for being there? I can fucking believe it, as well. This is the reason I packed it all in.'

'Why?'

'Because people are bastards.'

Hopkins made sure the shotgun was out of sight, but reachable for McCole, should they need to make a getaway.

Inside, the tavern had oak beams, a slate floor, an open fire and bronze trinkets nailed to the walls. The young barmaid blushed as McCole caught her staring at his dog collar.

'I'll take it off, shall I?'

'It doesn't bother me, sir. Some of the folk round here, though ...'

She glanced towards a group of burly drinkers near the door. They looked Hopkins and McCole up and down, but soon returned to their furtive murmuring. They were standing around huge casks on which they rested their pints and whiskies.

'What about you? Do you ever go to church?'

'I used to. When I was a little girl. Before—'

'Totem?' Hopkins interrupted.

'Don't get me wrong, I love Totem, but people have changed.'

'What do you mean?'

'All they care about is their fix. A few years ago, no-one would have stood for that boy's transmission,' the barmaid whispered. 'Now, they can't wait to tune in.'

'Ever get any hospital workers drinking in here?'

'Everyone who isn't working on a farm or on national service is either working in the hospital or is just ... In the hospital. What can I get for you gentlemen?'

'One cider, one lemonade. And a table for dinner.'

Hopkins paid for the drinks and walked with the barmaid to a table by the window looking out over the beach.

Only a few slivers of red luminescence remained in

the sky. Two lovers walked along the shoreline hand-in-hand, making Hopkins remember his wife. She would have liked the place.

'And what about you? Will you be a farmer or a hospital worker?'

'I'm going to Grosvenor University in Sheffield to take Media Studies. Everyone knows that's where the real money is.'

McCole cocked an eyebrow at Hopkins and took a slurp of his cider.

'Smoked salmon on the specials there, Hopkins,' McCole said, pointing at a scrawled chalkboard hanging on the wall. 'Might rekindle your taste for the old firewater.'

'I'm not eating salmon or drinking whisky ever again.'

'Those days weren't all bad. Remember when the river was in flood?'

Hopkins rolled his eyes. 'Yes, McCole.'

'Remember when you were wading?'

'Yes, McCole.'

'And the fish bit your dick?'

'Thank you, McCole.'

'I'd never seen such a thing before.'

The barmaid cleared her throat.

'I'll take the smoked salmon, please,' McCole said, smiling. 'And a whisky. Laphroaig, if you have it.'

'No problem, sir. And for you, sir?'

'Smoked mackerel stuffed with raisins, pine kernels

and orange, please. Nothing else to drink, thank you.'

'Your meals won't be long,' The barmaid took their menus and adjourned to the kitchen.

'You're a saint, Doctor,' McCole said, draining his pint.

'I think you're just saying that.'

'Why'

'So that you can refer to me as Doctor in that condescending tone.'

'Come on, Hopkins. I'm trying to relax. Isn't my fault you can't handle your ale.'

'I have a job to do.'

McCole looked around the tavern's customers. 'How are we supposed to know which ones work at the hospital?'

'Look at their shoes. Most farmers won't bother with fancy shoes.'

'You're pulling my leg. What is it with you and shoes, anyway? You got a fetish?'

McCole returned to the bar for another pint of cider before his whisky arrived.

'Trust me, McCole. Eliminate the bad backs, bad hair and cheap shoes.'

'Man looks on the outside, but God looks at the heart.'

'We don't need to see his heart, McCole.'

'I'm away for a fag before the food comes. You keep looking at their shoes.'

The hot food sat on the table for ten minutes before Hopkins decided to start without the wandering McCole. After finishing his meal, he wiped off his plate with a napkin and placed it over McCole's untouched dinner. He wedged enough cash for the meals and a generous tip under the plates.

The path out the back of the tavern led down the steps and on to the beach. Looking down the shoreline, he saw two cigarettes glowing in the darkness. Drawing close enough to hear their voices, he recognised McCole's. He climbed over the rocks to reach their cove and jumped down on to the sand.

'McCole, you there? What's that smell?'

McCole emerged from the darkness.

'Who was that?'

'One of your locals,' McCole said, smoking the pungent-smelling cigarette

'Farmer? Is that this year's crop you're smoking?'

McCole shook his head and held the smoke a little longer. 'Hospital cleaner. Biggs was transferred to Exmoor to make up short numbers. About the same time Muldoon arrived.'

'Short numbers?'

'Bus crash. Two doctors, the driver, four orderlies and eight patients.' He offered the joint to Hopkins, who shook his head in response. 'About nine months ago. No survivors.'

Silence.

'Didn't I tell you I was a people person?'

'Did you ever hear anything about that on the news?'

'Never.'

'What did this guy say about Davis and Biggs? Did he say where they might be?'

'He said you've got more chance of plaiting your own piss than finding Biggs here.'

'Dead?'

'On the run. Probably didn't fancy the old bus crash scenario.'

'So, you're telling me we have no chance of finding this orderly?'

'He's gone, Hopkins.'

'And your new friend gave you no idea where?'

'Wouldn't tell me at first.' McCole tucked his hands into his jacket pockets. 'Until he clocked my forces tattoo.'

'Well?'

'Snowdonia,' McCole said, looking northwards. 'To find Lucky Newman.'

'I thought Lucky Newman was dead.'

'This guy reckons Lucky Newman is heading up a resistance, maybe even starting a coup.'

'We have to find them.'

'I'm not dragging my fat arse over a mountain range for a couple of ghosts, so forget that.'

Hopkins looked back towards the tavern. 'They served up your dinner about half an hour ago, by the way.'

McCole flicked the joint into the sand. 'Good. That walk's worked up my appetite.'

When they got back to the tavern, Hopkins saw that the full plate of food had gone from their table.

Three farmers in the corner kept looking over.

'Let's go somewhere else.'

'Fuck's sake. You're having a laugh,' McCole grumbled as he followed Hopkins out through the front door. 'I'll waste away to nothing.'

The barmaid shouted from the kitchen. 'Excuse me, gentlemen. Your bill's not paid.'

'I left double what the meal would have cost under the plate of salmon.'

The table of farmers laughed as they huddled tighter over their pints.

'That's my dinner,' McCole said, narrowing his eyes at the plate on the farmers' table.

With a mouthful of smoked salmon, the biggest one looked over and grinned, letting the juices run down his chin.

'Cheers, vicar,' he mumbled, as chunks of fish tumbled from his mouth. The rest of the farmers found this hilarious. They pounded the wooden table with their fists, causing a pint glass to smash on the stone floor. A cheer went up.

Hopkins walked over and spoke calmly. 'That belongs to me.'

The farmer spat out the chewed salmon on to Hopkins' shoes.

'You can have it, mate. It's fucking cold, anyway.'

His shoulders and arms were far too big for the gilet he was wearing. Hopkins knew that they could explode into violence against him at any second.

Hopkins touched his eyebrow nervously. 'And the

money I left for the bill?'

'That's your parking fee and I'm the parking attendant. You can afford it anyway, posh lad. Now pay the lady what you owe her.'

McCole took a wedge of cash from his pocket and handed it to the barmaid, not taking his eyes off the big farmer looming over Hopkins.

Hopkins held out his hand. 'My money, please.'

McCole took a single step forward, and the farmer's friends stood up.

The farmer spat in Hopkins' open hand and elbowed him hard in the head, sending him straight to the floor. He kept his arms high as muddy boots started flying towards his face, their steel toecaps threatening to break bone. Meanwhile, McCole charged headlong into the men. Their boots lifted off the floor and bones cracked as the reverend laid into the trio.

By the time Hopkins had pulled himself to his feet on an upturned chair, McCole was already finished with them. The three farmers lay on the cold stone floor of the tavern, two of them snoring; the other groaning in pain. The rest of the tavern remained frozen as the wild-haired, red-faced chaplain rummaged in the snoozing skinhead's pocket for the cash. He gave it to the open-mouthed barmaid and apologised. Despite the chaos, the plate of salmon had remained intact apart from the few pieces that the farmer had eaten. McCole picked up a fork and scooped a large piece into his mouth as Hopkins beckoned him outside.

McCole gave a thumbs-up to the slack-jawed diners while Hopkins dragged him through the front door. 'That's good cold, even.'

As they growled through the dark countryside in the Mercedes, the two men did not speak. He didn't know what to say to McCole until they arrived at a small guesthouse, recommended to them by one of the hospital guards. McCole struggled to get out of the passenger seat, so Hopkins walked around the car to help.

'Thanks, McCole.'

'It's alright. Watch my ribs though, aye?'

As he reached into the back seat of the Mercedes for the Beretta, Hopkins stopped him.

'That can stay there. We're leaving for Snowdonia.'

'We've no idea where we're going once we get there. And what about the kid?'

'We don't know how long it'll be before he comes round. We need Biggs' testimony to stop the transmission.'

'Back at the beach, that guy mentioned Davis, too.'

'Why didn't you tell me? Where is he?'

'He said that Davis is off suspension and back on C-wing. But I get a bad feeling about this guy.'

'He could be on a night-shift,' Hopkins replied. 'We could have been there by now. You should have told me.'

'He got Biggs fired by telling a pack of lies about him. Doesn't sound like your most reliable source of information.' McCole winced and held his ribs.

'Why don't you go and have a bath? I'll call your room when I'm back.'

'Get to fuck.'

'I'll be fine.' Hopkins lifted the centre armrest's cover to reveal a Smith and Wesson .357 magnum revolver. 'Being a doctor's a dangerous job on this island, it seems.'

'That's an old gun. And you're an old man.'

'Said the pot to the kettle.'

'Hopkins, you're so old,' said McCole, buckling up his seat belt. 'You used to get seaties on a fucking Penny Farthing.'

Hopkins rolled his eyes.

'You're so old, Julius Caesar used to steal your lunch money.'

They followed the bullet-holed signs. Exmoor Hospital 12 miles.

'You're so old–'

'I get it, McCole.'

By the time they'd parked the Mercedes and negotiated the maze of hospital corridors and checkpoints, McCole was breathing hard.

'Might have cracked a rib there.'

'Maybe.'

'Want me to call someone when we reach C-block?'

'What they gonna do with it? Kiss it better?'

'Get some painkillers at least.'

'My painkiller's waiting for me in a bottle on the sideboard back at the guesthouse.'

'Did you bring the money from the room?'

'In the boot.'

'I should have enough on me,' said Hopkins, feeling a wedge of notes in his inner jacket pocket.

'For what?'

Once they arrived at C-wing, Hopkins noticed the same guard as the day before at the security gate. He stood to greet them. 'Evening, sir.'

'Evening. I believe Davis is back on duty?'

'He signed in after you left, sir.'

'So where is he now?'

The guard checked his clipboard down and then across, then his bank of screens.

'Says here he's supposed to be in sector C9, where your John Doe is, but I only see the inmate,' said the guard. 'Unless he's in one of the other cells.'

'Can you access the cell cameras?'

'Not without Chandler's clearance.'

'We need to have a quiet word with Davis, so maybe you could let us down there. Hopkins slipped a wad of cash underneath the clipboard on the desk and pushed it in front of the guard.

'If it means Davis might get caught red-handed—'

McCole sneered. 'Get caught doing what?'

'I've caught him doing weird stuff with patients a few times. Restraining them and force-feeding them when there's no need. I think he gets some kind of kick out of it, sir,' the guard replied, taking the cash from beneath the clipboard.

McCole sighed. 'Just what we need: another fucking weirdo.'

The guard buzzed them through the gate and they walked down the dim corridor. The further they went, the quieter the screams from the rest of the hospital became. As disturbing as the sounds of torment were, it was the deathly silence in the depths of the wing that made Hopkins shiver.

They found Davis in a dark, disused shower block, surrounded by cigarette smoke. He'd heard their shoes on the hard floor and was trying to wave the smoke away, but the moonlight caught it as they both entered the tiled room. McCole even recognised the brand of tobacco.

'Got any more of those? Been years since I've had a Camel.'

Davis handed over the soft packet from which McCole withdrew a crisp, white cigarette before offering one to Hopkins. He shook his head, so McCole handed them back to Davis.

McCole loomed over him. 'Are you Davis?'

'Who's asking?'

'I'm Reverend McCole and this is Doctor Hopkins.'

'I didn't do anything. What do you want?'

'We want information.'

'About what?'

'About patient John Doe in C9. And your ex-colleague Biggs.'

'What's in it for me?'

'Keeping your job.'

McCole clenched one his bruised fists. 'Keeping your teeth.'

'Don't think you understand,' Davis said, removing another Camel from the pack for himself. 'I have an arrangement.'

'With whom? Charles?'

Davis rolled his eyes towards the damp ceiling. 'Please.'

'Chandler?'

Davis shook his head and pointed upwards with his finger.

Hopkins had no time for the theatrics. 'What do you want?'

'Cash.'

'Cash this,' McCole said, surging forward with a head-butt to Davis' nose. In the moonlight, the eruption of blood looked black. Davis fell to the floor, holding his face, while Hopkins struggled to hold McCole back.

'We're on a mission from God here and this cunt's fuckin' round about money.' The chaplain wiped the blood from his forehead and picked up his still-smoking cigarette off the damp tiles.

Davis snorted through his bloody fingers. 'A mission from God?'

McCole broke away from Hopkins grip and grabbed Davis by the collar, lifting him off his feet.

'I haven't had my dinner, so fucking answer his question.'

'Let him go, McCole. Go and smoke your cigarette in the corridor.'

McCole let go of Davis and walked out of the shower block, steaming with anger. Once the heavy door had clunked shut, Hopkins turned to Davis.

'Is he really a priest?'

'What can you tell me about the John Doe in C9?'

Davis cocked an eyebrow at Hopkins.

Hopkins took the rest of the cash from his pocket. 'Tell me everything.'

Davis' eyes focused on the wad of money. 'That buys you three questions.'

'Done. I already know that you work for Alice Grosvenor, so we won't bother with that one.'

'I don't know who that is,' Davis shrugged, thinking that his performance was convincing.

'Did you hurt that boy on purpose?'

'The Horseman? I'm a professional. Of course not.'

Hopkins scanned Davis' rat-like face and shook his head. 'If you don't tell me the truth, we don't have a deal.'

'I would never harm anyone under my care.'

'Davis, I haven't the time to waste. I'll give you this money if you answer just one question truthfully,' said Hopkins, looking at his watch. 'If you don't, you'll have to speak to the reverend again.'

Davis' eyes widened no more than a micron, but

Hopkins knew what he was thinking. He was weighing up the situation like a good little sociopath.

'Some doctor. What's the question?'

'Are we agreed on these terms?'

'Agreed,' Davis said, itching his nose in his most obvious giveaway yet.

'Where is Biggs?'

Davis fell silent for a moment before a look of triumph lit up his face. 'I don't know. I actually don't know.'

'You have no idea where Biggs is?'

Davis laughed. 'No-one does.'

Hopkins heart sank as he realised that he was telling the truth. He stood up, handed over the money and walked towards the door of the shower block.

'Why is he called The Horseman?'

'Before he went back to la-la land, he kept asking for his horse,' said Davis as he counted the cash. 'Or it could be a reference to how many people he's killed. Or his fucked up face. Who cares?'

Hopkins turned his back on Davis counting his money and walked out of the block without another word.

Hopkins rejoined McCole in the silent corridor. 'Mission from God? Are we due a sermon?'

'All this is the work of science.'

Hopkins glanced at the catatonic patients in the cells, surrounded by plumes of orange gas. 'This isn't science.'

'It's evil. Life is cheap here.'

'But profitable.'

'You don't talk like a scientist sometimes, Hopkins.'

'And you're the village vicar, I suppose.'

'So, what did you get?'

'Well, Davis is a sociopath, but not a very bright one.'

'And?'

'They call the boy the Horseman because of an hallucination he had when he was in Dartmoor.'

'From Dartmoor? Why the fuck was he in Dartmoor?'

'It's the expression they use for medicating patients into catatonia,' Hopkins said, as they hustled towards the security gate. 'He kept asking for his horse when he woke up.'

The guard stood up in anticipation of their arrival. Hopkins sensed that something was up with his body language. He was holding a clipboard and a pen.

'Please sign out here, gentlemen. Night-time policy.'

Hopkins signed the sheet and handed the pen to McCole. As he went to sign, the guard encircled several items with the pen on the paper. He said something to McCole, but Hopkins couldn't catch it on account of the creaking gate. McCole took the sheet of paper from underneath the signature list and stuffed it into his trouser pocket.

'Good night,' the guard said, tipping his hat as they

left through the gate. 'And good luck, sirs.'

'What the hell was that, McCole?'

'A warning to leave the island tonight. He gave me this, too.'

Hopkins read the scrap of paper. 'Co-ordinates?'

'Co-ordinates and a frequency.'

'A frequency?'

McCole turned over the scrap of paper and read the guard's instructions. 'It's an invitation to Lucky Newman's hideout. We get to Snowdonia and tune our radio to this frequency. Then we transmit a beacon signal and wait for instructions.'

'I'll get the stuff from the car. You head to the roof and start the rotor.'

Davis' girlish hands fumbled with the heavy tools that the Grosvenor agent had given him. He blamed his dead mother for her fine bone structure.

In the pathetic light of a pen torch clamped between his teeth, he struggled to read the scrap of paper that had come with the tools. He sighed and walked around the metal and glass eggshell of the helicopters cockpit and opened the pilot's door. The instructions were in some kind of military short-hand that he couldn't read, having ducked his national service on a medical blag. He only had twenty minutes before the doctor and the chaplain would be at the helipad and he wanted to do this job right.

He couldn't wait to see this thing go down in a ball of flames with Hopkins and that fucker McCole inside.

Davis ran his tongue over the hot, coppery seam that had formed on the inside of his lip. He could still make it ooze blood into his mouth if he pressed his tongue hard enough against the split.

Shame that it would be over so fast. He would have loved to have seen the fear in the reverend's face. Eyes widening, sweat slickening his skin, heart beating faster. The same way he liked his inmates when he was kneeling on their faces.

Davis found the panel named in the instructions and prised it open using a crowbar. After he jammed the sharp end into the circuit Board, he spat on it for good measure.

Grosvenor always paid well, but he would have done this shit for free. As the circuit Board fizzed and released a plume of smoke into the cockpit, Davis felt that warm glow of satisfaction that he got from sabotage. The fact that this one would be lethal made him giddy.

His delight was short-lived, as someone yanked him backwards through the open door and hurled him on to the cold tarmac of the helipad. The crowbar clanged, but he managed to keep hold of it and swung blindly into the night. It connected with something hard and his assailant let out a gasp. The hands tightened their grip on Davis and smashed him into the helicopter's shell, causing him to fall unconscious.

Hopkins arrived at the helipad to find McCole sitting in the back of the Lynx with Davis duct-taped at the hands, feet and mouth. The chaplain leant against the pilot's door, trying to staunch the bleeding from his head with a dressing from the helicopter's first aid box.

'What the hell happened?'

'This little shit was trying to sabotage us. I stopped him before he got any further than this panel.'

Hopkins inspected the damage, reaffixed the panel's outer casing and sat in the pilot's seat, reaching up for his headphones.

'Can we still fly?'

'Can you live without heating in the cockpit? He took out the wrong circuit.'

'What are we gonna do with him, anyway? I say we drop him on Grosvenor's office roof from 500 feet. Make a point.'

'Take him with us.'

'Fuck that. Why?'

'We can't leave him here and we can't kill him.'

'Fucker crowbarred me in the head. Why can't we kill him?' McCole dug Davis in the ribs with the bruised and bloody knuckles of his right hand.

'McCole, you won't even kill fish when we catch them.'

That's different: they're not trying to kill us.'

'We take him with us.'

McCole strapped himself in the back seat with Davis lying next to him. 'Fine. Give me one of the guns then.'

Hopkins handed him the .357 and started the rotor. 'Be careful: it's loaded.'

McCole pulled the revolver from its holster and rested it across his knee with the barrel pointing at Davis's head. As he cocked the hammer, Davis' eyes widened.

'Careful not to go over any bumps now.'

'Don't mess with that thing.'

McCole uncocked the revolver with a sigh. 'The loonies in C-wing would make me a saint,' he said, waving the barrel at the hospital.

'There are no saints anymore, McCole.'

'There'll always be saints. Isn't that the whole fucking point of saints?'

The helicopter's rotor whined ever higher as both men put on their headsets.

Hopkins looked at Davis' duct-tape bound face. 'Why do you want to kill him so badly?'

'Because he can't be saved.'

Now that the rotor was up to full speed, Hopkins peeled the helicopter off the hospital roof and took to the skies, bound north by north west for Snowdonia.

28

Saturday's transmission of a disgraced judge had been one of Totem's most popular transmissions yet. The depravity behind the wrinkled, kindly old face. The desperate protests of innocence. The right honourable Judge Higham's conviction had sent the public's morbid curiosity into overdrive. Strapping the old boy down to that gurney in an orange jumpsuit had definitely been one of the highlights of Alice's year.

Those quivering, burbling lips.

Liver-spotted hands trembling at his sides.

Old and salty tears running over paper thin eyelids as the electrodes stuck to his shaven scalp.

It was his own fault for turning against her. For trying to shame her. Her ambition sickened these patriarchal old fools, whom she had been sweeping away for the past decade. He should have stood aside: apart from anything else, the big pharma buyout was none of his business.

When Judge Higham's dream turned out to be a shade too tame, she thought that Totem had failed her for the first time. Until she summoned the archaic might of her radio and print companies. They chewed up the judge's dream and spat it out as something monstrous. She could always trust the mob to believe what they wanted to believe.

They didn't vote him back to prison, either. They voted him free, hunted him down and strung him up in his seaside bed-and-breakfast hideout.

Just like Alice had strung up Andrew Hopkins in the woods.

It was something of a turning point for Totem.

And for the British public. Her loyal little savages.

Higham's family were still in hiding.

Alice just hoped that the social fabric wouldn't completely tear asunder before they transmitted the Horseman.

She couldn't wait another sixteen years to rear a new sacrificial lamb.

Some of the things the boy had experienced had been unsavoury, even by her standards. But that was the point. It was the only way she would finally get her place on the Board: to push beyond her own boundaries. These were the requirements of his martyrdom and her ascension. The Board wanted a dream that would traumatise Britannia, instilling a fear so powerful that the citizens would do anything to be set free from it. They would kneel before her and

Britannia's only major pharmaceutical company, which was now hers in the wake of the judge's death.

And then she would be rewarded with her long-awaited promotion.

But first she had to find another way to kill Hopkins.

29

The box of grilled, green metal and glowing valves squelched as Lucky Newman signed off and removed his headset. The other faces in the room stared at him.

Biggs stared at Lucky. 'So?'

'They're landing in the old quarry to the north.'

He sent McClane and two new recruits on their way to fetch Hopkins, McCole and–to Biggs's chagrin–Davis.

'We should get rid of Davis. He's a snake.'

'We need intel on Grosvenor.'

'Do you think Hopkins will help us?'

'We can help each other.'

'What does he want from me?'

'What Grosvenor won't give him: the truth.'

'About The Horseman? But I hardly know anything.'

'You know enough to keep him sweet.'

'What if he asks about his son?'

'Don't tell him. Not yet.'

Half an hour later, McClane returned with Hopkins and McCole.

'Clark and Evans have taken Davis to the brig,' McClane said, locking the weapons in a safe.

'These are friends of ours.'

McCole caught Lucky's eye. 'What happened to you, Newman?'

Hopkins realised that McCole was not talking about crucifixions, beheadings, IEDs or POWs. He was asking about his disappearance.

'I thought you were dead.'

'Grosvenor made an example of me. After the article about Totem ran, she dissolved my bank account, revoked my citizenship and labelled me an enemy of the state. Then she bought up every last printing press in Britannia. Except one.'

Hopkins and McCole followed Lucky into the bowels of the bunker, down staircases and tunnels that seemed to turn back in on themselves. As they progressed down the final passageway, the mechanical clunking and hissing became louder. A young man with a rifle welcomed them into the room.

'Our job is to print the truth. His job is to protect it until it's delivered.'

The guard saluted. 'Morning, sir.'

'Don't salute me and don't call me sir. How many times? Call me Lucky or Newman.'

'Yes, sir,' he said, dropping his right hand back to his side but hardly standing at ease.

'He's only been here a fortnight,' Lucky whispered to Hopkins. 'Good lad, but he's puddled.'

'You mean PTSD?'

'Bit of a dirty word round here,' said Lucky, meeting McCole's stare. He nodded in understanding.

As they progressed further into the room, the press became so loud that they had to shout above the working machinery. Two men stood on the other side of the press, both cradling levers. Meanwhile, other personnel maintained the machinery that wasn't running. It was so clean that the oil lanterns reflected around the room every time they spun or clanked.

'We Frankensteined it from old parts. Shipped them into town with the help of a few locals. Carried them up the mountain piece by piece.'

Hopkins seemed impressed by the machine: the chaplain less so.

'Is something the matter, Reverend?'

'I'm just tired,' McCole grunted. 'And hungry.'

'We've arranged sleeping quarters for you here in the bunker. I'll ask one of the men to bring you some food, if you would like?'

'Bless you.'

'A little bedtime reading?' Lucky suggested, handing the two men a copy of The Serviceman. 'Hot off the press, as they say.'

The paper was cold now, but it was true: it had

been hot when Lucky Newman had given it to Hopkins in the printing press room. As he lay in his bunk, even with McCole snoring across the corridor from his room, he struggled to keep his eyes open long enough to read it. The gentle flicker of the paraffin hurricane lantern lit up the crisp, black ink on the page.

INVENTOR OF TOTEM COMES OUT OF RETIREMENT TO PROTEST TRANSMISSION OF MENTAL PATIENT

The headline was true enough. Hopkins went on to read how he had once been one of the leading minds in neuropsychiatry until the tragic death of his son.

They didn't once use the word suicide when referring to Andrew's passing, which Hopkins found strange.

He doused the hurricane lantern, closed his eyes and began to dream.

Hopkins wandered a barren moor at dusk, dressed in a black cassock, like the moth-eaten one McCole kept in his wardrobe at the distillery. But he was not in the Highlands. This was not Scottish soil. The heather didn't purple the hills and the setting suns felt warm.

He looked in every direction for a landmark, but there was nothing.

All the gulls stayed silent as they watched him fade into the moors.

After a mile or so, the suns were lower and shadows longer.

A young man on a horse watched him.

The rider headed south and Hopkins followed for what seemed like hours.

Finally, the horseman stopped at a tall wire fence. Hopkins slowed down when he realised that it wasn't Andrew riding the horse, but John Doe from Exmoor.

Hopkins approached as the horse's bulbous, wet eye watched him from behind a stray lick of white mane. The horse grunted and backed away as he reached out his hand.

John turned the horse towards the prison. 'Follow me.'

Hopkins obliged, weaving through a maze of tall wire fences until they could see the main building. Half the west wing had crumbled away in the Atlantic winds. The jail loomed in the dusk like a giant, crumbling sandcastle.

'I've been waiting. I thought no-one would come and see.'

The waves crashed beyond the prison.

'Have you seen Andrew Hopkins?'

'I'm mad, not dead.'

John turned his horse for the east wing, while Hopkins followed behind. By the time they reached the flattened wire fences and battered walls, it was dark.

'Is this Dartmoor?'

'Yes.'

'The real one?'

'Does it matter?'

Hopkins woke from the dream to knocking on his door. He opened it to see Newman standing there with a cup of black coffee in hand.

'I was hoping for a chat over breakfast.'

'Let me shower first, Newman.'

'As you wish, Doctor.'

'Call me Hopkins,' he said, taking the coffee mug and closing the door in Newman's face.

He heard Newman mutter through the door. 'Arsehole.'

It wasn't that Hopkins disliked Newman or even that his request was unreasonable. His nightmares preoccupied him until noon or his first drink - whichever came first. And his drinking days were gone. He also didn't like to be reminded of the past, which Newman would want to talk about.

He swilled the coffee, threw the towel on the radiator over his shoulder and stepped out into the bunker's warren.

Already the corridors were alive with boots thumping along them like blood through an artery. Hopkins could hear the faint clatter of old-fashioned typewriters through the walls. All trying to revolutionise Britannia one keystroke at a time. Radios squelched and buzzed around the tunnels, making Hopkins feel like he was deep in a giant insect colony.

On the wall was a map of the bunker, showing which direction to walk for the shower block. Personnel wearing headsets and clutching wads of loose documents ran past him, but each took the time to wish him a good morning as they went.

The shower block was spotless, like everything else in the bunker. The mirrors by the sinks were still steamed but there was no-one else in the tiled room. Hopkins stripped off, threw his stuff in one of the lockers and stood under one of the old-fashioned heads, which reminded him of watering cans. The steel Twyfords taps turned until hot water came out, prickling his nervous system to life.

Hopkins hoped that a good night's rest might have calmed McCole's alcohol withdrawal. He always knew that the chaplain was capable of violence, but the display in the tavern had still surprised him. Those farmers were half McCole's age and only one had time to land a blow before he'd wiped the floor with all three. Through countless whisky-marinated conversations, Hopkins thought that he'd had the measure of McCole.

The chaplain often claimed to hate violence. He used to say that just the thought of it made his hands shake and his skin go cold. But he'd also said that life cannot exist without it; that the act prerequisite for life is an act of violence in itself.

Hopkins remembered McCole's suicide bid in the out-house. The thought of life alone on that rock—

forever to be mocked by ghosts in the stills—still made him shiver.

He unwrapped the soap in the tray, folded the brown paper neatly and wedged it behind the pipe.

Once showered, Hopkins hurried back to his room to get dressed so that he could go and check on the chaplain. Buttoning his shirt with one hand and knocking on McCole's door with the other, he received no answer. None of his hideous snoring came from within, either.

He opened the door and peered inside. The bed was made and the room was tidy. Most unlike McCole.

Hopkins closed the door and sniffed the air. Smoky bacon.

As he headed down the corridor towards the canteen, he heard people laughing hard. Hopkins turned a couple of corners and swung open the heavy door marked CANTEEN.

Plates and pans clattered in the open kitchen where several men were manning the stoves and the sinks. In the centre of the room was a long table, either side of which everyone was sat on benches, which looked like old church pews. Convenient, since McCole seemed to be delivering a booming sermon of smutty jokes.

'Ah, good morning, Doctor.'

Everyone stood and saluted like the guards at the lab used to. Hopkins could feel his cheeks turning red.

One of the men whispered something about a helicopter in Newman's ear.

'Let the man have his coffee first. The helicopter can wait. Grosvenor's team won't be here until tomorrow.'

'Grosvenor's sending reconnaissance?'

One of the soldiers shook his head as he chewed his bacon. 'Nice euphemism, Doc. Read that in the Grosvenor Mail, did you?'

A leather-faced man in his forties continued speaking from the far end of the table. 'They're death squads. I was in one sent to Snowdonia to find the printing press and wipe out the resistance.'

'Why did you defect?'

'When I found out Lucky Newman was the leader, I turned. The Serviceman changed everything.'

'To truth and the sovereign state of Snowdonia, where we are all free men.'

Some of the men were pale and twitchy from substance abuse. Others were scarred, disfigured, even missing limbs, but all of them were smiling, including McCole, who was still stuffing his face. He looked up from the full English breakfast

'When was the last time we had black pudding, Hopkins? Actual black pudding?'

Hopkins didn't respond, being somewhat aggrieved by this. Years of counselling. Free room and Board. Gallons of whisky. Litres of antiseptic to treat the wounds caused by the whisky. For nothing. All he had to do was fry up some congealed pig's blood and serve it up on a plate to stop the ape from killing himself.

'If you'd wanted black pudding, I'm sure we could have found some.'

'Banned on the mainland since Swine Flu. Don't think I didn't try.'

'So you two lived on that island for how long?'

'Sixteen years.'

'In a whisky distillery?'

'Oh, aye,' McCole said, raising his mug of steaming black coffee with a shaky hand. While the men fantasised about living in a distillery, he looked at Hopkins to see if he had noticed his delirium tremens. Hopkins—falling straight back into their habitual routine—pretended not to have seen it and flicked his eyes away. The embarrassment wasn't helpful to McCole. Neither of them thought that they were ever going to leave that island anyway, so it had become a routine that was hard to break.

Newman nodded at McCole's shaking fingers. 'Most here know what it's like.'

Hopkins was envious of the camaraderie McCole had struck up with the ex-servicemen. There had been no voices of encouragement in the doctor's ear when he gave up drinking so that they might both survive the winter. Quite the opposite, in fact. McCole had been most vocal in criticising his abstinence. He often referred to a blood oath on the island's mountain, which neither of them could ever remember.

Hopkins sighed. 'Good for you, McCole.'

One of the men presented Hopkins with his own full English breakfast, but he had lost his appetite. He sipped at his fresh cup of coffee to get it kick-started again.

'Where is Davis?'

'Stockade. We'll be questioning him later. You're welcome to sit in.'

'And Biggs?'

'Biggs is sat right there,' Newman replied, pointing his finger at a robust young man with black hair and red cheeks. He was wearing a lumberjack shirt and was sat halfway down the table on the opposite side from Hopkins.

'I need to speak with him.'

'And I need to speak with you, Hopkins. For The Serviceman.'

Hopkins nodded in agreement as he chewed on a small morsel of toast and egg.

Newman leaned across the table. 'Biggs, go with the doctor to the War Room when you've both finished breakfast. He has a few questions about the Horseman.'

30

The War Room was full of radios, switchboards, maps, projectors, blackboards and boxes of documents. Back up batteries for the radio units sat amongst loose scrolls of blueprints on metal shelves that ran along one wall. Hopkins picked up a stray walkie-talkie unit, pressed a button and it crackled to life. He put it back on the shelf and sat at the round table, which took up the centre of the room. Biggs stood behind one of the chairs, looking nervous.

'Sit down, Biggs. When did you first encounter the patient?'

'I was working at the Leeds Borstal for Boys and they brought him from a care home out on some island off Scarborough. He was the talk of the place. The way I heard the other lads talking before he arrived, I knew there was gonna be trouble.'

'Why was he the talk of the place?'

'Because of what he was supposed to have done in

the care home.'

'What was that?'

'Taken out the eye of a Grosvenor agent. With a garden fork.'

'And what do you think?'

'The agent probably got what was coming to him.'

Hopkins had been reading Biggs since he sat down. There was nothing to suggest that he was lying. 'You're saying that the boy was abused in the care homes?'

'Show me a kid that wasn't abused in the care homes. But he got it worse than anyone I've ever seen. Showed me a scar from a whipping. Told me he was seven when they did it.'

'What happened at the Borstal?'

'Chaos.'

Hopkins saw black clouds of guilt gathering over Biggs. 'What do you mean?'

'There was a bounty for slashing him up. All the inmates were talking about it. I told the warden and he locked the kid in ISC for his own safety. Banned Grosvenor's security agents from the grounds.'

'The warden who was crucified?'

'After that, they threw away the key on the kid. I got a commendation and a visit from Grosvenor's security, warning me not to talk to anyone about him.'

'So he didn't crucify the warden?'

'He was in an ISC cell at the time. There's no way he could have done it.'

'You said Grosvenor's security agents came to visit

you?'

Biggs took a deep breath and rubbed his neck. 'After the warden got killed, the kid changed. Kept screaming to me through the walls of his cell, but I couldn't make out what he was saying. I had the tray halfway in the food hatch one morning and he told me that he's Arthur Muldoon's son.'

'The first man ever transmitted by Totem?'

'The only person I mentioned it to was Davis. Next morning, we're all on a helicopter to Exmoor. At first, I thought we were just escorting the inmate. Didn't realise we'd be staying.'

'You were always going to be staying.' Hopkins leafed through his documents. 'You're lucky you weren't in a bus crash or some other such unfortunate accident.'

'Grosvenor's men were always around the borstal from the day he arrived there. When the new warden arrived, we were told to give them access to all areas and not to ask any questions. I always knew that there was something wrong about it, but I–'

'Can you tell me why the patient is still in a catatonic state even though his medication has been cut?'

'You can thank Davis for that. He screwed in a high-dosage wake-up canister before Muldoon was ready. He's always doing it. Gets a thrill from watching them fit. Kid'll be lucky if he's not a vegetable.'

'Why didn't you report him?'

'I did every time, until I found out he was on Grosvenor's payroll. After that I didn't bother. That day he did it to the boy, I knocked out one of his teeth and ran from the hospital. Didn't stop until I got here.'

'I couldn't get anything out of Dr. Charles. No paperwork, no interviews, not even a diagnostic sheet. Just a few scans which make no sense.'

'Charles is just another scarecrow.'

'He used that word, too.'

'All the hospital workers call the doctors that.'

'Why did you put your neck on the line for this kid?'

'Muldoon? I grew up in the care homes myself. Felt sorry for him.'

'So you came here for protection?'

'I'd heard rumours about the printing press. And I served two tours with Commando 42. Thought I could be of some use.'

'When's the boy likely to pull out of the catatonia?'

'Could be days before he comes round, if he comes round at all. I don't think they ever wanted you to speak to him.'

Hopkins opened the door of the War Room. 'I think it's time we had a word with Davis.'

'Doctor?'

Hopkins closed the door. 'Yes?'

'Don't take your eyes off him.'

31

Hopkins followed Biggs to the stockade where they found that the prisoner's interrogation was already underway.

He entered the room to see Davis naked and duct-taped to a small wooden chair, trembling like a pig in a slaughterhouse. There were four other men in the darkened room. McClane stood in the corner, casually sharpening a knife as if he were a vaguely interested butcher. Newman held a lit hurricane lamp aloft which cast strange shadows on the walls. Tears rolled down Davis' face as one of the men loomed over him with a lump hammer. He lifted it above his head, lined up with Davis' right knee.

'Stop this at once.'

The man with the hammer turned around with it still held above his head.

'McCole, put that hammer down right now,' Hopkins sighed.

'Are you serious? Apart from trying to kill us, do you know what he did to that boy? Did you tell him, Biggs?'

'I told him, McCole.'

'Put it down.'

Newman stepped forward from the shadows and confronted Hopkins. 'This is not your area of expertise. I suggest you leave if it makes you uncomfortable.'

'It's wrong, Newman.'

'I know it is. But we're at war, Doctor,' Newman replied, fitting a brown paper bag on to Davis' head. 'You've never been to war, have you?'

McCole whispered in Hopkins' ear. 'I'm not going to use it.'

'I have not been to war,' Hopkins replied to Newman. 'What's that got to do with anything?'

'Then with all due respect, you're not experienced enough to moralise with us on this scenario.'

Hopkins cottoned on to the game and reluctantly went along. 'He'll be in a wheelchair for life.'

Davis sobbed from within the paper bag and trickled urine on to the floor.

'If you won't leave, we'll have McClane here escort you.' Newman winked at Hopkins, while McClane smiled uneasily.

'Fine, but this is on you, Newman. I'm leaving the bunker and heading back to the mainland. You're all going to Hell.'

Hopkins opened the door and slammed it without

leaving the room. He took little pleasure in watching Davis lose control of his bowels as he spilt every lurid detail of his wrongdoings. The sordid confession fluctuated between blaming others and pleading for his life, turning Hopkins' stomach.

'Did Alice Grosvenor tell you to use that canister on the patient during his extraction from Dartmoor?'

'Yes.'

'At that dosage?'

'Yes.'

'She wanted him catatonic. She didn't want him talking to Hopkins. I told her I could stop him from talking by using the canister.'

Biggs closed his fists. 'You piece of shit.'

McCole glared at Hopkins as if to say he told him so.

'And what about the reverend's Lynx helicopter that you tried to sabotage? He's still upset about that.' Newman rustled the brown paper bag while McCole rested the lump hammer on the apex of Davis skull.

'Go like a fucking coconut, that. Do I win a prize if I smash it first go?'

Hopkins' felt queasy as the other men laughed at Davis thrashing against the duct tape. He rattled and scraped the wooden chair on the concrete floor while the brown paper bag shook from side to side. Newman blew out the hurricane lamp and ushered everyone out of the cell. McCole exited after Hopkins, cradling the hammer and looking pleased with himself. When the door to Davis' cell was locked, the group began walking back towards the War Room. McCole whistled the tune to Jerusalem, stopping Hopkins in his tracks.

'Who are you?'

'Don't fucking start with me, Hopkins. I told you I wasn't gonna use it,' he said, offering him the heavy hammer. 'It's true: you know nothing about war.'

'I know it killed my son slowly. And in disgrace.'

McCole dropped the hammer to his side. 'Hopkins, you'll never know until you've been there. You might get the chance if Newman's right about the radio transmission they intercepted.'

'What do you mean?'

'Grosvenor's sending a team into the town. Newman thinks they're gonna squeeze the locals to give us up.'

'So you want me to head into a gunfight against a team of professional mercenaries?'

'Professional bufties.'

'What is the plan?'

'We're heading to the war room now for a briefing. Sounds good that, aye?'

'You're loving all this, aren't you?'

'Keeps us out of trouble, doesn't it?'

The War Room was already packed with the same men who had been sat in the canteen, as well as a few Hopkins didn't recognise. A dozen or so bodies strapped in various types of special-forces gear murmured while they waited for Newman to deliver the briefing. Meanwhile, the presses hummed and clanked at the other end of the bunker. Newman broke off from the conversation he was having with one of the soldiers and cleared his throat.

'Close the door, please,' Newman said as he moved behind a desk covered in documents. 'We can expect two teams to infiltrate the town of Betws-Y-Coed from the east and west on the A5. They will seek to block the road in and out of the town with a machine-gun equipped guard post. The other units will likely move into the town to press locals for information on the location of the printing press, unless we can intercept. As always, we must make every effort to ensure that no harm comes to any local civilians, especially children. Green and Galley, you'll be working the radios.'

The pair grunted past their folded forearms, while a thick-necked, square-headed man behind them smirked.

'We need that intel on the team members. Someone here must have history with one of them, at least. Use your powers of deduction, gentlemen. Jameson: OP west by the bridge. Lynch: OP east at the A5/A470 junction, by the river,' Newman said, handing them maps and relevant documents. 'Read those quickly and leave them in that waste paper bin on your way out. Camo up, tool up and get to your post. McCole, you're on armoury duty. Here are the keys. Double-check ammunition before it goes out and make sure you hold something back for yourself:

you'll be coming with us.'

Newman continued to assign various tasks and posts to each person in a whirlwind of documents, radio crackle and nylon webbing. In the end, only he and Hopkins remained in the War Room.

'What about me?'

'Guard duty. Keep an eye on Davis in the stockade. Take whatever you know how to use from McCole at the armoury. Food and water from the canteen. Make yourself comfortable. Maybe you'll get some more information out of that snake.'

'What's going to happen to Davis?'

'That's up to you.'

Hopkins stood alone in the corridor outside the cell, listening to the last of the boots thudding out of the bunker two levels above. He opened the observation slot in the cell door and peered inside to see Davis still duct-taped to the chair. Hopkins could see that his ribs were still rising and falling, but the lack of response to the clank of the observation slot was a bad sign. Had Newman gone too far with the interrogation? Hopkins hadn't lasted long as an agent of vengeance: he was already back to being a physician, concerned for the man's welfare.

He called through the slot. 'Davis?'

No response.

'Davis?'

His head didn't move as his ribs rose and fell.

Hopkins took the cell key from his pocket and unlocked the door, cocking the magnum that he'd retrieved from McCole at the armoury. He moved inside the cell, keeping the barrel of the revolver pointed in Davis' direction. He reached out his left hand to check Davis' carotid pulse in his neck. Weak and shallow. After taking a small torch out of his pocket, he lifted Davis' chin and shone the torch into his eyes. Slightly delayed pupillary response. Mild shock, most likely.

Hopkins picked up a bottle of water and encouraged him to drink. After some initial spluttering, he began slurping at the bottle like a lamb sucking at its mother's teat. His translucent frame was held firm by the duct tape.

Davis' eyes were alive now and staring back at Hopkins.

'More water.'

Hopkins obliged.

'Thank you.'

Hopkins didn't say anything.

Davis began sobbing. 'Are you going to kill me?'

'I'm not going to kill you. McCole, I can't speak for.'

'Why don't they just get it over with?'

Hopkins rooted in his bag for the sandwiches he'd brought from the canteen. He pulled out a large triangle and held it up to Davis' mouth. Davis eyed the sandwich with suspicion, so Hopkins took a bite himself and offered it again. Davis took a small bite and chewed.

'Why are you doing this?'

'Beloved, never avenge yourselves, but leave it to the wrath of God.'

'Learn that from your friend, did you?'

'I did.'

'In the end, it's all a big black hole.'

'What is?'

'Everything. Life is meaningless.'

Hopkins took a drink of water. 'Is that why you've done the things you have?'

'I do those things because I get paid for doing them.'

'You don't care that your actions have hurt others?'

'Why should I?'

'And God's wrath? Doesn't bother you?'

'As for the cowardly, the faithless, the detestable, as for murderers, the sexually immoral, sorcerers, idolaters, and all liars, their portion will be in the lake that burns with fire and sulphur, which is the second death. What a load of horseshit.'

Hopkins took another drink of water. 'Horseshit enough that you memorised it? Ever strangle a kitten when you were a boy, Davis? Drown a puppy?'

'You do know that Grosvenor will kill you all, don't you? You think that this lot and some rag newspaper is enough to take her down?'

'I didn't come here to fight. I came here to help that patient, but you took that away from me.'

'So now you're playing soldier.'

'I'm no soldier. I came here because I need help.

Tell me about the boy.'

'If I tell you, Grosvenor's men will kill me. If I don't tell you, your friends will kill me.'

'I won't let them.'

'You won't have a say. If you let me go now, I'll disappear. I won't even go back to the mainland. Then my blood won't be on your hands.'

'You do know what a neuropsychiatrist is, don't you, Davis?'

'It was worth a try.'

Davis thrust forward out of his chair and aimed a long splint of wood at Hopkins' left eye. He staggered backwards and caught Davis' wrist before the sharp point could make contact with the soft jelly of his eyeball. The pair fell over the bag of food with Hopkins on his back and the splint only inches away from his face. Davis was pushing down with all his weight and reaching for Hopkins' holster with his other hand. He pushed a thumb into Davis' left eye, making him recoil. As Hopkins drew the .357 from the holster, a pain flashed through his leg. He looked down to see that Davis had buried the splint in his thigh. When he withdrew it to stab him again, Hopkins lifted the gun to Davis' face and pulled the trigger. In the deadened room, the shot felt like it burst his eardrums. And for a split second, the flash illuminated the hole where Davis' face used to be.

His ears ringing, Hopkins holstered the gun and heaved himself out of the cell, leaving a thin trail of blood behind him. He reached down and ascertained that his wound wasn't arterial, so he tied a simple dressing around it. He concentrated on his breathing and tried to ignore the blood and bone fragments splattered on the wall.

He hadn't expected Davis' head to explode like that. He couldn't wrap his mind around what had just happened.

His hands and arms shook until his whole body was trembling. He looked at Davis' corpse lying in the cell and felt his guts plummet, then a surge of nausea. He vomited on the floor and remained in a recovery position until the shock had passed. Finally, he was able to sit himself up against the wall, albeit soaked in a cold sweat.

He had killed a man. Somebody's son.

Hopkins had dropped into the darkest, deepest well on Earth.

Evil or not. Another human being.

He stood up on shaky legs and retrieved the revolver from the cell, holding his breath as he went in.

He didn't want to know what the room smelled like: what he could see in his peripheral vision was bad enough.

Davis' body had folded back on itself at the knee, still holding the bloody splinter of wood in a stiffening hand. Hopkins swept around the floor and found the revolver, its muzzle still warm. He picked it up and put it back in his holster before staggering out of the cell and taking a breath. He caught the tail end of the smell he'd wanted to avoid: somewhere between a butcher's shop and a firing range.

Meat and gunpowder. Blood and sulphur. He climbed the ladder out of the stockade with quivering arms, and hauled himself through the hatch. He collapsed and lay there on the concrete in silence, overwhelmed by the finality of what he had done.

32

John Muldoon staggered into the wire fence, almost blown off his feet by the wind. The rain lashed into the soaked white pyjamas, making a patting sound against the fabric. Every droplet whipped into his back like a tiny, cold bullet.

Ever since he'd arrived back on the island, things hadn't been the same. He couldn't find his horse. No matter how far he walked, he couldn't even find the town, let alone the forgery or the blacksmith's house. All that remained was this building he was too scared to enter. He knew that there was something in there that would change everything. Something dark and painful.

He tried to find shelter from the storm in a beach cave, sharing a bed with the crabs and the sand flies. All night, he could hear fat conger eels slurping through the gully above him to mate in a nearby rock pool. He moved on to another cave higher up in the cliff face, away from the sea and sand. After throwing a rock inside, he discovered that it was home to a few thousand bats. He pinned himself to the cliff face as they swarmed out of the cave.

When the bats' squeaking had died down, John took his arm from his eyes. He looked out to sea where lightning was thrusting its white fingers into the froth. It illuminated the entire cliff face, allowing him to see the sheer drop below.

It'd be quick.

And the waves would wash away the mess.

No need to bother anyone.

Like he'd never even been here.

John pushed his bare, bleeding foot to the edge and held on to a vine protruding from the mouth of the cave.

And let his weight hang on the vine.

All he had to do was relax his muscles.

Just open his fingers and it would all be over.

Forgotten. Like a dream.

Row, row, row your boat gently down the stream.

As long as he got to see his mother and father, it would be a fair trade.

But what if that wasn't the deal?

It was worth taking the chance.

The muscles strained in John's forearm as he let his weight hang further over the precipice.

Merrily, merrily, merrily, merrily.

He let go of the vine and felt his entire weight plummet down the cliff face when lightning struck him right down his middle.

Life is but a dream.

Two white-masked faces stared down at him.

'He's come to. Make sure of those restraints.'

'Shouldn't we report this to Charles?'

'Orders are to report everything on John Doe here directly to Chandler. You want to get suspended like Biggs and Davis?'

'But Charles is a doctor. I mean, this guy needs care.'

'He's a maximum security risk, which means minimum exposure to staff and other inmates. We only take him out of this bubble if we have to.'

'I've had to stand here lighting him up like a Christmas tree for the last three days. I didn't sign up for this. Why don't they choose someone else for the transmission? I'm sick of the smell of this guy's brain cooking.'

'Gotta be this guy.'

'Why?'

'Who knows? Help me wrap this up. Don't let the electrodes touch: it still holds a charge.'

'I mean, I'm not saying that I won't be tuning in, but still – he's only a kid. Why don't they transmit that other guy in ISC waiting to go to Dartmoor?'

'He's Mother Teresa next to this guy. You know what this one did, right? The crucifixion?'

'This is that guy?'

'This is him: the Horseman. But we're not

supposed to know that.'

'Thank fuck this placement is only temporary. This whole place creeps me out.'

'Listen, you're gonna have to change him.'

'Why me? Why don't you change him?'

'I did it last time.'

The two orderlies leapt back as John strained against the gurney's cuffs. 'Get me out of this.'

'What do we do?'

'Go and get the taser.'

'Joking, aren't you? Kid's probably fucking immune to electricity, the amount that's gone through him.'

'And the spray. And the net.'

'He's not a fucking bee.'

'You won't fucking be in a minute. Get them. We've got to get him on his feet as soon as possible.'

'Why the big rush? Transmission's three days away yet.'

'Chandler's orders.'

John couldn't work out what they were talking about. He was too busy sweating from the pain in his bones. The room was halfway between a cell and a grimy hospital bay with its padded walls and Plexiglas.

He assumed that he was back in Exmoor in some kind of ISC unit for lunatics, but he was still couldn't work out how he got from Dartmoor to that padded cell.

Or what had happened to Arthur.

'My horse. What happened to my horse?'

'Mother of God, he's asking for his fucking horse. We're all gonna die.'

'Don't be ridiculous. Call Chandler and tell him that the Horseman is awake. I'll stay with him.'

'Am I back on Exmoor? Where's Biggs?'

'Some nice people from Totem will be here soon to tell you everything. We're just orderlies.'

'Do you know my name?'

'John Doe.'

'My name is John Muldoon. Tell everyone. Arthur Muldoon was my father.'

'Arthur Muldoon. Why do I know that name?'

'She killed him with Totem. And now she wants to do the same to me.'

'I'm just an orderly,' the white mask said, looking up at the two-way mirror. His forehead had become shiny with sweat. 'I don't know anything.'

'You do now.'

What a mess the boy was making for Alice to clean up, even as he lay prone on that gurney, cuffed and shackled to its steel frame. She picked up the small walkie-talkie device on the table in front of her and ordered agents to intercept the orderly as he left the wing.

'Leave no trace of his body or uniform near or around the hospital incinerator. No repeats of last time.'

John Muldoon was her martyr. And now he was hers to destroy before the baying mob, which couldn't wait for the transmission of a madman. If only they knew what horrors lay in wait for them. She'd have sent the whole country to Dartmoor if the Board demanded it, but her father had taught her:

Softly, softly, catchee monkey.

Or was it the one about boiling the frog? The only way that she could only get her place on the Board was by heeding his advice. She knew that much.

When she first visited John Muldoon in the care homes, he seemed helpless and naive. By the time he was five, Grosvenor began to see the change in him: a distance creeping in around the eyes. On her next visit when he was eight, she saw him fresh from a knife attack by an older boy. When the doctor pulled back the dressing, the wound seemed romantic somehow. The boy's soft, stitched-up face made her feel like the artist she never was, especially when it contorted in pain. It was the canvas on which she had been painting in blood and tears for sixteen years.

And he had turned out wonderfully. Her little masterpiece.

The boy had been trying to detach from his own existence since he was five years old and now she was going to give him exactly what he wanted.

By Sunday morning, his darkness would envelop Britannia. Everyone would seek to detach from their own existences, too. To whom would they turn? Grosvenor Pharma, of course.

After the Lord Higham wobble, she sought out the best neuroprogrammers to work on priming convicts.

Editing undesirable truths from the transmissions had become a necessity. Not only was a great deal of political ground covered to her benefit, but it made for some spectacular show business. Once Lucky Newman had disappeared, there was only one journalist who had picked up where he had left off. Alice threw her in prison for sedition and programmed her for a preoccupation with dead bodies, then transmitted her for all to see.

Nobody questioned it.

And nobody cared about the sedition charge. All they cared was that she dreamt about having sex with corpses and made them enjoy it, so down the Dartmoor pathway she went. Since Alice had made that example, no journalist had dared oppose her.

Alice couldn't wallow in her former glories all day. She had business to attend to, and that business had just woken up in the plexi-cell. She gathered up her things and left the observation booth to enter the room.

'I'm afraid you can't go in there without protection, marm. It's protocol. He's a category A patient.'

'Get out of my way, or I'll have you thrown in the cell next door. I am protocol.'

The orderly stepped aside and opened the door for her while Muldoon stared at her from the gurney.

'I know you. You were at the care home. In the black car.'

'Tell me about your horse.'

'Why?'

'Because I'm here to help you find him.'

John's face chewed up on its scar tissue even more when he frowned.

'Come now. They must call you that name for a reason.'

'What name?'

'You mean you don't know? Everyone calls you the Horseman.'

'Like who?'

'Everyone. Out there.'

Muldoon eyed her, still frowning. 'I don't believe you.'

'It's all over the papers. All over TV, radio ... So, it must be true.'

'You don't want to help me.'

'What makes you say that?'

'You killed my father.'

'Why would I do such a thing?' she said, smiling and stroking his hair. 'It was all just a bad dream, darling.'

The boy flinched and turned his head away as Alice traced the outline of the most disfiguring scar on his face.

'Why don't you kill me?'

'I need you for something. You're a very special boy. No easy ride for you, I'm afraid'

'There's nothing else you can do to me. You've done everything you can.'

Alice arched an eyebrow. 'I do love a challenge.'

The anticipation of stripping away these last few shreds of innocence filled her with joy. She left her creation strapped to the gurney in the centre of the cell, shaking with fear.

33

Hopkins was sure that he had opened his eyes, yet he could see nothing.

'Doctor, wake up. We're on blackout. We have to head to the armoury and take as much stock as we can,' said a voice in the darkness. 'Then we have to evacuate to higher ground. There's a hut further up the mountain.'

'What's going on?'

'Grosvenor's deployed her foreign mercenaries. Our code words didn't work. They're on their way into the town now.'

'What about McCole? And Newman?'

'They're dealing with the situation, sir.'

'The prisoner … I killed him.'

'We know,' said a different voice in the darkness. 'Green heard the shot through his headphones while he was manning the radio. Came running and found you passed out. We cleaned and glued your leg up, put a new bandage on it.'

'But ... Davis …'

'Sir, you did what you had to do. There's no time to dwell on this. Everyone else is already on their way to the hut. Galley, you got that lamp sorted yet?'

A hurricane lantern glowed in the darkness. 'It's a new wick. Gotta soak up the paraffin.'

'Where are we going?'

Green hooked his arm under Hopkins' and lifted him to his feet. 'Galley and I are under orders to escort you to our secondary base, sir.'

He tried to walk and collapsed from the shooting pain in his leg.

'Any painkillers in your kit?'

'All the medical supplies have gone ahead with the rest, sir. You'll have to stick it.'

'It's started bleeding again.'

'Galley, get round the other side of him. Keep all his weight off that leg, We'll work it out, Doctor: there should be a surgical kit in the armoury.'

There, he found a plastic green box with a white cross. Hopkins stumbled through the armoury, trying to open it. In his frustration and agony, he smashed it off the wall and rifled through the contents on the floor. Finding some morphine capsules, he opened the packet and gulped them down.

The pain began to subside after a few minutes of lying on the floor of the armoury. Meanwhile, Green and Galley loaded up on weapons, tools and ammunition.

'Ok, Doctor. We're ready to leave. How are you doing?'

'I can walk,' Hopkins said, grabbing the edge of the gun cabinet and hauling himself to his feet. 'Let's go.'

'Do you still have your sidearm?'

Hopkins pulled back his jacket to reveal the revolver in its holster.

Galley handed Hopkins two nylon pouches with belt clips and velcro. 'Take these.'

Hopkins ripped one of them open to reveal a speed-loader equipped with hollow-point rounds. He used the belt clip to hook them next to the gun.

'Best on the other side, sir. Too much weight. Easier to draw on that side, too. Let me show you.'

The young soldier showed him how to draw the speed-loader, empty the revolver and reload without dropping anything.

'It's what God gave us opposable thumbs for, sir.'

'I think anthropologists might argue that point, Green.'

'Sorry, sir. I thought that because you were a scientist—'

'I still am, Green,' Hopkins said, adjusting the belt and holster. His face still had some of Davis' dried blood on it. 'Still am.'

Green helped him up the staircase towards the bunker's exit. 'No disrespect intended.'

'I get it, Green. Probably best not to kid too much with McCole, though.'

'Agreed, sir.'

'You can drop all the sirs. I never served.'

'Newman says that you're the most important man in Britannia. He says that you're the only one who can help him bring down Grosvenor. That's good enough for me.'

'He says what?'

'He says that you'll back us because of your son; that the truth will turn the whole of Britannia against her.'

'Oh, he did?'

'You'd better speak to Newman about it, sir.'

'If he makes it back.'

'Newman always makes it back, sir. He's Lucky.'

The trio hacked through undergrowth and crossed sheer ridges to reach the mountain hut. Hopkins' leg jolted with pain as the wind sent him staggering backwards. The snow felt like it was slicing into his face as they slogged the last few hundred yards.

They poured into the stone structure to find the press operators huddled around a pitiful fire. Galley and Green set about building it up, while Hopkins sat at the long, heavy-looking dining table. He looked out of the window at the entrance to the bunker half a mile below. Keeping his injured leg straight eased the pain.

Galley and Green were handing out the contents of the holdalls to everyone in the hut when Hopkins noticed his Beretta.

'I'll take that, Green.'

Green handed the shotgun to Hopkins while Galley fizzed and crackled the radio in the corner, trying to contact Newman.

Galley turned away from the radio, his headset dangling from his ear. 'Green, we could be on our own.'

'Alright. Steady on. We don't know anything yet. McClane and Dickinson could have taken out Grosvenor's men already.'

34

McClane's dead eyes stared at Lucky as he and McCole entered the Royal Legion Social Club. His body was slumped against the bar in a pool of blood alongside Dickinson's.

There was no time to grieve.

He had to find and kill Grosvenor's men before they reached the farm. Their next stop after that would be the bunker to kill everyone, as they had already done in the Legion. Other veterans lay slain about the bar, under the dartboard, slumped over the pool table, some of them still clutching their cues. Lucky was enraged, as were the rest of his team. Or what remained of it, at least.

McCole pulled the latest edition of The Serviceman out of a man's mouth and straightened up his medals. 'Let's kill them all.'

'We need photographs before we do anything. Get me a camera.'

'We haven't got time for fucking snapshots, Newman. Let's get after them.'

'Use your head. Grosvenor will use this to turn the people against us. And we need evidence for the top brass or they won't back us for the final push.'

'They're helping you take down Grosvenor?'

'We've got a general and a few colonels on our side already. Where do you think we get our intel?'

McCole looked around at the dead bodies. 'From the land of fucking Oz, by the looks of it.'

'We've got to get to the Kennedy farm. They've been helping us since we arrived. Grosvenor's men could be on their way there now.'

'How many you think there are?'

'OP post reported eight. Took three of them out. Could be another team we didn't account for. Estimate ten left,' replied Jackson, an ex-Para from the mining town a few miles away.

'Is everyone reloaded? Move out through that exit and head east up the hill towards the farmhouse.'

Sirens rang through the deserted streets as he led the men out of town towards the woods by the farmhouse. He instructed them to turn off their radios and to spread out as they walked up the hill and through the trees. Every man had his MP5 at the ready as they swept through the wood, pausing for every rustle of leaves in the darkness.

They arrived at the border of the farmhouse land and climbed over the wooden fence. The grass leading up to the centuries-old house seemed bright green, even in the dying light. And the air stank of manure. Lucky worried that this heightening of his senses might be ominous. He instructed the four men to wait at the boundary while he hopped through the fence and walked up to the front door.

Lucky shouted through the letterbox.

A man in a muddy and oily tracksuit opened the door, turning his lumpen 60-year-old hands in a rag.

'I'm fixing the tractor. What do you want?'

'Is Lea home? You two might want to hit the road for a day or two.'

'She's up at her mother's in Windermere. Is that blood on your jacket?'

'Remember that ammo you stashed for us a few weeks ago?'

'Yeah, it's in the old coal bunker. Why?'

'Because we're gonna need it,' said McCole, wiping blood off his eyelid. 'Team of Grosvenor's men just shot up the Legion Club in town. Killed everyone in there. We think they're coming here next.'

'Shit. Looking for you?'

Lucky signalled to his team to enter the house. 'And the printing press, the whistleblowers and everyone else holed up in the bunker.'

Once Kennedy had recovered the boxes of ammo, he put the whole farm into blackout. The men operated by the light of a paraffin lamp in the farmhouse's hallway.

Kennedy kicked the bag of guns. 'What have you

got for me, then? You youngsters still using those wimpy nine-mils?'

'Take whatever you want.'

The farmer opened a cabinet to retrieve a cannon of a shotgun, to which Lucky raised an eyebrow.

'You should see the size of the geese this year.'

'Do you have floodlights in the cattle barn?'

'Don't I know it. Costs me a fortune.'

'Take us there.'

As they reached the barn, the sun sank behind the mountains. The birds stopped singing to make way for the howling and cooing of the nocturnal creatures. Lucky instructed his men to hide in the hayloft with their sights trained on the barn door. Kennedy called him over for help with hooking up the flood-lamps.

'So, you're gonna lure them in, blind them and kill them? Just watch my cows, right?'

'They'll secure any outbuildings like this barn before they go for the main house. Dickinson radioed that they had night vision on them … Before he got taken out.'

Kennedy climbed the ladder to the hayloft. 'What if they don't use it?'

'They'll use it. No moon and we've blacked out the farm. They're not going to wander up flashing torches about: they're professionals.'

'Christ, Newman. How professional exactly? You'll have to explain to my wife if she comes back and finds me dead.'

Lucky didn't smile because he was thinking about

the men that he had lost already. He rested his MP5 on a bale of hay and aimed his sights over the barn's entrance.

'You used to have a better sense of humour. I liked you better when you were a cocky little bootneck.'

'I hear something in the woods.'

The men lay still atop the bales of hay, looking down on the cattle shed floor, while the inhabitants of the stalls farted and pissed. Lucky kept his hand on the switch for the lights as he saw a shadow float by the entrance.

The adrenaline made his throat thud.

He sighted up three Grosvenor mercenaries seeping into the barn like deadly inkblots.

Lucky switched on the floodlights, causing the mercenaries to stagger and claw their night vision units from their heads.

Before any of them could fire off a round, Lucky and his men dropped them with a barrage of bullets from the hayloft. Lucky stamped on the bale set alight by McCole's muzzle flash.

Lucky heard something drop on the soft hay behind him, as Kennedy smothered the fire with his jacket.

It was a familiar sound. Heavy and metallic.

Lucky knew exactly what it was.

Searching the floor with his bare hand, he brushed the cold metal of the grenade with his fingers. He wasted no time in throwing it out of the hayloft hatch.

The explosion echoed through the woods. Through the smoke, he could see and hear all the roosting birds taking flight from the trees.

Peering downwards out of the hatch, he saw the bodies of two mercenaries slumped against the barn wall.

Silence.

They stripped the mercenaries' bodies of equipment, weapons and ammunition. It wasn't difficult to tell where Grosvenor had sourced them. Eastern European or Czech sidearms and German boot-knives. There were five of them, which made the bodycount ten, but Lucky didn't want to take any chances. He handed out the dead men's night vision units and ordered a sweep of the perimeter.

'We should bury them.'

Kennedy snorted. 'Don't bother. Got the pigs round the back.'

'Last time I buy bacon from you.'

'You still owe me for last week's and the week before, by the way.'

'We owe you a lot more than that, Paul.'

'You're not getting off that easy. Give me a hand with this,' Kennedy said, dragging a dead mercenary towards his tractor's bucket.

35

Hopkins was envious of the others who were sleeping comfortably in the hut.

No such luck for him. Anywhere he positioned his freshly-stabbed leg resulted in a burning ache. And every time he drifted near sleep, the smell of meat and gunpowder came back to him, reminding him of Davis.

With Galley having fallen asleep at the controls of the radio, only Green was still awake, sat at the table by the window looking down over the bunker.

Hopkins found a bottle of whisky in the cupboard and bit his lip as he felt the thirst. He took a glass and poured himself a large whisky before offering the bottle to the young man.

'No, thank you, sir. On duty.'

Since the snow had subsided, Hopkins could now see the stars out of the hut's window. The Milky Way arched across the sky and down out of sight behind the horizon.

Hopkins' sleeve failed to wipe the window clear, so he stepped outside with his glass. Green followed and stood next to him, scanning the darkness all about them.

'Look at those stars.'

'I can't, sir,' the young man said, his eyes glistening as he searched for the enemy.

Hopkins handed the soldier the whisky tumbler. The young man took it, but did not drink.

'It smells good, but I can't, sir.'

'You want me keep watch for a while?'

Green smiled and shook his head.

'And you won't look up? Even for a second?'

'I saw enough stars out in the desert.'

'You remind me of my son.'

As he stared into the Milky Way above, Hopkins felt the distance between him and Andrew.

Lost to him forever in the cosmos.

Nothing he could do.

This was all a fool's errand, his return to the mainland. He would never find redemption here. He should have stayed on the island with the ghosts in the stills. Should have let himself sink into the peat bogs of the distillery island. Should have blown his head off with the shotgun in the out-house.

McCole had been on to something there.

He smelled the amber liquid in the glass.

Reconsidered it.

Poured the untouched whisky over the edge of the

cliff.

Put the empty tumbler on the table.

He was too tired to do anything other than collapse in his bunk, despite the persistent burning in his leg.

Hopkins' dream began in the observation room next to John Muldoon's cell in Exmoor. There was no air and the sounds of his actions came a split second afterwards.

Paper rustled in front of him.

A knock on the wood.

Another on the window.

Instead of John Muldoon, his son Andrew came shambling into view. He wore a dirty straitjacket with rusted buckles. Most of his skin was gone and so was his left eye, but Hopkins still recognised the corpse sitting on the other side of the glass.

'Hi, Dad.'

'I still have your letter here.' Hopkins reached into his pocket and pulled it out. 'Still read it every day.'

'I didn't write that.'

'The police found it on your body.'

'I didn't write it.'

'What are you saying?'

'That I didn't write it.'

'And that's all you can give me, Andrew?'

'You'll find out the truth. But you won't thank me. No-one will.'

'What happened out there in Damascus?'

'Give me the letter, Dad.'

Hopkins pushed the letter edgeways into the window. Instead of folding, the letter passed straight through as if the glass were liquid.

Andrew shook off his rusted, mouldy straitjacket and plucked the paper from his side of the glass.

'Thanks, Dad.' Andrew disappeared before Hopkins could protest.

John Muldoon spoke into his ear, startling him. 'He'll be ok. You'll be with him again. If you come and see.'

Hopkins jumped back at the sight of Muldoon dressed as an orderly. His eyes shone and there was no slur in his voice.

On closer inspection, the skin on his face was smooth: no great seams of scar tissue dividing his handsome features.

'John? Is that you?'

'This is what I would have been. Without Totem.'

'What do you want from me?'

'I want you to come and see.'

Hopkins woke up to the squelching of the radio. Hopkins rubbed his face and yawned: he had fallen asleep on the bunk fully-clothed, with the smell of whisky in the air. Roused by the radio noise, everyone else began to sit up in their bunks, too. Galley was already wide awake, listening intently to the transmission.

'Sir, we've received word from Newman. The

threat has been neutralised. I hope you don't mind: I packed up your things. We're all-clear to go back to the bunker'

Hopkins took his bag, put on his shoes and pulled on his jacket. Checking the pocket for his son's letter, panic shot upwards through his body as he realised that it wasn't there. He scrabbled around on the floor, searching under the bunks and between the feet of the others.

'Has anyone seen my letter? Please, it was a letter from my son.'

'Don't you remember, sir?'

'Where is it, Galley?'

'You got up from your bed and put something in the fire last night, sir.'

Hopkins hobbled over to the wood-burning stove and opened the grill. He ran his fingers through the warm ash, but there was no sign of the letter.

When they arrived back at the bunker, Newman was in the canteen, patching up his injuries alone. Two steaming cups of black coffee stood on the table.

'So ... Davis?'

'He would have killed me.'

'You alright about it?'

Hopkins sighed.

'We need to talk, Doctor, so that if anything happens to either of us,' Newman said, taking a dictaphone out of his pocket. 'All this won't have been for nothing.'

'What about Davis? I should clean up.'

'You get a pass on this one. I shovelled his brains into a plastic bag and hosed down that cell before you arrived.'

Hopkins balked.

'A thank you wouldn't go amiss, Hopkins.'

He tried to stave off the lurching nausea. 'Thank you.'

'Let's begin.' Newman clicked the record button on the dictaphone and put it on the table next to his coffee. 'What was Totem originally designed for?'

'For treating PTSD victims like my son. I planned to sell it to the military.'

'So why didn't you?'

'My son committed suicide and the military withdrew their offer, forcing me to sell to Grosvenor.'

'And what did you sell, exactly?'

'The lab and the research.'

'So you never dreamt that Grosvenor might use Totem as she has?'

'Its application was always meant to be therapeutic.'

'In its current application, does it pose a danger to the public?'

'Yes.'

'Please explain why transmitting the criminally insane might be dangerous, both for the patients and for the public.'

'Totem was designed to be used between

individuals or small groups, not an entire population and certainly not for recreation.'

'So what danger does it pose to those tuning in?'

'The trauma of seeing and feeling such a disturbed patient's consciousness might leave permanent damage to the psyche of anyone who has tuned in. Potentially this could create mass psychosis across Britannia.'

Lucky Newman leaned back in his chair. 'So, you're saying that this transmission could drive people insane?'

'To the point where reality becomes entirely insufficient. It's the same principle as Cold Shock Response: their minds might not be able to cope with the sudden and drastic change in their perception of reality. The consequences of such a mass psychosis would be devastating.'

'Were you given the chance to counsel the inmate proposed for transmission?'

'He was deliberately stupefied by a member of hospital staff under the orders of Alice Grosvenor.'

'So you made no evaluation?'

'He was catatonic during my visit to Exmoor.'

'Is it true that attempts have been made on your life?'

'Yes.'

'And can The Serviceman and the resistance count on your support?'

Hopkins looked at the dictaphone.

'Your endorsement would mean a great deal,

Doctor. To the people involved here, especially,' Newman said, wiping a spot of blood off his sleeve. He appeared unsurprised by Hopkins' attitude, as if he had somehow made provisions for it already. 'We need your statement for the brass: they won't lift another finger for us unless you're on board.'

'I'm no soldier, Newman. And I wouldn't have the first idea about how to stage a military coup.'

Newman clicked off the dictaphone. 'There's something else you should know. About your son.'

Hopkins sat up straighter in his chair.

'We have intel telling us that Grosvenor had him killed to get you to give up Totem.'

A block of ice enveloped Hopkins. He stopped tracing his eyebrow and let his hand drop to the table. 'How can you be sure?'

'Another whistleblower.'

'Did the whistleblower do it?'

'No. He was just her driver. We questioned him like we questioned Davis.'

Hopkins remained silent.

'Do you want a drink? Smoke?'

Hopkins shook his head.

'Why don't you go and get some rest?'

'Where's McCole?'

'In the canteen.'

'Does he know? About Andrew?'

'I thought it was better to tell you first.'

Hopkins nodded and tried to hide his shaking hands.

'I understand if you would rather go back to your distillery. But just a few words would make all the difference. What she did to Andrew will turn everyone against Grosvenor.'

Hopkins picked up the dictaphone and recorded his statement endorsing the resistance and their plan. Without another word, he walked out.

He showered, redressed his wound and retired to his room to lie on his bunk. Staring up at the ceiling, Hopkins flashed from sorrow to rage to gratitude for the truth at last.

A knock at the door. 'It's me.'

'Come in.'

McCole entered, dressed in jeans and a woollen jumper.

'Clergy casual: I love it.'

'Newman just told me about Andrew. Sorry, Hopkins.'

'I don't even know how to feel, McCole.'

'Come on, up you get.'

'Why?'

'You know why.'

Hopkins stood up and begrudgingly acted out the ritual. He kept his arms by his sides while McCole hugged him like a large child.

Hopkins sighed.

'Well, it makes me feel better.'

'I heard McClane and Dickinson got killed.'

'I heard the same about Davis. Sorry you had to, you know.'

'I had no choice. He was trying to kill me.'

'No, I meant because I wanted to do it.'

Hopkins noticed that McCole was bleeding from the ear. 'You got hit?'

'Scratches. So, we're gonna kill her, right?'

'Grosvenor? We won't get anywhere near her.'

'Newman is working with the brass who want Grosvenor dead. Things are changing.'

'When is this coup taking place?'

'If Grosvenor finds out about the generals helping us, all hell will break loose, so we have to keep it cloak and dagger. On Saturday, Newman's going on patrol at Totem HQ with Her Majesty's.'

'She still uses them for the transmissions?'

'Has to, otherwise the coup would have happened already. They're a skeleton crew. Scarecrows to keep the brass and citizens off her back.'

'So Newman will take the boy during the transmission?'

'That's our only chance: while everyone's tuned in. They'll only wake up from the transmission when the charges go off.'

'Charges?'

'We're going to plant explosives on the mast, bring it down and take The Horseman—'

'John Muldoon.'

'We take Muldoon down to the docks where you'll be waiting on a boat to get him out of there.'

'Blowing things up doesn't sound very covert to me, McCole.'

'They're going to take out Grosvenor in her office in Totem HQ. I'll do it for you myself if I get the chance.'

'It's a suicide mission.'

'As if you'd be bothered anyway. Have the island all to yourself then.'

'You're mad.'

'Is that your medical opinion, Doctor?'

Hopkins shooed his friend out of the room. 'I'm gonna get some more sleep. Good night, Reverend.'

'It's 2 p.m., Hopkins.'

'Good afternoon, then,' he said, closing the door.

36

If not for the straitjacket, John Muldoon would have found a way to kill himself already.

He didn't understand why they would take him away from his horse, who was probably dead by now.

What kind of God could just stand by and do nothing while this went on?

John had tried to tell himself that every awful thing that happened to him was a test.

That every cry turned inward was a sacrifice.

That every cheek turned would be another step closer to Heaven.

But it never ended.

If anything, his trial had only grown worse.

Now, it had come full circle: he was about to be degraded like his father. By having his soul stretched out in the sun like a wet, bloody hide for tanning.

For all to see.

For all comers to wrap themselves up in it and

become him.

And unbecome themselves.

To know how it feels to slip in hot blood on a cold, shower block floor, or the smell of your own strangled breath.

To know the intoxication of madness.

To be an agent of chaos.

To matter to the cosmos.

Even if through destruction.

John knelt and prayed.

To whom, he wasn't sure.

Maybe Doctor Hopkins.

Maybe Biggs, the orderly who was kind to him.

Any of the gods he had read about in the bookshop on Dartmoor.

There had to be someone out there who could save him.

37

Dinner in the canteen was a quiet affair. No-one mentioned the fallen and when there was conversation, they talked about the coup.

It reminded Hopkins of his old lab's canteen, causing his appetite to wane.

'McCole, you'll go with the doctor to the harbour at Bala, where you'll board the boat for Sheffield.'

'Understood.'

'Biggs, Jackson, Green and Galley: you're all coming with me to Totem HQ. The rest of you should remain in the bunker, operating as normal. The transmission begins in 48 hours. McCole, you should be gone within the hour to make your rendezvous at the harbour wall in Llangollen. Take Kennedy's Defender and an extra jerry can of fuel. I'll get him on the radio now and tell him you're coming.'

They walked down to the farm, where Kennedy let them into the bullet-riddled barn. Hopkins hauled himself into the Defender, throwing his bag in the back. There was a noticeable creak in the suspension as McCole did the same. The stink of death that hung in the barn also permeated the vehicle.

'Old car,' McCole said, acquainting himself with the dashboard and the controls. In the damp, oily Defender, Hopkins could smell the freshly fired guns McCole had stashed in the back. He considered asking him how many of Grosvenor's men he had killed in town, but thought better of it.

The 4x4 chugged to life and roared away from Kennedy's barn. The farmer held his shotgun in one hand and waved with the other as they drove off his land, towards the harbour.

'Haven't you been drinking?'

McCole shook his head, not taking his eyes from the unlit, narrow roads.

Hopkins shrugged and tuned the radio to Grosvenor News.

Today in the heart of Snowdonia, a terrorist group struck a veteran's legion bar, gunning down seven ex-servicemen before engaging in a fire-fight with Grosvenor Security, who forced the attackers into a retreat. Doctor David Hopkins is believed to be in collusion with the terrorists.

'She's going to make herself into a saviour once everything's gone to Hell. Do you believe in evil yet, Doctor?'

'I'm coming around, Reverend.'

'You know what has to be done, then.'

'I can't condone murder, McCole.'

'She can't be saved.'

'She had a mother and father. She's a human being.'

'Andrew Hopkins had a mother and father, too. So did John Muldoon.'

Hopkins said nothing.

'How many more will it take?'

'I get it, McCole.'

In other news, preparations have begun for what is being described as the most controversial transmission ever at Totem headquarters in Sheffield. The inmate at Exmoor, known only as John Doe, has no next of kin and is deemed to be one of the most dangerous men in Britannia. Known as The Horseman by staff, John Doe was sent to the high security hospital for the crucifixion of a warden at a Leeds borstal.

Experience the borderlands of reality through the consciousness of the unhinged in this special transmission on Saturday at 10pm, live from Totem HQ, Sheffield. Will he be rehabilitated or sent back to Dartmoor? Cast your vote by telephone or by radio. Grosvenor 24-Hour News 90.1 - 97.3FM. No fake news: all real news.

'Think this is going to work?'

'The brass know that this could be their last chance to take Grosvenor down before her mercenaries start seizing their remaining bases.'

'They want her prosecuted?'

'They want her dead.'

He pictured Alice Grosvenor on her knees with his .357 magnum pressed to her forehead. The hot muzzle branding her skin. Closing her eyes in anticipation of the bullet. Tears escaping from the corners of them as she says her mother's name.

'I'm not cut out for it, McCole.'

'Did a pretty good job on Davis.'

Hopkins felt queasy at the thought of how much blood there had been. 'McCole, please.'

When they arrived at the harbour wall, Hopkins took out the radio and the scrap of paper that Newman had given him. He read out the code and within seconds, received a coded response to which McCole nodded. He never imagined that McCole's whisky-pickled brain could process so much new information.

'The boat will take us to Sheffield Docks. We'll lie low there until Newman arrives with the boy.'

They left the Defender on the harbour wall by the old bandstand and took the bags from the vehicle. McCole removed the Beretta. He broke the barrel and loaded it with two bright red cartridges.

'I thought these people were allies.'

'Well, they won't mind then, will they? Better safe than sorry.'

Hopkins removed the .357 from his bag and reloaded it before holstering it on his belt. Shockingly, the gun still felt comfortable in his hand, despite having killed a man with it. He picked up his bag and headed towards the dilapidated bandstand, lit only by the moon.

'We'll hide out in here until they arrive. Anyone comes looking for us, we'll see them go to the car first.'

Hopkins found it difficult to navigate the cobbles with his injured leg. He hobbled up the bandstand steps and brushed aside the mounds of dead leaves and litter before sitting against the railings.

In the moonlight, they cast finger-like shadows that tried to grab McCole as he joined Hopkins.

'Do you think that there'll ever be music in this bandstand again?'

The two men sat in silence as the Earth turned and the breeze rustled the dry leaves.

'When this is all done, let's go fishing and have a drink like we used to.'

'I'll be treating Muldoon if this plan succeeds. That's going to be a full-time job.'

'We'll take the lad fishing. It'll be good for him.'

'McCole, you saw him. It's not like he's had his heart broken by the girl next door.'

'Well, if I was his doctor, I would prescribe fishing and beer.'

Hopkins sighed. 'What time is this boat getting here?'

'Should have been here ten minutes ago,' McCole said, looking out to sea.

The night was clear and the horizon still held a smudge of red from the sunset. Hopkins closed his eyes against the warm breeze and inhaled the salty air. A deep thud from further down the harbour wall made him draw the revolver. McCole crouched in the centre of the bandstand, took a radio out of his pocket and switched it on. He pressed his ear to the device and looked up at Hopkins, who was pointing the six-shooter into the darkness.

'It's them. Let's get to the pontoon.'

Hopkins followed McCole out of the bandstand, looking both ways before he left cover.

'Where are they?' Hopkins strode to the end of the floating walkway.

'They'll be here.'

The rushing sound of water broke the silence around the pontoon. The beams of timber sloshed and heaved, threatening to throw them in. Hopkins and McCole steadied themselves against each other while the sea gave way to the rising, riveted steel.

'You're kidding me, McCole. A submarine?'

'Don't tell me you haven't always wanted to have a go in one.'

The 50-foot long submarine groaned as it settled. As the rushing of water ceased, the hatch opened and a man climbed out on to the deck. He was in his forties with long, unkempt hair and hard eyes.

'Step aboard, gentleman.' The submariner pointed to the steel rungs protruding from the smooth black flank of the vessel.

McCole hopped from the surging pontoon on to the tiny metal bar and heaved his body up the ladder and into the hatch. Hopkins holstered his revolver and tried the same, but lost his footing on the first rung. He held on by his right hand to another rung, but his legs were now wet and cold and his shoes full of water. He pulled himself up and into the submarine, spitting out brine that had splashed into his mouth. Crashing to the floor of the sub, Hopkins winded himself and landed on his wounded leg, making him gasp.

The weather-beaten commander stood over him, his wild hair silhouetted against the caged red light.

'You alright there, Doc?' He reached down an oily, calloused hand to help Hopkins to his feet.

'I'm Commander Gorrie. We'll be taking you to Sheffield's Victoria Docks,' he said, introducing two crew members sitting at a bank of glowing dials and levers. 'While these men will take your vehicle back to the bunker.'

McCole handed the keys to the men as they climbed out of the sub, closing the hatch behind them.

Hopkins' skin began to prickle and cold sweat dripped down his back as he contemplated being stuck in the sub for any longer than half an hour.

'You want to lie down in your bunk for a while?'

Hopkins staggered to a seat and collapsed into it, removing his wet shoes, socks and trousers. 'I'll be fine.'

'McCole, good to have you aboard. We have everything manned already, but should we need to surface in an emergency, there's some protocol I need to run through with you and the doctor. If you would follow me, it won't take long,' Gorrie said, edging past the crew. They gave a headphoned nod to Hopkins and McCole as they squeezed into the jungle of gleaming brass pipes and gauges. The tang of oil and diesel hung in the air, what precious little there was. The commander explained the different emergency procedures in case of engagement. In the next breath, he assured them that they were undetectable by radar.

'Are we armed anyway?'

'Of course,' the commander replied. 'Limpet mines and side charges.'

Hopkins tried to fend off his claustrophobia with a deep breath. 'How long will it take us to reach Sheffield?'

'Fifteen hours or thereabouts. Feel free to sleep in your bunks. We've got everything under control. Orders are to dock at Victoria, where we'll wait for Newman and the boy.'

'And after that? Where do we go once we've got Muldoon?'

'We don't know: it's classified until after the mission. We'll hide in deep water off the east coast somewhere until the generals contact us.'

'Where is command HQ?'

'We don't know that either. All classified.'

Hopkins breathing returned to normal, but he felt drained. 'Is this my bunk?'

'Take that one,' the commander said, pointing to the smartest, cleanest looking cot. 'Sweet dreams.'

38

In his dream, Hopkins was back in Exmoor, looking into a padded room.

'John? Andrew?'

Nobody answered from the corners of the cell. They were darkened on account of a flickering light that made the shadows expand like a breathing ribcage.

Long, black shadows scraped down the glass of the cell window. Hopkins looked down at the clipboard on the table in front of him.

On it was written:

Dock 22.

The breathing he heard from the seat next to him turned his skin cold. He looked up at the glass and caught the reflection of his son sitting next to him. Hopkins didn't dare look directly at the boy's face, because his hands were so hideous. They were bloodless and unnatural, as if compelled by electricity.

The blue fingers jerked as they fidgeted with a length of string, tying it and untying it.

Hopkins rested his own hands on the table, noticing the obvious genetic similarities between his and Andrew's.

He looked into his son's black eyes in the reflection. The lips moved, but no words came.

'I can't hear you,' Hopkins said, even though his son was sitting right beside him.

One of the blue hands placed itself on top of Hopkins' own. Sand piled up where the cell used to be. An intense heat began to radiate from the glass, as if hot sun were shining through it.

Curious, Hopkins entered the cell and immediately felt heavy in his new clothing.

Screaming in his ears.

Sand in his mouth.

A strange smell in the air, like metal.

And gunpowder.

He looked down at his assault rifle while an officer screamed at him. Move out. Clear the next one.

The name on the officer's uniform read Tappin.

Women and children ran screaming through the smoke cloud, some missing limbs or struggling to carry the broken bodies of their loved ones. Each face that came out of the smoke accused Hopkins through their tears. Some were too hysterical, their minds shredded by the horror all about them.

Hopkins let go of his rifle, allowing it to hang at his side by its strap. Hands grabbed him and propelled him forwards into the smoke and screams of the street.

A building with a wooden door emerged from the dust.

Get in there and clear it, Hopkins. Now!

Hopkins adjusted his ballistic helmet and raised his rifle, stalking around the edges of the building.

Grenade, Hopkins! What are you waiting for?

He looked down at his assault vest to see two grenades clipped to it.

Now!

Hopkins pulled one of the grenades from his vest, activating it. He drew his arm back to throw it into the ground floor window of the building. As the grenade left his hand, a baby cried from within the room.

He tried to kick down the door, but his commanding officer pulled him to the ground before the explosion.

Face down in the dirt, splinters of wood and bits of concrete smashed against his ballistic helmet, but his ears took the worst of it.

A piercing pain. Ringing.

Hopkins tried to stand up, but fell back to the dusty street again.

He ran his hands over both of his legs, fearing for the worst, but he was not injured anywhere except for his ears. Both of them were wet with blood.

Steadying himself against the wall, Hopkins climbed to his feet and waited for the smoke to clear.

The CO shouted from beyond the dust and smoke. *Don't go in there, Hopkins!*

Tappin's red and wide eyes appeared in front of Hopkins' face.

We can't afford to lose any more men.

No-one will gain anything from going in that room.

Move on to the next one.

But Hopkins had to know. He ripped away from his commanding officer's grip and walked through the doorway into the plumes of smoke and dust.

There was that smell again.

Gunpowder and meat.

A wet, gasping sound came from the corner of the room, beyond the smoke and shadows. Hopkins walked closer, his nervous system bristling with horror at what he might have done.

Hopkins found himself in a quiet room with fizzing, broken lights and padded walls.

His senses were transposed: some of them heightened, some of them dulled.

He placed his hand on the Plexiglas window of the cell and saw that it was much younger than the one from his waking life. The small mark from a broken test tube during his university days was no longer there on his palm, but instead, his hands were bubbling with scar tissue. As he flexed his fingers, he noticed that the joints were painful.

A terrible loneliness descended upon Hopkins as he remembered:

A white horse called Arthur.

A lonely moor.

A black building on the coast with truth inside it.

He had to know what was inside that building.

Then he would be fearless.

Then he would be free.

As he woke from the dream in his tiny bunk, Hopkins dinged his head on a pipe. Looking around, he could see that the submarine had not been an hallucination. The crew continued steering the vessel towards Sheffield docks. The large screen lit up the bow's control room, which crackled and beeped. On the screen, he saw the underwater ruins of a church bell tower and a bank of Georgian houses' relics. Beyond the searchlight, a bridge emerged from the gloom. As they drew closer to pass underneath it, it seemed to Hopkins like a cast iron web with its centre missing. The many beams and curves of the iron created odd geometric patterns, lit up by the sunrise refracting through the water. McCole and Hopkins watched the screens while the submariners kept the vessel on course.

'Doesn't seem real, does it?'

'I've got to tune in for the transmission. I have to see.'

'What if you turn into one of these schizophreniforms or whatever you said?'

'It's the only way I'll be able to help him. I need to feel what he feels. And I know to know what's in that building.'

'What are you talking about, Hopkins?'

'The black building on the moor. I saw it in my dream.'

'You sure you know what you're doing, Hopkins? You haven't fallen apart on me, have you? What if Grosvenor's men recognise you when you're ashore?'

'I'll find a Totem pod in the backstreets near the docks, out of the way.'

One of the submariners interrupted. 'The hotel in the docks has a facility I believe, sir.'

'Oh, great. Why don't we organise a day trip?'

'I'm going alone.'

'If Grosvenor's agents catch you, this operation is over,' the commander said. 'You're only going to see what they want you to see, anyway.'

'How do they fix it to transmit what they want?'

'They don't fix Totem: they fix whoever's being transmitted,' replied Hopkins. 'They have to be programmed.'

'Subliminal programming?'

'That's what they start with. What comes later is worse,' said Gorrie, handing McCole a copy of The Serviceman. 'It's different for everyone.'

'You got all that from this?'

'Lucky Newman is a great man, sir,' said another of the submariners. 'If it wasn't for him, there wouldn't be a coup at all.'

Gorrie frowned at the use of the word. 'There'll be no coup yet, Williams. This is a covert mission, which is why we can't breach until the last minute in dock

22.'

'I have to see.'

'We have all the medication you requested to treat him post-transmission. In that briefcase stowed above your head there.'

'It's not enough. I have cash. You can have everything I've got with me.'

'We're not mercenaries, Doctor. There's one other way,' Gorrie said, glancing at the engineer. 'Still remember how to do it?'

Williams sweated behind his thick glasses. 'Commander, please. The Admiral said he'd court-martial me if I ever did it again.'

'Did what?'

'Williams here worked out how to turn the sub into a Totem pod back in Leeds.'

Williams spoke sheepishly. 'The hull acts as a resonator. Like a pod.'

'Does it hurt?'

Hopkins looked at Williams. 'Does it work?'

'You'll get what you need.'

'What about Totem juice?'

'There's a dimethyltryptamine-based serum in that kit: it'll work the same way,' said Williams, reaching up for the medical briefcase. He opened it up on his lap, withdrew the bottle of dark liquid and handed it to Hopkins.

The commander interrupted in a brusque tone. 'It's noon now. E.T.A. Sheffield docks twenty-hundred hours. Transmission begins twenty-two-hundred hours. Williams, you'd best get to work while I help Archer. McCole, help the doctor prepare for the casualty.'

Hopkins watched the ruins of a cathedral bell-tower drift by. 'Trying to convince him that this is actual reality is going to be a hard sell.'

McCole grunted in agreement.

'You've been quiet, McCole. Something the matter?'

'I'm not sure about this.'

'You don't have to drink the serum: only me.'

'You said that it could be dangerous for the public and they ain't stuck on a sunken fucking tin can with four other blokes. They could go mental and plough this thing into that,' McCole said, pointing at the screen while the relics of a motorway flyover passed beneath them. 'No offence to you lads, but I'm starting to feel a bit claustrophobic.'

'You have a better idea?'

'I'll go ashore with him to find a pod and stretch my legs a wee bit.'

'Two of you will attract more attention. The most that'll happen is you'll feel your chest vibrate a bit and you'll have a few hallucinations. It won't be the full thing, as long as you leave the juice alone.'

'Christ help us.'

Williams spoke without looking up, one headphone held to his ear and his pencil scribbling away on a pad of paper. 'We need all the help we can get.'

'I don't want my son to have died in vain.'

'We're all sorry about your son.'

Williams and Archer nodded in agreement. McCole looked at Hopkins, waiting for his reaction, but the doctor refused to meet his eye.

Archer spoke without turning away from his station. 'When I read the story about your son in The Serviceman, I wanted to kill her myself, doing that to one of our own.'

'His blood is on her hands.'

Hopkins thanked the men as he pulled at his right eyebrow. With no desire to dwell on the subject, he carried on organising the medical kit.

As requested, there were also documents detailing the technical specifications of the transmission. The information was as he expected, but the power supply figures seemed too high. Hopkins turned another page, but they were the same. He stared at the data, trying to make calculations in his head.

'What's the matter?'

'These parameters could kill the boy before I even get a chance to treat him. I hope Newman can get him out of there before it's too late.'

39

The voice crackled through the old radio receiver. 'Marm, we have a problem.'

'Show me.' Alice leant back in her glass throne and swiped around the screens on the armrests.

The picture from the lab camera fizzled before blooming into clarity. Muldoon lay on the gurney, watching the men in white coats surround him. One of them pushed a button on the main lab console and spoke in a panicky, thin voice.

'The subject is not responding to the stimuli, ma'am.' On the screen, the scientist held the button with one set of fingers and tugged at his already thin red hair with the other. Alice thought that he would look pretty on his knees, pleading for his life, but there was no time for that.

The Horseman's smile was flawed, just like his simpleton father's. The vulgar genes that had created the uneven teeth and dark, coarse hair shone through the scar tissue like sunlight through a cheap lace curtain. The same genes that had infected Jennifer, tainting her beyond redemption. She could never have been the same after that. She saw nothing to remind her that this piece of meat on the gurney was her grandson. He was her golden ticket to a place on the Board and nothing more.

Soon, this unpleasant little archipelago would be washed away by the sea anyway. Bones picked dry by the omnipresent seagulls plaguing the nightmares of any survivors. Before that happened, Alice was offering them ignorance at a price. Alice would sell them paradise in a pill or canister, so that they would know nothing of their brutal deaths. Once such a great empire, now this tiny collection of islands clung to a precarious existence. Everyone was too busy salvaging what they could of what they had left. Too busy to notice another oil field grab with conscripted cannon fodder. Or the bonfire of human rights acts that had been burning since the floods.

She pushed the talk button. 'And you've tried electro-therapy?'

'He blew every battery we have. We should postpone, pending new brain scans.'

'Nonsense. Have you tried the videos of his father's transmission?'

'Yes. No response.'

'His suicide?'

A short pause before the scientist answered in a flat tone. 'Yes.'

'Nothing?'

'Nothing. He's shut off from us completely.'

'You're saying he's catatonic again?'

'None of his readings suggest that. Also, he seems to be … smiling.'

'Call Farrell to get things ready. Looks like we'll need him after all,' Alice said, feeling her stomach knot with excitement. 'And get me a clean-up team: there'll be a lot of blood.'

'Who do you want to do it?'

'I'm coming down: I'll do it myself.'

As Alice thought about seasoning her little lamb for the spit, she started to tingle again.

Flanked by six security agents, Alice waited in Totem's basement car park for the delivery to arrive.

None of them spoke English, which was just fine with her: there was never any of the pathetic moralising as with veterans of Her Majesty's forces. The foreigners took the money and did as they were told, no matter how grim the task. Soon, Alice would have enough of them to arrest the remaining generals she hadn't already bought out.

And there was nothing they could do about it. Lucky Newman's efforts would amount to nothing once she'd decapitated the rebellion. From his mountain bunker, he'd put up more of a fight than she'd expected, but he couldn't hide in there forever.

Someone should have told these idiots that Her Majesty, her crown and her throne were leagues beneath the sea and were likely to stay there forever.

They were trying to piece together the shards of Britain like a smashed china teacup; to reinstate the stiff upper lip on a head with its brains blown out. Newman had done considerable damage by circulating The Serviceman in the Royal Legions. Who would have thought that amidst the whisky farts and sweet pipe smoke, that there would be enough hot blood to raise a rebellion? Who would have thought that the crew-cut young drunks could take their heads out of their pints of beer and bags of powder long enough to tie their boots?

It was nothing more than a tin-pot army, but she would still make examples of them, especially Newman. In the past twenty years, Alice had put some of her best men on to killing him and they'd all come back in body bags, but Newman's lucky streak was due to run out soon.

The truck pulled up in the loading bay and two grunts got out of the cabin to unlock the back door. A white horse cowered in the darkness of the vehicle, until they led it down a ramp and on to the concrete of the loading bay. The handsome creature staggered under the weight of the sedatives she had ordered as Alice lifted a hand to its face.

'Sssh, settle down,' she cooed, stroking the horse's white mane. 'Take him to the cell and wait for me there.'

The security detail looked at the delivery men and the delivery men looked at them. The humps looked away first.

Every time Alice tried to touch the horse, it recoiled. Its brown eyes watched her until she gave up and walked away through the warm monoxide breeze of the loading bay.

Back in the lab, Grosvenor approached the boy on the gurney. Looking down into the eyes of the Horseman, she could see that her little martyr was playing possum. There were faint movements and twitches in his facial muscles that gave Alice some satisfaction, but it was the smell of the boy that got her. That unmistakeable aroma of trapped prey made her shudder. She closed her eyes as she inhaled the scent from his scalp.

This was pleasing to Alice, but the boy was too calm. There was none of the rage required by her engineers for the transmission.

Alice had made provisions for this, of course. Leaning away from the wretch, she stood upright and instructed the white coats to bring in the horse. Muldoon turned his head to the sound of hooves on gorilla glass. The beast's nose twitched as her programmers led him to the table. Alice stepped away from the gurney and instructed them to let go of the reins, allowing the horse to draw near of its own accord. She raked her fingers around on a screen until the cell vanished all around them. The white coats exited the cell through its main door.

In the darkness, there was only the sound of the horse's breathing. She prodded the tablet's screen and the cell slowly illuminated. This time, rolling fields and leafy trees appeared all around them in the gorilla glass walls, floor and ceiling. The result was a seamless illusion of Dartmoor. As the room grew in brightness, Alice could see that Muldoon was looking at the clouds and landmarks: a tree, a fence and a river. He lifted his head off the gurney as the white horse grunted.

He looked at the creature and he tried to lift his shackled hand to no avail. The horse inched closer to the gurney.

Muldoon's voice was thin. 'Arthur?'

Grosvenor remained out of his field of vision in the corner of the cell as the horse nudged his hand.

A tear ran down the scar seam on Muldoon's left cheek.

'Where have you been?'

Alice watched the animal react with none of the fear it had shown towards her in the loading bay. Her patience already wearing thin, she allowed the horse to nuzzle the boy a few more times before she withdrew the scalpel from her pocket. Searching the horse's neck with one hand, she found the artery and plunged the scalpel into it. She drew it lengthways along the rubbery vessel to open it up and the horse reared. Blood sprayed all over her, Muldoon and the glass screens showing the digital Dartmoor.

Alice spat out the horse's blood as she stepped out of range of the red torrent. To the white coats and security crowded around her, she disguised the spasms of pleasure in her groin as heaving nausea. She clutched her stomach and fell into the waiting arms of her faithful mercenaries. Two of them carried her through the cell door, hot and wet with blood. Looking back over her shoulder through sticky eyes, she could see the Horseman thrashing against his restraints. The arteries in his own neck were bulging and his mouth, agape in despair.

With her own blood-slick lips, she smiled to no-one in particular.

40

Lucky sweated even in the draughty confines of the chopper. It had been a while since he had worn standard issue uniform, and he didn't remember it being this uncomfortable. Pulling at the neck of his ballistics vest allowed some air to circulate, but he was still stifled. Thunder rolled somewhere behind the clouds as the pilot banked towards Church Street.

The blue glow of masts had appeared across the islands during the journey, but the one at Totem HQ dwarfed them all. It was an old TV antenna salvaged from Winter Hill, stretching a kilometre-high into the clouds like a giant needle. The blue glow made the pilot squint, even from a distance. Having requested landing clearance over the radio, the pilot shouted over his shoulder to Lucky.

'Good luck, sir.'

Lucky nodded at Biggs, Jackson, Green and

Galley, who were all pale with adrenaline.

'We've only Grosvenor's men to worry about once we've got the kid,' Lucky shouted above the blades. 'We'll have enough numbers for a fighting chance once our boys turn on the mercs. You should be able to tell them from Her Majesty's easily enough. '

'How?'

Galley stuffed some kevlar back in a bullet-hole. 'Their body armour hasn't got holes in it for a start.'

Green adjusted his webbing. 'They've got Steyr rifles.'

'Proper roiders some of them. Fucking massive.'

The undernourished, under-equipped men looked at each other, then down at their old guns.

'How are we going to pull this off?'

Lucky lit a cigarette and winked at his pale comrade. 'It's a good plan: stick to it.'

As Totem HQ came into view, everyone in the helicopter peered down at the armour-clad security. The blue light from the mast reflected off their helmeted, insectoid heads.

'There's dozens of them.'

Green sighed. 'They've got full ballistic gear head-to-toe.'

'Well, it's a good job we brought loads of fucking bullets then, isn't it? All that kit will just slow them down: it's better for us.'

Lucky tried to bury his concern inside his hot and bulky armour. He knew Green was right. If they fired a single shot too soon, they wouldn't even make it out of the transmission hangar.

'Don't engage Grosvenor's men in any way until you hear the blast. And don't get too pally with any of the servicemen, either: we don't know who we can trust. I'll meet you all back at the bunker in a few days when things have cooled down. I want detonation six minutes after the transmission begins. When Grosvenor finishes her countdown, start your watches. Good luck.

'Good luck, sir.'

The helicopter touched down under the watch of a dozen six-foot guards lined up on the roof. A colonel and a staff sergeant waited to receive them by the door. Lucky and his team jumped down on to the concrete and scurried over. He recognised the colonel from his second tour of Syria. The man reached out his hand to him and smiled from behind a short-cropped, grey moustache atop a pencil neck.

'When I heard it was you, Newman, I couldn't believe it. Just had to get on Board, old chap,' Colonel Tappin said, shaking Lucky's hand. He didn't remember the colonel being this flamboyant when they were in the field. He'd seen the overcompensation with the jolly-good-old-British-Army-Officer bit in many a killer. 'Everything's in place. You'll have no bother from our boys. Watch out for Grosvenor's lot, though: bunch of heathens and miscreants.'

'Where is my station, Tappin?'

'Straight down to business, Newman. You always

were. You come with me: Sergeant Rowley will assign your men.'

Lucky addressed the sergeant. 'Make sure they're in the east wing of the grounds, where the graveyard used to be.'

The sergeant nodded and took the men to a fire escape on the east side of the building.

'My goodness, Newman. That old crone got under your skin. So serious these days. Looks like you're taking it personally.'

'I take it personally whenever someone tries to kill me, Tappin. Don't you?'

'I suppose I do, old chap. Suppose I do.'

'I know you do, Tappin.'

Tappin punched Lucky on the shoulder. 'Like the good old days hey, Newman?'

'Which good old days were these?'

Tappin ratcheted up the questions as they approached the lift. 'What's the plan anyway? Are you going to sabotage the mast? Obviously, you're taking Grosvenor out?'

'Just keep me covered on the west wing by the transmission hangar. Jesus, I can't believe they didn't brief you.'

'Only kidding, Newman. Might want to keep everything on the QT from now on, old boy. The games are about to begin.'

Although Tappin was working his last nerve, Lucky was glad to have a somewhat known quantity in his midst. But how did he know that taking out

Grosvenor and the mast had been on the cards? Lucky supposed that any seasoned soldier might see them as primary targets. Tappin continued smiling at him as the lift descended to the transmission hangar.

'Is it because of what happened in Aleppo, Newman?'

'Huh?'

'You don't like me because of Aleppo.'

'Aleppo, Damascus, Homs ... want me to go on?'

Tappin's smile twitched. 'They were all legitimate targets.'

'Women and children?'

'They were our orders, Newman. Insurgents come in all shapes and sizes: you know that. Would have lost a lot more men if I hadn't done things the way I did.'

'I never found a bomb strapped to any six-year-old kids hiding under their beds in all my time in Syria.'

'Maybe you weren't there long enough. I got tired of shovelling my mens' guts out of the dust.'

The lift stopped and spat them out into a grey, concrete loading bay area. Between the trucks and coaches, Lucky could see more mercenary guards. They stood by the entrances, except for four men trying to drag something big out of one of the vehicles. The men must have been the roiders that Jackson had referred to earlier. As they heaved on the ropes, they cast enormous shadows across the loading bay.

'They pop out of shrapnel wounds in bright pink.

Always remind me of those kids' animal balloons.'

'Alright, Tappin.'

'Sorry, old boy: these things just come to me sometimes. Get your pass ready.'

As they rounded the corner, Lucky could see that the mast was throwing a soft blue light over the grounds. Behind the cathedral, the converted Winter Hill mast stretched into the night sky, pulsing blue with energy amongst the stars.

On the exterior, the cathedral had been infected with Totem. Gorilla glass panels covered the walls, running endless promos. Panels of circuitry clung to the stained glass windows. Even the gargoyles spewed cables from their mouths.

The rumble of the waiting crowd grew louder. Lucky looked up at the transmission countdown projected on to the cathedral's roof: 22 minutes 31 seconds.

Her Majesty's checkpoint waved Lucky and the colonel straight through, but Grosvenor's guards took their ID tags, making Lucky sweat. When they checked out, the guard let them into the transmission area: a colony of metal eggs surrounded by soldiers loyal only to their queen.

'Come on, I'll show you the escape route.'

They walked through a stone arch into the cathedral. The nave was lit only by candles and the mast's light filtering through the stained glass windows.

The voices echoing around the cathedral sounded

procedural, like surgeons in an operating theatre. Lucky followed Tappin past a group of the white coats around a gurney on the altar. The stained glass windows and blue light from the mast projected oily shapes and colours on to their crisp lab coats. Lucky's standard issue boots squeaked on the marble floor, causing the kaleidoscopic scientists to notice them. He tightened his grip on the Heckler and Koch hanging from his shoulder.

Tappin waved to them. 'Everything's fine. Routine patrol. Carry on.'

They looked back down at the gurney, on which Lucky caught a glimpse of Muldoon's limp body. Alice Grosvenor appeared from the darkness of the choir stalls, stalking her way towards the altar. She nodded at one of the neuroprogrammers, prompting him to swipe his finger around on a wall-mounted glass panel. A grinding, creaking sound came from the cathedral ceiling, making Lucky look up. He flinched at the sight of a 20-foot-wide brass mouth lowering towards the altar. The strange object reflected a microcosmic Milky Way on the cathedral's grand ceiling. On the gurney, the boy remained still as the giant bell descended closer to him. Lucky saw that above the bell, a jungle of cables twisted around the brass pipes like vines.

'They melted down every last church bell on the mainland to cast that. Except this one over here in the chapel of St. George.'

When he'd climbed the steps, Lucky saw a large

bronze cross: a memorial to the members of the York and Lancaster Regiment. He wondered how this had survived the ruthless iconoclasm that had swept through Britannia in the wake of the floods.

Tappin pointed at a freshly-polished ship's bell engraved with HMS Sheffield. 'That bell is the reason you're here.'

'What are you talking about, Tappin?'

'The Navy wouldn't let them melt that one down. You might think I'm exaggerating, but that's when it all started. When the admirals refused to budge on the bell, Grosvenor started bringing in the mercenaries.'

'Think there's a bit more to it than that.'

'Of course there is, dear boy, but it's rather poetic, don't you think? Without this bell, the military might still be co-operating with Grosvenor, and you might still be eating seagulls out of alleyways.'

'Who told you about that?'

'You're kidding, aren't you, Newman? Everyone knows, old chap.'

Lucky read the brass plaques in the stone walls and stared up at the curious stained glass windows.

'Bet you've never seen a polar bear in a stained glass window before. Or a tiger.'

'The Sheffield Pals. The tiger represents Salonika and the polar bear, the Allied landings in 1944.'

Lucky ran his hand over the brass tips of the sabre scabbards, which made up the memorial fence. Facing downwards was a row of unsheathed bayonets, polished and sharp.

Two guards opened the main doors. The elite lined up in their expensive eveningwear, eager to be stuffed into their pods. Lucky observed their ruddy faces and haughty affectations as they slithered by. While Britain sank in the floods, these people had remained untouched by the waters. Now they only ever left the capital to satiate the dark tastes they could not within its limits.

The white coats hovered by the gurney while a screen sprang to life above the altar. Grosvenor's smiling face appeared, her eyes as black as ever.

Lucky felt his heart quicken. The backdrop on the screen was her office, hundreds of feet above where they stood. At the sound of Grosvenor's voice booming through the cathedral, the guests looked up, each clutching their drained flute of Totem juice. The kaleidoscopic light seemed to seek out every carat of diamond in the room, casting a refractive shimmer over the nave.

'Good evening and welcome to a very special Totem transmission.'

A raucous cheer from the crowd went up as they raised their flutes.

'Please make your way to your designated pod. Be advised that any unrecognised DNA material present in the vessel will alert our security, so double check your tickets.'

Couples separated without so much as a word and strode to their pods before anyone else could claim them. Some couldn't get inside quickly enough. A beep went up from the countdown clock, indicating five minutes to transmission. The white coats shrank back from the gurney into the choir stalls and the hum began making Lucky's teeth buzz. When he looked at the bell, it seemed blurred to his eye, as if it were vibrating. The light from the mast burned brighter, illuminating even the pods at the back of the nave. A bell chime cleaved through the cool air of the cathedral, creating another pitch above the low hum. Tappin stuck his bony finger in his little ear and wiggled it about, then opened his jaw a few times.

'Always gets me.'

Tappin led lucky to a large plaque in the floor, out of sight of those in the nave. He squinted and leaned down to read the inscription.

Honi soit qui mal y pense.

'French?'

'Evil be upon him that thinks evil of it.'

'We don't really have time for this, Tappin.'

'Hold your horses,' he said, heaving off the brass plate to reveal a ladder stretching down into darkness. 'This is your escape route. Leads down into the crypt, comes back up through the graveyard or you can carry on all the way to the docks if you cross into the old drainage tunnels. Come on, I'll show you.'

Tappin took the machine gun off his shoulder and laid it on the stone floor, then gestured to Lucky to do the same.

Lucky had that bad taste in his mouth.

Reminded him of seagull blood.

With no other way out of the cathedral alive, he unhooked the weapon from his shoulder and laid it down.

'You first.'

'Naturally, Newman.' Tappin wedged himself through the gap and down the ladder.

Lucky looked around to check that they weren't being watched, then up at the countdown clock: three minutes and fifty-two seconds.

When he had descended, he was in total darkness except for the psychedelic glow from the hatch above, which seemed miles away. Lucky searched his assault vest, checking the pockets for his torch to no avail.

'Tappin, you got your torch there? Looks like your boys scrimped on my kit.'

Silence.

And that bad taste.

'Tappin?'

The darkness crowded up against Lucky, making his heart thud and his mouth dry up.

He tried again. 'Tappin?'

His boots echoed on the stone floor as he took a few steps away from the ladder. He listened hard for breathing or boots scraping.

Silence.

He needed his weapon. As he stepped on to the first rung of the ladder, he felt a heavy blow to his ribs, followed by a sharp pain. His knees buckled, but he stayed on his feet and drove backwards with his elbows into his assailant, connecting with a thump. Lucky pulled out the hot and sticky knife from his side and surged towards his assailant. In the sultry darkness of the crypt, the two men snarled against each other.

He could feel the blood in his boots now. His heart pumped it ever more quickly out through the hole in his side and down his leg. He knew that he would soon pass out. And then he'd be finished. The mission would be a failure.

The humming escalated and the kaleidoscopic light from the far-away hole became as bright as daylight. It chased downwards into the crypt and lit up Tappin's wiry frame against the brickwork of the tunnel, allowing Lucky to aim the knife for his heart. The double-crossing colonel collapsed in the dirt.

He removed the knife from Tappin's twitching body, and listened to his last words in the strange light:

'Evil be upon him that thinks evil of it,' he rattled.

As Lucky climbed the ladder, each rung brought a flash of pain that made him nauseous. His vision closed in as Grosvenor counted down. After struggling with the last few rungs, he spilled out into the chapel, striped by the long, thin shadows of the memorial bayonets and sabres. He picked up his MP5, hooked it on to his shoulder and leant against the wall. An arc of blue electricity fizzed down the nave. Lucky's ears felt like they were going to burst, so he clamped his hands over them and lay on the chapel floor. He had to catch his bubbling breath before the transmission started.

5

4

3

2

1

Hopkins held the small vial of Totem juice to his lips and drank its contents. He had always relished the prospect of altered consciousness, especially as a medical student. While his colleagues were too conservative for that kind of thing, Hopkins always wanted first-hand data. He had often volunteered for such experiments when others would not.

Even so, his hands were trembling. He felt like God was watching. Every move. Every thought.

'You want a wee dram to go with that,' McCole said, holding up his flask. 'This is my last. You can have it.'

'No, thank you, McCole.' Ho0pkins winced at the idea of mixing whisky with the bitter dimethyltryptamine elixir.

'You sure you know what you're doing?'

'I invented the thing.'

McCole rolled his eyes.

'Williams, run one last check on it.'

'Diagnostics appear to be fine, sir,' Williams replied as he read the screen in front of him.

'Commencing manual check.'

Williams ran to the back of the submarine and disappeared through a hatch. He returned fifteen seconds later and sat back down in front of the screen. 'All wired up and ready to receive transmission, sir. Countdown: three minutes to transmission.'

Williams switched the radio from his headphones to the sub's speaker system, introducing a low hum into the confined space. Hopkins leaned back in his bunk as the vibrations intensified.

McCole looked at the commander. 'I only came to keep him out of trouble.'

The vibration intensified again, rattling things off shelves. The bank of screens in front of Williams glowed blue and began to flash, building up in tempo.

Commander Gorrie shouted above the loud hum. 'Everyone in their bunks, now!'

'I hope this thing can take it, Commander!'

A metallic rattle skewered through McCole's prayers. The chaplain clambered on to his bunk, his every move strobed by the flashing screens.

The smell of brass filled the air and Grosvenor's smug voice crackled in the blue light.

5

4

3

2

1

Alice listened to herself barking from the cathedral square far below her office window. She'd made the recording days before in preparation for Muldoon's transmission, so that she wouldn't miss out on the fruits of her labours. Leaning against the smoked glass, she looked down at the deserted streets, cradling her own flute of Totem juice. She often came to the window late at night, hoping for some voice from the wilderness to whisper in her ear, imparting all the secrets of the universe. Maybe a whisper of regret or remorse for all the things she had done. An affirmation that she was actually a warm-blooded human being. In part, at least.

But it never came.

The blue glow of her pod drew Alice away from the window. Cast from the same metal as the Totem bell, the pod would resonate in exact unison during every transmission, affording her the purest signal. The finest artisans had engraved it with the Board's symbols between the crystals and gemstones. She was almost as proud of the pod as she was of John Muldoon. The mast grew brighter, encouraging Alice to spare a thought for her little martyr. She might have said a prayer if she'd known how, just for the fun of it.

The people of Britannia would know true suffering once they'd been dipped into the hellfire of Muldoon's dream. Then her ascension could begin. The Board's promises would finally come true. Maybe they would send someone to give her the news in person this time, instead of a phone call. Alice tingled with excitement at the thought.

She observed the sacrificial lamb on one of her many screens. Eyes glazed over, breathing shallow, heart rate high and still covered in horse blood, Muldoon twitched beneath the Totem bell. The light was now so bright that she had to shield her eyes. Alice thought about who she might fire for choosing the wrong filters.

She ran her fingers over the pod's sparkling cocoon of expensive minerals and metals and unbuttoned her work suit, letting it fall to the floor. She performed the short ritual of placing her underwear and jewellery in her desk drawer before climbing inside the pod. Once inside, the heavy latch locked with the sincerity of a guillotine.

Alice nestled her naked body against the pod's cool horse-leather lining and closed her eyes.

5

4

3

2

1

THE HORSEMAN'S DREAM

John Muldoon wandered up the high street of the deserted town, watching the snow melting on the cobbles beneath his feet. The wet stones reflected the few Christmas lights that he had hung in the shop windows the previous year. Nothing fancy, just a few nine-volt fairy lights, but it reminded him that Dartmoor was the closest thing to a home that he'd ever had.

Past the butcher's and the bookshop, John stopped outside the old barber's and listened for Arthur in the stables down the side street. He heard a rustle and the clunk of the door, followed by the creak of it swinging open. Taking care on the slick cobbles, he set off down the road and headed for the dim light, his heart quickening at the thought of seeing his horse again. The familiar, severe camber of the old road pushed him into the gutter, so he steadied himself with one hand on the windowsill of the cottage. Snow fell on his eyelashes in thick flakes.

Inside the stable, there was nothing apart from a flickering hurricane lantern hung on the doorpost and a few of the hay bales lying around. Holding up the lantern to the dark street revealed nothing, so John headed to the Army and Navy shop.

The place was still lit with the fairy lights he had found and strung up the previous Christmas. The door loosed a cloud of dust as he closed it behind him and the wind sighed against the murky glass. In the back room, he found a thick woollen army issue sweater, which clung tightly to his torso. Searching the shelves for a heavy coat, he dug out a brown, waxed jacket with tartan lining.

When John returned to the main area of the small and jumbled shop, he noticed something that wasn't there before. A Beretta shotgun sat on the glass counter, with a dozen or so red shells next to it. He looked around the place and opened the door to check the street, which was becoming white with snow.

No-one there.

Finding warm clothes in a basket by the rattling door, he removed his hospital pyjamas to put them on. He had to look over his shoulder first, as had become habit since he was seven years old. He peeled off his hospital slippers and replaced them with the paratrooper boots that shone like the shell of a beetle.

Drawing the lantern close to the shotgun, he saw intricate engravings of shapes and words on it. John recognised but couldn't decipher the strange code. With the shells all stuffed into the left-hand pocket of his jacket, he picked up the shotgun and left the shop. The old hurricane lantern lit the way and it swung from the crook of his elbow.

A few steps down the high street took John to the edge of the moor, where he could see the prison. A single window glowed through the darkness, but disappeared when the wind sighed and the snow thickened. He knew that Arthur was in the prison grounds somewhere. He stepped forward into the blackness of the moor, tightening his grip on the shotgun.

When he arrived at the small wood, John saw faces in the trees and brambles, illuminated by his lantern. Vines twisted around each other in the darkness like malnourished limbs, blanched by the acids of time and weather. He tried to look away from the faces, but couldn't help recognising a cheekbone here or a decayed eye socket there. A snarled lip or a bloody strand of hair stuck to the porcelain smoothness of an exposed skull.

Keeping his eyes fixed on the prison through the thin, leafless trees, he tried to ignore the moans coming from the darkness. Searching with his hands out in front of him, the ice-cold wire fence came within his grasp. He raked his fingers through the diamond holes as he walked along the fence until he found a gap and pushed through. When he arrived at a hole in the concrete wall of the prison itself, he entered the building with the shotgun raised.

The corridor was peeling green and black and John could feel the curled vinyl floor tiles trying to trip him with every step. Every wire-glass security window was smashed in circles like ice in a puddle, and drips of water echoed in the corridor's ruined chamber. He followed it until he came to an electronic security door, which glowed blue amidst the decay.

He tried the door, but it would not open. As he positioned himself to shoulder it, the symbols on the shotgun passed through the light and the door clacked open. It revealed a small metal room with another glowing panel.

His knees buckled slightly as the lift moved upwards. The door slid open and as John stepped out on to the metal floor, the lantern flickered. A nest of girders and beams moaned and creaked ominously above him. The skylights beyond them were smashed like the security windows in the corridor. Water droplets squeezed through the cracks. Their descent from the wired glass to their obliteration on the prison floor seemed to take minutes rather than seconds.

John noticed a break in the hypnotic pattern of bars at the far end, indicating a cell door left open. His footsteps thundered on the metal staircase as he approached it.

When he reached the open cell, he held his lantern up, but the room appeared to stretch into a long, dark corridor. As he walked further into the darkness, John felt hot, so he removed his jacket and jumper. Wiping the sweat from his eyes with his bare forearm, he continued to search for the back of the cell without success. He kept walking until the stone floor made a different sound under his boots.

In the light of the lantern, a precisely laid mosaic floor shimmered golden under his feet. The sweet smell of burning wood reminded him of before he met Arthur, hiding out in the barn in Dartmoor. The air was hot and dry and when he looked up at the myriad golden surfaces in the cell. John dropped the lantern so that he could shield his eyes. He kept the shotgun raised and pointed into the light, which revealed an ornate domed hallway before him. Figures dressed in white moved about, but it was too bright for John to make out their faces. The mosaic floor fell away, pixelating everything with their reflections flashing this way and that. John fell into a black hole with the thousands of small tiles.

Hot sand blew into his face, sticking to the sweat already on his brow.

Men shouted.

Women screamed.

He looked back to see that the cell had vanished: there was only sand and dust behind him.

The assault rifle was heavier than the shotgun and he was further restricted by the ammunition clipped to his vest. An explosion showered him with tiny fragments of rock. Through the dust, John staggered towards the only building he could see. At the door, two men with the same rifles and uniform crouched, one shouting at the other.

Clear it, Hopkins. Now! Grenade, Hopkins! What are you waiting for? Now!

The young soldier threw the grenade inside and a baby cried.

He tried to kick down the door, but the officer pulled him to the ground before the explosion.

The officer shouted again from beyond the dust and smoke.

I can't afford to lose any more men. No-one goes in that room. Move out.

The soldier ripped away from the officer's grip and walked through the doorway. The next sound to come from within was a young man's scream of despair, which was all too familiar to John.

He walked to the doorway to see Andrew Hopkins huddled in the corner by a gasping pile of bloody meat and hair. The dying remains of a mother and her baby who had been hiding in the building. An officer stood over Hopkins shaking his head. The ID patch on the officer's uniform read Tappin.

No-one goes near them: they could be booby-trapped. Are you going to clean up your own mess, Hopkins? Or do I have to do it?

The officer aimed his assault rifle at the mother and child still clinging on to life.

Hopkins jumped as the shots rang out and his eyes rolled upwards in their sockets.

The room smelled like sulphur and blood.

Muldoon, drone strike's due in thirty seconds. Leave Hopkins: there's nothing we can do.

We can't leave him behind.

He's done. Better off dead, trust me. Move out.

The officer disappeared into the dust cloud, continuing to shout orders at the rest of his men as if nothing had happened. John ran inside the hellhole to find the young soldier slumped against the wall.

Shouting at him didn't work.

Shaking him by the assault vest didn't work.

Slapping him in the face just turned his skin red, so John grabbed the shoulder of his vest and dragged him outside. As he pulled him towards an alley, the injured man's boot-heels carved clean trails on the blood-covered street.

He pulled Hopkins into the gap between the buildings, barely able to see for the sand and smoke in his eyes. An explosion sent both men crashing to the stinking floor of the alley. Though winded, John managed to summon help on his radio. Fragments of the building they had just escaped lay all about them.

Medics are 90 seconds away, Muldoon. Hold on. Over.

He tried to get Hopkins to take some water from his canteen, but it dribbled out of the side of his mouth. Boots clacked down the alleyway. John raised his rifle, but lowered it when he saw that they were the same boots that he was wearing.

The men got in his face, pulling his eyelids up and

checking his pulse.

This one's fine. Other fella's gonna need a holiday. Bring the truck.

Man, they'll court-martial you for this. You disobeyed your CO.

They ought to give him a medal. What's your name?

Muldoon, sir. Private Arthur Muldoon.

As John followed the medics down the long alley to the waiting ambulance, darkness fell The sound of his footsteps changed as he pushed through another storm of mosaics and light, bringing him back to the cell in Dartmoor.

He picked up the lantern and the shotgun from the rusty skeleton of the bed. To his relief, the sliding metal bars were still open, so he stepped through them and back into the main hall of the prison. There, he climbed a staircase to the next level of cells, the tang of wet rust rising from the handrails.

John peered down the row of cells, searching for any reflections of light.

Nothing.

He looked across the deep and wide rift, crosshatched with metal beams the same as that on which he was standing. One of the beams bridged the gap, so John stepped on to it, nervously watching the green and rusty spot in the middle. The bridge clanked in the silence high above the wipe-clean floors: the same floors they had in the borstal. He stepped over the middle of the bridge, trying to ignore the groaning metal. After he'd made it to the other side, the beam folded and crashed into the darkness below. The echo seemed unending as John continued searching along the row of cells.

He hurried along the platform towards a glimmer of light, keeping the shotgun pointed into the cell as he approached. When he realised that someone was in the bunk, he stepped back to a safe distance. The inmate's ribcage was rising and falling as if he were asleep.

John saw something under the bunk. Something metal. He reached his arm between the bars to retrieve it. Thinking that something had bitten him, he let go of the object and pulled back his hand to examine it. A perfect sphere of blood appeared from a clean cut on the edge of his finger. John rested the lantern on the ground and lay on his front, so that he could see right underneath the bed. The blood was still wet on the blade of the weapon: a toothbrush with the bristles melted and a razor jammed into the middle of it. It was even the same colour bristles as the one they'd used on him in the borstal.

A bit further under the bed were other small improvised blades. He'd seen them all before.

All variations on a theme.

A body in the bunk turned over, revealing to John a face so familiar that it made his heart rattle.

Morning, son.

John didn't know how to answer.

Get yourself some breakfast.

His father climbed out of the bunk and came face to face with him, then pointed towards the rear of the cell.

A table appeared out of the shadows. His father sat down in the chair nearest the window that looked out on to a meadow. John took the seat opposite and asked the man if he really was his father.

I'll always be your Dad. And she'll always be your Mum.

John felt like his heart was going to stop. His mother's floral dress undulated as she turned to a cabinet above the kitchen work top. Her voice trickled through his nervous system like cool water when she spoke.

Oh, you've cut your finger, John. Let me get you a plaster.

Let me stay here with you.

His parents looked at each other.

You can't. You mustn't.

Please let me stay.

Things will be different when you go back, John.

You have to trust us.

Something thundered in the open space of the main hall.

John pulled the shotgun off the bed and pointed it towards the door as the footsteps drew closer. His father lowered the barrel, reassuring him that it would be alright. A famished, bloodless face appeared in the darkness beyond the bars, making him shiver.

He's late.

He'll be leaving soon, said John's dad. He's not staying.

There'll be a penalty.

The man's arms were so thin that they looked like they might snap as he rooted around his library trolley. He withdrew a book and stepped closer to the bars, revealing more of his thin, translucent face. His bald head wobbled atop the prison uniform like a wooden puppet's. The pencil neck that connected it to the withered torso was mottled with dark veins and indecipherable tattoos.

John lifted the shotgun and told him to leave them alone.

Don't shoot the messenger.

The pale, hunched twig of a man put the book back in his trolley and smiled at John. Maybe later.

John lifted the shotgun barrel between the bars, pointing it at the cadaverous face. The librarian laughed and shuffled back into the darkness. As John turned around to sit back down at the table, he saw that it was no longer there and neither were his parents.

He ripped the mouldy mattress off the bunk and kicked the walls where the kitchen window had been. After that, he searched every cell up and down that side of the wing, then leant over the top metal balcony to look for any sign of them over on the other side.

Nothing.

He ran to the lowest level, trying to find a way out

of the wing. Kicking through a rusted shut door led him out into the dawn. Snow was underfoot, and concrete under that. At first it looked like part of the recreational facilities, but as John moved forward into the sunrise, he realised he was elsewhere now. Spirals of metal and tiny wooden castles appeared everywhere. Weathered advertisements for ice cream, lolly ices, burgers, hot dogs. Beyond them, rusty-shuttered stalls with flaky signs that read coconut shy, test your strength and tattoo parlour. No sign of his parents, though.

Working his way through the fairground, he saw a ride with painted, wooden horses. He rested his lantern on the weed-ravaged concrete to inspect it. Keeping his shotgun in his right hand, John circled the ride, brushing off any snow off each horse as he passed by it. He stopped at the white one, leaving his hand to linger on its painted wooden mane.

Tinkling, tuneless music echoed off the castles' wooden ramparts and metal shutters. He followed the sound to the Tattoo Parlour, but stepped back as something rattled from within. A withered, inked hand slithered beneath the shutter and forced it upwards with a squeal that could have shattered his teeth. The smell that came out of the crumbling stall made John balk.

He ran, not wanting to look back. Up ahead he saw a wood and broke away from the concrete to weave between the trees, away from the tattooist. Further in, he heard voices and slowed to a creep, trying not to snap any twigs underfoot. Snow fell from the branches overhead, but every time he glanced upwards, there were no birds. Through the trees, three men and a woman encircled a large oak. A body hung from the tree by its neck, steam coming from the open, upturned mouth. Squinting against the brightness of two bright red suns on the horizon, he saw the dead face of Andrew Hopkins: the soldier who had thrown the grenade.

John moved through the wood to gain a clearer view of the woman and saw that it was Alice Grosvenor. A twig snapped and the group turned in his direction. He ran, but the snow slowed him down, deepening with every step. He dropped the heavy shotgun as he lost his footing. Leather-gloved hands grabbed his clothes and Grosvenor was staring down at him, looking as if she wanted to peck his eyes out. She walked onwards, leading the way for her ghouls to drag him back towards the tattooist's stall.

John writhed and struggled to free himself as they dragged him towards the source of the stench. The tattooist leant on the counter, waiting for his prey to stop struggling. John cried out when he saw that the man's frail arms were inked with patterns like those on the shotgun and the gate.

The leather gloves grabbed John's head and forced it down on to the counter, holding a knife to his neck to keep him still. Dazzled by the red light of the twin suns, he turned away.

Make him face me.

The stiff leather fingers gripped John's skull as they turned it to face Grosvenor. Meanwhile, the tattooist librarian wheezed foul breath as he inspected a patch of skin above his right eyebrow.

Why are you doing this to me?

The tattooist rattled amongst the array of old-looking instruments on his mouldy shelves until he settled on a needle.

What are you doing?

He leant closer to John's ear.

Something that will set you free.

The inked fingers flicked a few switches on some rusted machinery. The needle whined at a higher pitch as it came closer. When it made contact, the pain was excruciating. John's eyes watered and he thrashed his legs against his captors. He was helpless as the needle dug deeper into his flesh. He called out for his mother and father, but he only heard cruel laughter from Grosvenor in response.

Don't think they're coming.

Through the agony, John called out for Arthur.

Grosvenor stopped laughing.

Hooves thundered towards them. Hooves that he had heard a thousand times before on Dartmoor. His captors jumped at the sound of boughs and twigs cracking in the frosty air. Through the trees, John could see a large horse approaching at speed, his white mane aflame in the dawn's golden suns.

Arthur.

The tattooist withdrew the filthy needle as

something exploded in the distance. The ground shook and colourful shards of stained glass fell silently into the snow at John's feet.

42

Those six minutes seemed like forever to Lucky. The explosion from outside had scattered the white coats around Muldoon's gurney. Still conscious, one of them scraped his hands across the shards of broken stained-glass, painting blood all over the altar steps.

All but four of Grosvenor's men ran outside when the mast blew. The sound of gunfire lured the stragglers to the door, allowing Lucky to sneak up from the chapel to the altar. He unstrapped Muldoon and the semi-conscious white-coat groaned. With half of his face encrusted with bloody stained-glass, the programmer grabbed Lucky's ankle. After pistol-whipping him, Lucky was able to free the boy. No time to check for a pulse, but his chest was rising and falling, which was good enough.

The pods remained locked as a siren began to wail through the cathedral. Harrowed, screaming faces pressed up against their port-holes, all bearing the same bloody wound above their right eye. He put Muldoon over his shoulder for the ladder descent into the crypt. The punctured lung that Tappin had given him was painful, but the adrenaline and a double dose of codeine from his kit took the brunt. Lucky kicked the covering plate aside and eased himself down. With his left arm clamped around the boy's legs, he managed to climb down to the bottom.

His breath gurgled as he heaved the unconscious boy down the tunnels of the crypt. He headed east to the docks by the light of his small vest torch that dangled from its clip, creating giant shadows on the tunnel walls. Above them on the streets, Lucky could hear car tyres screeching and women screaming. Sirens rising and falling from every direction. He stopped to catch his breath for a few seconds, listening to the symphony of panic in the city. Just as he rolled the Horseman on to the stone floor, voices rose in a distant part of the tunnel. He wasn't going to be able to outrun them, so he rigged a grenade and paracord as a trip wire across the ground. He stuffed his assault vest into a crevice a few feet beyond the wire, so that the mercenaries would keep their torches high as they walked into his trap. The boy murmured and touched the skin above his right eye as he drifted in and out of consciousness.

'Can you walk?'

The boy wobbled on his feet. 'Who are you?'

The radio crackle and hushed voices drew nearer. 'Someone else Grosvenor screwed over. You coming?'

The boy looked both ways down the tunnel, and then back at Lucky, who sighed.

'I know your father was Arthur Muldoon,' Lucky said, the boy's blood-encrusted eyes brightening at the mention of the name. 'And I know about everything that's happened to you. We're here to put things right.'

'Do you know Hopkins?'

Lucky pointed down the tunnel. 'I'm taking you to him now.'

The young man staggered off in the direction of the docks with Lucky following behind.

'You see or hear anyone up ahead, get down and keep quiet.' He looked over his shoulder, unsure whether he'd seen the flash of torches in his peripheral vision. 'Won't be long before the trip wire goes off.'

They followed the tunnel for another three minutes before arriving at another hole in the wall. As they climbed into the parallel tunnel, an explosion shook the ground. Seconds later, bits of rubble came spitting down the tunnel after them. They hurried through the filth underfoot, gagging on the smell of something that had died in there. Eventually, they came to three shafts of streetlight shining through the holes in a manhole cover. Lucky hoped that the rungs of the rusted, barnacled ladder would hold his weight while he heaved the cover open. He pushed with everything he had left, but couldn't move it.

He came down the ladder and took John by the arm, leading them further until he could hear waves rolling against the dock wall. A chorus of gurgles sang out as the seawater drained from its various cavities. As they progressed, the wind blew into their faces from a distant opening in the concrete.

Lucky staggered towards the dim light of the exit. 'Come on, we're nearly there.'

The boy dragged like a dead weight. Lucky shone the torch into his eyes, which were rolling back in his head.

'Not yet, John,' said Lucky, slapping his face. 'Hopkins will sort you out.'

The boy's eyes had glazed over. Nobody home.

'Come on. We're right there. Don't give up.'

Nausea washed over Lucky as the knife wound ached. He had nothing left. He could accept losing his life there in that stinking tunnel to Grosvenor's soldiers, but he wasn't going to let her have the boy's. She'd done enough to him. Beneath the dried blood flaking away from the boy's face, Lucky could see the scarring that he'd heard about. He regretted that he probably wouldn't be around long enough to make Grosvenor pay for that. Gritting his teeth, he lifted John for the last fifty yards of the tunnel, trying to ignore the sensation of his lung collapsing.

As they birthed into the salty air of the deserted dock, sirens rose higher in the distance. Lucky rested against the cold wall, listening to the sounds of civil unrest. Above the noise, he heard something behind them in the tunnel. Rocks falling and boots clumping.

He headed for dock 22, gasping and retching for air under the floodlights. He peered down the side of every ship until he came to the Eddie Stobart and noticed a dark protrusion from the water near its stern. He hobbled down the steps to the floating pontoon. Drawing closer, he saw that it was the submarine, breeched and ready to take them aboard. He unclipped a carabiner from his vest and threw it at the hull to get their attention. The hatch opened and McCole emerged, looking shocked as Lucky collapsed to the concrete with the boy.

'They're coming down the tunnel. Get me a rifle.'

'Just get on board, man.'

'Take him and give me a rifle. Now.'

McCole emerged from the hatch and crossed to the pontoon with an M16 for Lucky. He took it from McCole and watched him lower the unconscious boy into the vessel before sighting up the opening of the tunnel.

'Fuck's sake, Newman. Get aboard, you bawbag,' said McCole, but Lucky didn't take his eye away from the scope, keeping the tunnel exit in his crosshairs.

'I'm done, McCole. Get the boy out of here.'

McCole dragged Lucky across the pontoon, his boots thunking against the hull of the submarine. The chaplain handed him down to the submariners, who hoisted him on to a bunk.

Lucky saw Hopkins sitting at a table, inspecting the wound above his right eye in the reflection of a gauge's glass window.

'Hand me that rifle.'

Hopkins grabbed his Beretta and a rifle before climbing through the hatch and on to the deck with the chaplain.

In between the bandage-ripping and the vein-slapping by Williams, Lucky could hear the skirmish through the open hatch. Gunfire cracked and boomed across the empty docks. McCole's rifle and Hopkins' Beretta each answered from the deck of the sub.

'We have to keep the boy safe.'

Archer reached for a lever. 'We should dive now.'

Lucky grabbed his arm. 'We're not going anywhere without them. We wait.'

The gunfire stopped. The men looked at each other as the silence continued. As the commander reached for the hatch, Lucky gasped. 'Wait.'

The two men climbed back into the sub and pulled it closed behind them. Hopkins dropped the shotgun in a locker and set about fixing up John Muldoon with his medical kit.

'Ok, fucking dive or whatever,' McCole said, filling the submarine with smoke from his rifle's muzzle. 'Unless you want this thing turned into a sieve. There'll be more of them.'

Lucky knew something wasn't right aboard the sub. Apart from the fact that his lung was having a plastic valve inserted into it while he was all hopped up on morphine. When things started to get weird, he wondered what drugs they'd given him.

The men leaning over him both had numbers above their right eyebrows. No more than a millimetre high. They stared at each other in disbelief as each crew member caught sight of their strange tattoos, almost losing control of the sub and crashing into the dock. Lucky clenched his teeth as the IV needle pulled in his arm.

The commander spoke sternly. 'Pull yourselves together.'

Archer's trembling finger pointed at Gorrie's right eyebrow. 'Commander, you've got one too.'

'Your only concern right now is this dive.' The commander sat at the controls and tried not to be too obvious about checking his own eyebrow in the radar screen.

A sweaty silence fell over the crew until they had made it to open sea. Lucky stared at the riveted metal plates above him, glad to be able to breathe again. But Archer could contain his questions no more.

'What the hell's going on, Commander?'

'I don't know.' Gorrie kept his eyes focused on the gauges in front of him.

The submarine was deathly silent until Archer spoke again. 'It was Death. We all saw it. We all felt it. The prison was a gateway.'

McCole's words struck through the air of the tight sub. 'And I saw when the lamb opened one of the seals, and I heard—as it were the noise of thunder—

one of the four beasts saying come and see.'

Even Hopkins and Gorrie looked up from what they were doing as the chaplain rose from his bunk. His frame filled the gangway, the red light behind him lending him an unholy air. With the Bible gripped between bloodless fingers, he walked towards the boy. Lucky saw Archer unclip his Colt .45 from its holster as the chaplain approached. McCole kneeled and began to pray alongside Hopkins. Archer clipped his pistol back up and held his shaking hands to his face.

'What does it mean?'

McCole smirked. 'It's an expiry date.'

Lucky pointed to his tattoo. 'What does mine say?'

'You haven't got one, Newman. You weren't in a pod.'

'Oh, God,' said Archer, still holding his head in his hands.

McCole caught Archer's eye. 'Have you seen what it says?'

'Of course I have, you Scotch twat. I'll be dead by tomorrow.'

Hopkins' concern was for the younger man's safety. 'Calm down, Archer.'

'Listen to the doctor, Archer,' McCole said, rifling through a tool box. 'Hopkins, help me tattoo over the numbers. You'll need this wire brush and that pen in your top pocket.'

'How come he gets it covered up?'

'You've already looked at yours. Too late for you.'

Archer leaned forward and squinted at McCole's tattoo. 'Well, how about I tell you yours, McCole? It's—'

McCole barely threw any weight into the punch, but it was still enough to put Archer to sleep and send one of his teeth rattling to the steel floor.

McCole held out the wire brush. 'If you wouldn't mind, Hopkins?'

Hopkins took Muldoon's pulse. 'I'd prefer it if you did it yourself. I'm busy.'

'What's your problem?'

'I'd rather not know yours.'

McCole raked the brush with his thumb and turned to Lucky. 'Sentimental old bastard, isn't he?'

'I'd do it for you McCole, if I wasn't seeing double.'

'Fine.' McCole took the pen from Hopkins and emptied a pool of ink on to a laminated chart. After swirling the wire brush about in it, he pressed it above his right eyebrow and pulled the brush back and forth until a trickle of inky blood ran into his eye. He dropped the makeshift apparatus to the steel floor with a clang. After dabbing a spot of ink on his right index finger, he rubbed it into the raw wound for good measure.

McCole held out the brush to the commander, who went through the same procedure before offering the apparatus to Hopkins.

'I've already seen it.'

McCole gave him a look. 'Well, I don't want to

know yours, either. Might get my hopes up and turn out to be bullshit.'

Hopkins accepted the grim tattoo removal kit. Teeth gritted, he jammed the sharp metal bristles into the numbers above his eyebrow. 'Who's the sentimental old bastard now?'

43

Alice Grosvenor knew that the boy's dream had doomed her even before she read the tattoo. As she stood her naked body in front of the huge Georgian mirror in her office, she considered the myriad signs of decay, despite scrupulous maintenance of both. She stepped closer and wiped away the blood to inspect her eyebrow.

A sequence of numbers.

A date.

Today's date.

She flinched as another explosion boomed around the grounds of the cathedral. Gunfire peppered the air and muzzle flash scorched the square below. VIPs ran from the cathedral, clutching their bloody foreheads and screaming like the inmates at Exmoor. The lights on the Totem mast extinguished as the high-tensile cables snapped like cotton thread. The towering structure swayed to one side, threatening to demolish a swathe of the new banking sector.

Alice had always found tattoos to be vulgar, but she knew that she wouldn't have it for long. She could already hear gunfire in reception and jackboots rising in the stairwells.

She fumed at the sight of the white coats duct-taped to their chairs in the lab. Flicking through the different screens, each image was more disheartening than the last. Dead security, smashed windows, Bentleys aflame in the parking garage and swarms of Her Majesty's marauding through Totem HQ. On the cathedral's altar: an empty, bloody gurney.

Newman was responsible for this. Not many people had ever said no to Alice, but Newman had. Not once, but twice. She should have tied up that loose end.

As for Hopkins, she couldn't believe it took him this long to work out that she'd killed his son. Alice could hear Andrew Hopkins' death rattle as she watched the moth-eaten soldiers climb the stairs with their old guns.

Alice checked the clock on her desk: 11:43pm. As if late for a train, she strode across her sprawling office to her transmission pod and climbed inside its plush womb, closing the hatch behind her. She drew her bare knees up against her cold breasts and watched the screen showing the pod's exterior. Boots clattered on to her office floor and encircled her. The raggedy troops cocked their antique firearms and pointed them at the metal shell, ready to fire.

Ready to initiate her ascension.

44

As they glided down what used to be the Humber Estuary, the suspension bridge loomed out of the darkness, taking them by surprise. Commander Gorrie had to manoeuvre to avoid the cables, causing yet more tension in the sub.

Once they'd rounded Hull's muddy Atlantis, Muldoon stabilised. Hopkins applied antiseptic where the Totem engineer's razor had slipped and the brass electrodes had branded raw circles into his skin. It reminded him of when Andrew was six years old and he caught pneumonia. Hopkins never left his son's side for a week, sleeping on a mattress next to his bed.

He sat down on the bunk opposite the boy. When Archer came round from his McCole-induced slumber, he was only conscious for about 30 seconds before his hysteria resumed. This time Hopkins gave him a sedative via syringe to the buttock, rather than McCole's fist to his jaw.

Hopkins dabbed at his right eyebrow with his sleeve. After applying a smidge of the antiseptic to the wound, he handed it to McCole.

McCole thanked him sarcastically. 'Yeah, great. Some fucking trip, Hopkins. I thought we were visiting a kid in hospital.'

'You're alright, aren't you?'

'I'm down a fucking eyebrow here. On my good side and all. What the hell's going on?'

'Something crossed over. Something's different. You feel that? Like we're still in the transmission?'

Commander Gorrie removed his headset with a clatter. 'Her Majesty's have red-zoned the capital. Even in the provinces, people are looting. Mainland's gone crazy.'

'What about Grosvenor?'

Gorrie stared at the radio. 'She's dead. Intel said she had today's date tattooed on her right eyebrow.'

'Archer was right,' said Williams, glancing at the snoring submariner, tucked up in his bunk under a blanket of sedatives.

'What does the kid's tattoo say?'

'He doesn't have one. He wasn't in a pod, either.'

'And the meek shall inherit the Earth.'

Hopkins ignored McCole and continued monitoring the boy's pulse until it stabilised.

McCole raised his bloody eyebrow. 'Happy now, Doctor?'

Hopkins stood up and hugged McCole, who was so shocked by the gesture that he kept his arms at his sides.

'You're weird, Hopkins.'

Williams gave up on the radio and put down his headset. 'Where are we going, Commander?'

'Still no word from the generals. We're on our own.'

'But we only have enough fuel to—'

'Dartmoor,' John Muldoon whispered through the oxygen mask. 'Come and see.'

McCole looked at the commander. 'Dartmoor? What's he talking about?'

'The island is surrounded by mines and we have no intel on numbers of surviving hostiles or whether they're armed or diseased. Out of the question.'

Williams' voice faltered when he spoke. 'I heard the prisoners survived by eating the dead, but then got wiped out by typhus. That's why they red-zoned it.'

'The brass won't send us there anyway. Why would they?'

Hopkins took a bottle of whisky out of the medical kit and clanked it on the tray next to the chaplain.

'I'll have that drink with you now, McCole.'

Gorrie brought some glasses from the galley, into which Hopkins poured large measures for everyone.

The radio crackled, halting the toast.

The commander put down his glass, pushed the

ear piece harder against the side of his head and asked them to repeat, his eyes widening.

'Co-ordinates.' His face blanched as he scribbled on a piece of paper. 'It's just a voice repeating them over and over again.'

Everyone waited in silence.

'Well? Where are they for?'

The boy whispered. 'Dartmoor.'

'Williams, double-check these numbers,' the commander said, handing him the scrap of paper. He held his head in his hands as he waited for Williams to confirm.

The boy spoke more loudly this time, lifting his head from the bunk. 'Arthur.'

Williams took out the charts and placed the scribblings alongside, checking each one twice.

'The boy's right. These are the co-ordinates for Dartmoor. What should we do, sir?'

Archer stirred in his chemical sleep. 'He's taking us to Hell.'

The commander placed the sheets of paper back on the table, checked the screens and turned the wheel halfway to the right. He tapped on a dial and glanced at the inky wound above his eyebrow in the glass. 'What was my date?'

Lucky lifted his head off his bunk. 'It wasn't today.'

'Good enough.' The commander changed course for Dartmoor, glancing anxiously at Hopkins.

John Muldoon's repeated, masked whisper

sounded deafening in the close quarters of the submarine. 'Come and see.'

45

Williams broke the silence as they approached the red zone.

'No mines showing up on the radar, sir. Should we proceed?'

Gorrie wiped the sweat from his forehead and winced as he brushed the wound above his eye. 'That can't be.'

He hustled over to the radar screen and examined it for himself, his jaw fixed agape in disbelief.

'Should we proceed, Commander?'

'Any more radio contact?'

'The same co-ordinates for Dartmoor on a loop until a few minutes ago. Now, we can't even get static.'

'Proceed. But give me eyes out front.'

Williams flicked a switch to bring up the sub's nose camera. It showed a clear path ahead, verifying what the radar had already told them. The sub passed over the ruins of a church, the cross on its spire threatening to rake their hull. Gorrie cast an accusatory glance at McCole.

'That was a close one.'

Hopkins monitored John, who had fallen asleep as they thrummed over Bath an hour earlier.

'Doctor, we need all eyes on the screens. If we hit just one mine, we're finished.'

'There are no mines,' Hopkins said, refusing to take his eyes from the boy.

'Maybe we're dead already.'

'The navy warned us about Dartmoor from the day we signed up.'

McCole nodded. 'I'll bet they did. No-one ever returned from there because no-one ever dared go in the first place.'

'What about the survivors? How do we know we're not walking into a cooking pot?'

'We're about to find out. Prepare to breech, Williams.'

'Yes, sir.'

Gorrie pulled one lever and pushed another, making the sub slow down and lurch upwards towards the surface. 'McCole, get the guns into the life raft when we surface. Hopkins, bring the boy.'

Hopkins winced at the sound of crashing water and groaning steel. The sub sounded as if it were about to disintegrate as it broke the surface of the water.

'Williams, life raft,' said Gorrie, dropping anchor with one hand and giving him a bundle of yellow plastic with the other. Williams took the raft on deck, dazzling the rest of the crew with the morning sunlight streaming through the hatch. The raft hissed and inflated as Williams pulled the cord. When he threw it in the water, a fresh, salty breeze drifted into the submarine, cooling their sticky faces. Hopkins breathed the air and closed his eyes. When he opened them, the Horseman was staring back at him from his bunk. His eyes focused on Hopkins for a few seconds before rolling back into his head. Hopkins lifted him out of the bunk and waited by the hatch.

Williams reached down with both hands to haul the boy out of the sub and into the raft. 'I'll come back down for Archer.'

'Stay there, Williams. I'll pass him up to you. McCole, you bring the guns. Doctor, collect what you need to take care of the boy.'

Hopkins followed the commander's orders and started gathering the medical supplies. Meanwhile, McCole scooped up Newman and handed him up the ladder. Once the injured man was on deck, the chaplain set about gathering the various firearms strewn about the vessel.

'Don't forget the ammo.' He dumped the box in the raft and reached back into the sub through the hatch.

'Give me Archer.'

Williams dragged the snoring man from his bunk

and put him on his shoulder. He wasn't even halfway up the ladder before McCole plucked him from the submarine like a tomato from a vine and delivered them to the raft.

'That it?'

'We're at full capacity, sir.'

'It'll have to be. We'll come back for the rations.'

McCole reached a hand down to help the commander out of the sub, but he waved away the offer. He returned to the controls, flicking switches and pulling levers until everything had shut down. The engines stopped, leaving only the sound of the wind and waves slopping against the submarine's hull.

Hopkins took the boy into the yellow inflatable, squinting at the brightness of two suns. Hopkins assumed this was a simple case of diplopia, probably a side-effect of the transmission. But it was the first time in sixteen years that he had seen a cloudless sky in Britannia. He flinched when he heard Andrew calling from the shore. The sound was unmistakeable. A female voice called out John's name. He looked at the other men in the raft.

'You hear that?'

'What?'

'Voices. They're calling for the boy. And for me.'

'I don't hear anything,' said McCole, shaking his head.

'What's with the sun? Where the hell are we?"

The commander spoke quietly. 'We've all had a long night.'

Newman yelled with pain as the raft wobbled.

'You ok, Newman?'

Lucky gave the doctor an uncertain thumbs up as he lay flat on his back in the liferaft alongside Muldoon. 'Don't forget the drugs.'

The shores of white sands led up to green hills with not a single transmission mast in sight. Dartmoor looked nothing like the Hell it was supposed to be.

'Do you see anyone, Commander?'

Gorrie held a pair of binoculars to his eyes. 'There's a wild horse on the moor.'

Hopkins felt the hair on his neck stand on end. 'What colour is the horse?'

'What does it matter?'

'Just tell me.'

'It's white.'

John Muldoon smiled and opened his eyes, each reflecting two suns and an impossibly blue sky. 'Arthur.'